YA PAUL Marcy
3525100256
12ya
Paul, Marcy
Underneath everything

W9-ADJ-365

UNDERNEATH EVERYTHING

MARCY BELLER PAUL

UNDER NEATH EVERY THING

BALZER + BRAY
An Imprint of HarperCollinsPublishers

Balzer + Bray is an imprint of HarperCollins Publishers.

Underneath Everything
Copyright © 2015 by Marcy Beller Paul
Map art copyright © 2015 by Bill Davis/Yarbrough, Williams & Houle, Inc.
All rights reserved. Printed in the United States of America.
No part of this book may be used or reproduced in any manner whatsoever
without written permission except in the case of brief quotations embodied
in critical articles and reviews. For information address HarperCollins
Children's Books, a division of HarperCollins Publishers, 195 Broadway,
New York, NY 10007.
www.epicreads.com

Library of Congress Cataloging-in-Publication Data
Paul, Marcy Beller.
Underneath everything / Marcy Beller Paul. — First edition.
    pages cm
    Summary: Mattie discovers surprising things about herself and her long-term
best friends when she decides she has had enough of her self-imposed isolation
from most of the school and two of her three friends, reconnects with her
ex-boyfriend, and enjoys all the parties senior year has to offer.
    ISBN 978-0-06-232721-5 (hardcover)
    [1. Best friends—Fiction. 2. Friendship—Fiction. 3. Dating (Social
customs)—Fiction. 4. Conduct of life—Fiction. 5. High schools—Fiction.
6. Schools—Fiction.] I. Title.
PZ7.1.P385Und 2015   2014041056
[Fic]—dc23   CIP
                                                                      AC

Typography by Sarah Creech
15 16 17 18 19   CG/RRDH   10 9 8 7 6 5 4 3 2 1

First Edition

For Chris, who is the real thing

And for Stephen and Alexandra,
who asked for longer stories

CHAPTER 1

WE'RE RUNNING THROUGH the parking lot toward the smell of burning wood. I tighten my grip on Kris's hand as we weave through rows of empty cars, but our palms start to pull away from each other, forcing our fingers to stretch and twist to stay together.

We keep going, toward the field full of black shadow-bodies and smoke curling into the sky above them, until we're standing behind our old intermediate school, on the edge of dead grass, staring at the Thanksgiving bonfire.

Kris's fingers slip out of mine. My hand drops to my side.

"So." Kris crosses her arms and exhales through pursed lips. "Is it everything you imagined?"

"Are you going to be like this all night?" I search the faces in front of us. It's hard to see in the dark, but every so often the crowd parts and the shadows shift. Flames sneak through, throwing an orange glow on a nose here, an eye there. The same noses and eyes and cheeks and mouths I've seen a million times since nursery school.

"Don't act all surprised," Kris says. "You know I didn't want to come." She slides a pack of Camels from her pocket, and I reach for my lighter. She brings the cigarette to her lips and cups her hands in front of it to block the wind. I flick open the cap of my Zippo to light her up, which is when I notice—she's wearing lip gloss. A shade between brown and deep red, like her hair. Kris never wears makeup. Neither of us does. Then again, we don't usually hang out with anyone but each other after school hours, either. At least, we haven't for over a year.

I laugh, nodding at the heart-shaped stain on her filter.

"Yeah, sorry to drag you out of the house. Looks like you barely had time to change out of your pajamas." I reach up and grab the cigarette, take a long drag, then hold it out to her, my lips forming a kiss.

"Shut up." She snatches the cigarette back and tucks it into the curve of her smirk. "It's tinted ChapStick." She blows smoke out the side of her mouth.

"Then give me some," I say.

Kris pulls a round, thin tin from her pocket and unscrews the cap. I swirl my finger around the mushy wax, smear it across my lips, and rub them together. Then I turn to her for an opinion, since she knows my face as well as I do, or she should, anyway. She's been looking at it since the day Mrs. Singer assigned us seats at the same table in first grade. But suddenly she seems different—the light from the bonfire jumping over her face, lengthening her long red lashes, whipping up her thick, wild ponytail, highlighting her soft, round cheeks and freshly glossed lips.

I wonder if I look different, too, now that my smile is wet

and low-lit. But if I do, Kris doesn't mention it. After a careful survey of my face, she nods in approval and slips the tin back into her pocket.

"I don't know what you're expecting," Kris says, waving her hand in a wide arc over the huddled groups that make up our high school. Our class alone is at least two hundred people, which is sort of like a small forest: just big enough to get lost in, just small enough for a single mistake to burn down the whole place. "Bonfire or not, somewhere in there is the same crowd we ditched last year." She takes one last drag, then flicks the lip-printed cigarette a few feet away. "A flock of sheep that big can't lead themselves, you know. Wish I could stick around to see what happens after June, when they try. Actually, no, I don't."

"Hey, Smoky, put out that fire."

"Half the field is in flames, Mats; do you really think it matters?" But we watch the glowing ember anyway, until someone steps on it. "Problem solved." Kris sighs. "So what's the plan, now that we're here?"

Here: Westfield, New Jersey. Division 18. Block 273. At least that's where we are on my 1921 Sanborn—the coolest map in my collection. I pull myself out of the pepto-pink paper version and into the real thing: Black sky. Crisp night. Senior year.

"Don't have one," I tell her.

"You've been carrying a to-do list since second grade," Kris reminds me. "You're going to tell me you spent all that time convincing me to come, telling me we couldn't possibly miss our last bonfire, and you don't have a plan?" Kris asks, as if I'll realize how weird the words sound when they're coming from her mouth.

I shrug my shoulders inside my jacket. I *did* want to come. I wanted to do *something*. But I never thought Kris would agree. It's the one thing I hadn't planned on. Here's the thing, though: plan or no plan, we're sticking together. Not because we're "best friends." Kris and I are a lot of things—we're sleepovers and secrets, mind readers and fortune-tellers; we're unconditional— but we're not "best friends." We banned that phrase last year when we agreed: That's just a label. It doesn't mean anything.

"Okay," she says, eyeing me. "Then follow me. I'm freezing, and I hear there's a huge fire in Block two hundred."

"Two seventy-three," I correct her.

"That's more like it." Kris pulls me through the cold crush of arms and shoulders until we reach the center, where everybody glows. The charred pile of wood is twenty feet across and surrounded by a thick ring of blackened ground. We stare into the fire. Neither of us has been to a party in a while, and I'm not sure how to get started. I scan the crowd, but everyone keeps turning to talk, or lifting their chins to chug, or throwing up their hands to wave to someone; and when they turn or lift or throw, they lose the golden light, and I can only see half of them. One time I think I spot Jolene diagonally across from me. But then the girl turns, and I realize it's not her.

The wind blows black smoke in our direction.

I'm about to ask Kris if she sees anyone interesting when Bella barrels into us, throwing her arms around us both like she meant to meet us here, when the truth is we haven't hung out with her in over a year. But that's Bella for you.

"Whoa, down, girl!" I shout, digging in my heels and using all my strength to stay upright. But she's in full-on Bella mode, so there's no stopping her.

"You gu-uys!" she squeals, giving our necks one last squeeze.

4

"You're totally here!" Bella's lined lips stretch into a smile. Her big brown eyes go wide. "Wait"—she grabs our hands and pulls us through the tight-knit groups—"come this way. The light from that thing totally makes my bronzer look orange." She's walking backward into the cold darkness when she bumps into Scott Strickland.

"You know you want me, Bella!" he shouts. Doubtful. He's put on at least twenty pounds since he graduated last year. He reaches for Bella but grabs my arm by mistake. I pull it away, and he squints at me, racking his brain for a name; but nothing comes, because I'm nobody, so he lets me go and turns around to find his friends.

"Eat it, Prickland!" Bella screams to the sky. A freshman girl whips her head around at the sound and falls into her friend. The two of them topple and crash-land, asses on the ground, heels in the air. Bella doubles over in laughter, crouching down as far as her black, patent knee-high boots will allow. "I swear to god, you guys," she says, her voice a soprano shriek between fits of giggles, "I'm gonna pee my pants! The look on that girl's face! I can't take it."

Kris's smile bursts open and then mine does too, so that the three of us are standing in a small patch of dead grass behind Thomas Alva Edison Intermediate School, laughing about nothing. Because that's what hanging out with Bella is like. I'd almost forgotten.

"Oh my god." Bella sighs, gently blotting the tears beneath her eyes. "That was awesome!"

"Classic," I say.

"Vintage," Kris agrees.

Bella stands up. I forgot how short she is. Even with those

killer heels, the tops of her curls barely hit my chin. She puts her hands on her hips and gets all fake-serious.

"So, what's *up*, you guys? I mean, I just want to say that I totally called it. I knew you'd remember."

What Bella remembers: freshman year. The four of us on the floor. Me, Kris, Bella, and Jolene, giving up our deepest wishes to the dark. It was Jolene's idea. Most things were. She turned off the lights and tiptoed through the room to where we lay waiting. With bits of sleeping bag bunched in her fists, she asked us what we'd be if we could be anything. And with our wishes still fresh on our lips, she swore we'd make them real. Right before we all promised to meet here senior year.

What I remember: how Kris and Bella fell asleep in bags on the floor while Jolene wove braids into my wet hair and words into the pink underside of my skin.

"I told Jolene you'd be here and she didn't believe me, obviously, but I was so right and you're here and it's awwwwesome." Bella jumps up and down without leaving the ground, like the cheerleader she is, and grabs our arms again as if we'll disappear if she's not physically touching us. "So, you're coming over after this, right?"

I can almost feel the lashes that landed on my cheeks that night; Jolene had dared me to swing the finished braids back and forth as fast as I could.

I bring my hand to my face, smooth the stray hairs.

"Of course we're coming," I tell Bella. I don't have to look at Kris to know she's clenching her jaw. Not only because I said we'd go to a party at Bella's—something we swore we'd never do again—but because I didn't check in with her first. "Everyone who's anyone, right?" Our old motto. Which suddenly strikes me as hilarious, because me and Kris, we're no one.

"Yaaaayyyy!" Bella sings, as if she might actually burst from excitement. And the way she's jumping up and down in that deep-cut V neck, it certainly seems like a distinct possibility. Kris should be mad—I know she's mad—but Bella's energy is infectious. Soon we're both smiling and nodding. Bella catches us in another double-hug-sleeper-hold before running back into the mass of shadow-bodies, shouting, "See you two *la-ter*!"

We watch her tall boots and teased curls disappear into the crowd.

"Did that just happen?" Kris asks.

"'It's all happening.'" I put my hands up in front of her eyes and fan them out around her face. It's a line from our favorite movie, *Almost Famous*, and it gets her to smile.

"'You cannot make friends with the rock stars,'" Kris quotes back—her favorite Lester Bangs line. "'These people are not your friends.'" Then she leans her shoulder into mine. Not too hard, just enough to let me know she's pissed.

"That wasn't cool, though," Kris says in her own voice again. "To make Bella think we're coming. Now she's all excited." Kris digs around in her pocket for the half-empty pack of Camels.

"Bella is pretty much always excited," I point out.

"True." Kris slams the soft pack hard against the heel of her hand, then shakes out a cigarette and nips it between her lips. "Some things never change, huh?"

I light her up.

"Guess not." The end of her Camel sparks red. I snap the Zippo shut with a flick of my wrist, tuck it back into my pocket, and slide my thumb over the smooth metal. "But I wasn't kidding. I think we should go."

The smoke catches in Kris's throat. She's coughing and shaking her head. When she finally catches her breath, I can tell she's going to launch into the Are You Forgetting When speech; but she barely has time to open her mouth before Jim Maronack sneaks up behind her and snakes his arms around her waist.

"To what do I owe this pleasure?" he says, swaying her back and forth. "The elusive Kris McKittrick, showing up at Thanksgiving bonfire? I must be on stronger drugs than I thought."

Kris rolls her eyes, wraps her shiny lips around her cig, and uses both hands to squirm out of his grip. Jim and Kris have been fooling around since fall of freshman year. He's totally in love with her and she tolerates him. He's not a bad guy, which makes it even worse. I mean, it's not his fault Kris swore off serious relationships. She has one goal, and one goal only: to get the hell out of this town, no strings attached.

"Blame Mattie," she says, tossing her head in my direction. "Totally her idea."

"Well then, thanks, Mattie, for releasing the princess from the tower," he says, holding his long arm out to me.

"My pleasure," I say, shaking his hand and raising my eyebrows at Kris. She shrugs her shoulders at me, then leans back into Jim and pretends not to notice that his arms wrap back around her waist. As if she doesn't love it. Anyway, that's my cue, so I check my phone: it's 9:05 p.m. and I need to be home by midnight, 12:30 a.m. latest, so we're good.

"Meet you back here at nine thirty?" I ask Kris. Jim kisses her neck.

"Half hour?" Kris tips her head sideways to give him more skin. I nod. "Okay, don't be late," she warns. Not only because we haven't finished talking about Bella's, but because even though Kris likes Jim, she doesn't like to be stuck with him. My job is to rescue her—eventually—but for now I leave Kris and Jim to their thing and make my way to the outer edge of the circle, where it's not as crowded.

I flip my Zippo inside my pocket and run my thumb over it in small strokes. Jolene gave it to me in eighth grade. She had a habit of hoarding strange things: a blank check, a lighter, a bullet. She'd pluck something from her small, jeweled box and carry it in cupped hands across her room to me, where she'd pry her thumbs apart like she was holding a live butterfly. But I'd barely get a chance to peer in before she'd snap her hands shut again, telling me the same thing she always did: it wasn't about the thing but what that thing wanted to be: A cashed check. A raging fire. A shot bullet.

What do you *want to be, Mattie?*

I pass the soccer team, zipping their Windbreakers up to the collars; student council members stretching their necks and swiveling their heads, pretending to be responsible; gamers and vloggers texting and taping the entire event; the drama crew—they're singing, as usual—and, eventually, the staff of the school paper. We're not really friends, but they know me. I spent a lot of time in the journalism room last fall. Even took it as an elective once upon a time. Plus, Kris is the editor-in-chief of the paper this year, and I've been known to hang around and help out, especially before big deadlines.

They nod in my direction. I nod back.

I'm on the other side now, opposite Kris. From here I can see the bonfire unobstructed. It looks so big. So out of control. Like any minute the breeze could blow my way and I'd be part of the flame.

I step toward it.

And there she is.

Jolene stands a few feet in front of me, tossing her long, dark hair. I can't see the streak of auburn underneath, but I know it's there.

I haven't been this close to her in over a year.

I turn my cheek. Feel the heat. Her warm breath against my ear as she whispers:

What do you want to be?

But Jolene and I didn't *become* anything. We were born one night.

There was blood: Jolene's bootheel cracking glass; her fingers pressing the jagged halves of her mother's necklace between our hot palms until our skin split; her hand squeezing tight—tighter when I gasped—so the blood wouldn't spill.

There was a story: she said the first line, I said the next. The ending changed, but the beginning was always the same. It was our lullaby.

It was us: two little girls all alone in the world.

I make a sharp right and veer away from her, into another shade of darkness, and walk back and back and back until I can't feel the heat anymore.

Then I stop and listen. Brittle leaves scrape the trees behind me. Fire crackles in front. Silhouettes swarm. The white noise of distant voices runs beneath everything. But there's no trace of her words, not even a whisper.

EX. CB

CHAPTER 2

"DO YOU MIND?"

I whip my head around to see who's talking, but after staring at the fire, I'm night-blind for a few seconds. So I follow my ears. The voice came from below and behind me.

"Do you?" I ask it. My eyes begin to adjust. I see a pair of unlaced sneakers emerging. Loose jeans. A flannel—cuffs unbuttoned at the wrists—and a thick silver ring gleaming in the darkness.

Hudson.

I should have known. He's never that far from her.

"Yeah, actually. You're blocking the view, not to mention blowing my cover." His voice is low and raspy. It reminds me of an old recording. The hum it gives off. How he used to say my name.

I step to the side. He hasn't said it that way since summer after sophomore year.

"Sorry," I say. I stare up at the branches intersecting the

night sky, because it's easier than looking at him.

Hudson rests his elbows on his knees and hangs his hands together loosely in front of him, admiring the scene. "Sit down if you're going to stay." He nods his head toward the spot next to him on the ground.

"I don't want to interrupt—"

"All this?" he asks, spreading his arms out around him, then draping them back over his knees. "I mean, yeah, I didn't come back here to chat, but you're cool."

I feel a shiver that has nothing to do with the weather, and a weakness I want more of. Then I hate him for making me feel this way. And I hate myself more for letting him.

"Cool," I respond, because it's simple and meaningless—the opposite of how this feels. I sit down next to him in the frozen grass like this is normal, something we do every day. Like this isn't the first time we've found each other on the fringe of a crowd since he stopped speaking to me. My skin prickles. I can feel every inch of it. I need to move, to do something. So I stretch my legs out in front of me, position my arms behind me, and sink my palms into the ground.

The wind picks up, blowing my hair into my face. A few strands stick to my lips, caught in the lip gloss or ChapStick or whatever Kris gave me. I reach up, carefully pull the pieces away, and scoop them behind my ear.

I look at Hudson. He looks straight ahead. I follow his gaze until I see Jolene's hair flip, a swish of black shadow. Of course he wasn't looking at me. Not with her standing so close.

Jolene's the kind of girl people stare at: Hazel eyes. Honey-colored skin. Wide lips. Dark-brown hair so thick you can barely run your fingers through it.

She's the kind of girl people listen to.

She could have been completely self-centered and gotten away with it. But she wasn't like that. Not with me. She never talked about herself. Instead she asked me question after question. And when I spoke, she leaned in to listen, devouring every detail like she would never tire of mining me. Like I was fascinating.

My palms hurt. They're pressed flat against the frozen grass and solid dirt. But I don't move. We both watch her.

A few minutes go by, and I'm starting to wonder what time it is, how long it will take me to get back around the fire and find Kris, when I turn to speak and realize Hudson is looking at me. Not Jolene. Not the fire.

Me.

So I stare back. Really, I don't have a choice. It's his eyes. They pin me in my place. I see something move across them—the faintest reflection of the silver-streaked sky. And something else, too. A promise. A private joke. A recognition. But of what, I don't know. I can't feel anything except his gaze moving through me, haunting me, hollowing me out.

"Thought you didn't show up at these things." His voice is deep, easy.

"Oh, I'm not really here," I say.

Hudson laughs, but he doesn't smile. Instead he picks at the grass by his sneakers, rolls it between his fingers, throws it out into the field. "No, of course not. Not really one for showing up, are you?"

I stare at the spot where he tossed the tangled grass, because, really, what can I say? I said I'd meet him. I promised. I didn't show up.

Jolene did.

Hudson wipes his hands on his jeans. The silver ring glints in the moonlight.

We both face forward. The crowd is splitting up now. The bonfire is more smoke than fire.

"You got the time?" he asks. "Cal probably thinks I took off."

Cal plays soccer with Hudson. They've been on the same team since town leagues and traveling teams. Now they're cocaptains of varsity. Hudson may have a real-life older brother, but he and Cal are closer than blood.

"Sure." I slide my phone out of my pocket and turn it on, the glow of the screen lighting us from below. "Nine twenty-five."

He nods. And just when I think he's going to get up and leave, he glances over my shoulder. "Wait. Is that you and Kris? From, what, fifth grade?" He's pointing to the picture on my main screen, leaning over me to get a better look.

He smells like winter. Always has.

"Yeah," I say, fumbling to shut it off. But Hudson wraps his hand around mine and holds the lit screen between us.

I'm supposed to rescue Kris now, but I don't move.

"You look the same," he says, his breath white against the night.

"Hope not. That was, like, forever ago. Things have changed," I say, with quick eyes toward the fire. Where is Jolene? Is she waiting for him?

"But not everything." He lowers his chin to the picture of me and Kris.

"Not everything," I admit.

Kris has had my back since the day we traded shoelaces in first grade. She's my oldest friend. For almost a year and a half, she's been my only friend. And right now I'm late to meet her. "I should go," I say, tugging my phone toward my pocket. Hudson's hand hardens around mine, gripping it tight. I look up, and our eyes meet for a second before a lock of his brown hair swings between us. He's let it grow long, almost down to his shoulders, and even though it's pulled back, this piece has escaped. As he reaches up to push it behind his ear, my phone blinks off, and the night falls new around us.

Hudson drops my hand, gets to his feet, and turns his back to me. But he doesn't leave. I shove my hand—suddenly cold, still gripping my phone—into my pocket and stand up beside him. We walk in silence toward what's left of the bonfire: blackened wood, a dense cone of smoke, small clusters of seniors, and a mass of underclassmen trying to figure out where to go, what to do. I keep waiting for Jolene to materialize out of the night, as if the gray swirls of smoke and ash will suddenly turn solid and she'll be standing right in front of me.

"Cal wants to meet the team at Bella's after this. He's my ride home, so I guess that means I'm going. But you won't be there, right? You don't do parties." Hudson stops just short of the sidewalk.

I spot Kris up ahead, at the edge of the parking lot. Jim is behind her, rubbing her shoulders; she's shaking him off, scrolling through her phone, probably looking for a text from me, which she's not going to find.

"Right." I turn to Hudson and search his face. If only the smattering of freckles on his nose formed a compass rose, or the flat line of his mouth pointed true north. Maybe then I'd understand what direction he's going: Does he want me to come? Does he want me to stay away? But his expression doesn't change. He's no map. I can't read him. "No parties."

Hudson nods in response. The slightest dip of his chin, the faintest flash of lowered lashes.

It's a minuscule movement.

It's not enough.

"No bonfires, either," I tell him.

Hudson's eyes tick to mine. Blue. Inscrutable. Then he steps into the splash of yellow light spreading from the single bulb behind the school, and for a second I see something ease in the crease of his brow and the set of his lips; but I can't quite figure out what it is before he starts up with those long, easy strides of his, down the sidewalk, out of the light, into the parking lot.

Hudson doesn't turn around. He doesn't miss a beat. He just walks away, like it never happened.

LOT 1
MB:46—665
MB:51—10.
60' R/W
YOUNGBLOC

COS.
MB:46—66
MB:61—10
60' R/W
YOUNGBLO

EX. CB

CHAPTER 3

"I DIDN'T AGREE to this." Kris locks her car and flicks at the filter of her Camel, launching ash onto the sidewalk. Her wine-red Docs thud purposefully beside me as we walk up the hill to Bella's house, stepping in and out of streetlamp spotlights and past a few parked cars. There are obviously people here, but it's not the bumper-to-bumper scene I thought it would be, considering it's Thanksgiving weekend. The tight grip of my ribs relaxes, releases my lungs. I breathe deeply.

"You promised you'd come," I remind her.

"To the bonfire. Not Bella's."

I drop my chin to my chest and burrow into my jacket.

Most weekends we don't park; we drive—blasting heat and music, leaking laughter and smoke through slit windows. When I'm behind the wheel, we stick to Westfield. I tick off street names and lot numbers in my head as we pass them, marking and measuring the land like my '21 Sanborn map, coloring certain plots pink and others green, cruising past Xed-out rectangles with one-word descriptions: *Butcher, Library, Post.* We drive down dead ends that don't exist yet. We know the future.

In Kris's car we cross the town border for roads that dip and climb and wind around mountains. We leave Westfield for the Watchung Reservation—a massive chunk of woodland that, due to its historical significance, was preserved (and saved from its fate as a neon-lit strip mall) in the twenties, around the same time my Sanborn map was created. But that's where the similarity ends. The reservation map is no pencil-drawn grid, full of boxes and block letters. It's like calligraphy, covered in curves and loops and wavy elevation lines. One look at that map and it's easy to understand why Kris likes the reservation—for the same reason all those plastic-covered plaques around the grounds tell us George Washington did: its mountains create a natural fortress. The only difference is that Washington used the Watchungs as a barrier against the British. Kris uses them against everyone.

And right now we're in enemy territory.

"I mean," Kris says, "I'm going to need a pretty spectacular reason to risk our fantastic, untouchable status as Nobodies." Kris pauses at the end of Bella's driveway—which is not so much a driveway as a mailbox next to an open mouth in the woods—and takes a long drag. She's squinting, and not because of the smoke. She knows there's something I'm not telling her. She always does.

So I swallow, say it—"I hung out with Hudson at the bonfire"— and brace myself. There's a hierarchy to Kris's hate. Jolene is the clear winner (isn't she always?), and Hudson is a close second. I'm not saying I don't get it. I'd hate anyone who led *her* on, broke *her* heart, and ignored *her* existence. And the way Kris sees it, that's exactly what he did to me.

"Hudson," she says.

I nod and wait for the Hudson speech, but Kris doesn't say anything. Instead she takes a drag that singes her Camel down to its brown filter, then she flicks it. It burns a red arc through the night—the wrong kind of lightning bug—before it lands on the pavement, under the reinforced toe of her boot. Then she starts walking again. We pick our way over a mound of protruding roots bowed like muscles over the cracked cement skin of the driveway. Leaves rustle deep inside trees. Scampering claws scratch high branches.

Kris checks her phone, pockets it again.

And just when I'm thinking Kris might actually let the whole Hudson thing go, she says, "So, what's up with Jolene's boyfriend these days? Are you two *friends* now?" Kris leans on the *F* word like it's a curse.

"No." Hudson and I were never friends. Even freshman year—when Jolene got us into senior parties and Hudson and Cal were the only other underclassmen there—Hudson kept his distance. Not just from me but from everybody. The way he stood, slanted away. The way he sized up a room, silent. Like he was guarding something. Then one night he let me in.

Then came Jolene.

Then he was gone.

"But you still want to go," Kris says. "Even though you're not friends. Even though Jolene will be with him."

We're only halfway up the tree-smothered drive, but we can already hear it: not music exactly, but a strong, rhythmic bass beat mixed with a mess of voices. The farther we walk, the fuller and more distinct the sound gets. Drums and guitar join the bass. Shouts poke through the wall of voices.

A closed part of me opens.

The memories come quick, like punches: the four of us squeezing onto Bella's deck swing and pumping our legs in the afternoon sun; Kris sneaking cigarettes on the back porch; Bella in the hot tub; me and Jolene swinging in the hammock, limbs hot and mingling, matching words and breath. And back, before that. The beginning. Bella bringing her new neighbor the day we hiked the cliffs at the reservation, the summer before seventh grade. Kris's voice lost to the leaves. Bella's laugh floating back to us from between the branches up the path. Jolene and me climbing the thin strip of cliff that clung to the mountain. Me, carefully. Jolene, surefooted. My heart skipping as her sneakers knocked rocks to the street hundreds of feet below (my safe streets, suddenly dangerous). Jolene grabbing my hand as she ran, screaming "Let's race!" before I could say no—that the path was too narrow. Jolene running ahead as I followed. Terrified. Ecstatic. Laughing into the sky.

"Even though Jolene will be there," I confirm.

Kris sighs, stares up at the slate-gray sky. She never talks about the beginning, only the end: the rope around my wrists, the tape on my lips, the busted lock, the bang of metal.

"Remind me again why I'm here?" Kris asks.

"Because you love me?"

She waves me off. "Obvious."

"Because it'll be your choice," I say. Because this is what she told me the night we left the manhunt game. It's what she always says. "It'll be on our terms."

"Well, when you put it that way." Kris takes out the small

tin of goo, refreshes the red shine on her half smile, then offers me the container. I shake my head. She covers the tin and slips it back into her pocket. "Jim did say he'd make an appearance if we decided to go. And I have to admit, I'm not *not* curious about what goes on at these things," she says.

"Oh, you know, I'm sure it's all naked wrestling and champagne," I say, straight-faced.

"Bubbles and bathing suits!" she cheers. And we're laughing, because in eighth grade Bella spent most of her time imagining the crazy parties she'd have in high school. The guest lists, the bartenders, the bouncers, the outrageous themes. And we'd always laugh at her. Like that stuff ever happened. But what do we know? It's not like we've been to one of Bella's senior-year parties. Maybe we're about to walk into a sand pit or wall-to-wall foam. Anything's possible.

We're just shy of the moonlight, in the last stretch of tangled branches, when Bella's house comes into view: three massive cubes nestled together and topped with heavy, rectangular slabs. It cuts white angles into the black sky.

Parked cars pack the wide circle of driveway to our right.

Everyone who's anyone? I think. More like anyone at all. Half the school must be here.

We're here.

"Okay. Let's get this over with," Kris says, but she doesn't walk toward the house. She's waiting for me, to make sure I'm cool, even though she can barely keep her teeth from chattering. And that's enough to get me moving.

"Let's."

Together we step onto the lit grass.

As we climb the long flight of stone steps stretching up to the house, I recite the surrounding street names in my head. One for each red plastic cup I sidestep: *Hillside Avenue. Breeze Knoll Drive. Roanoke Road.* It settles the nervous spark in my chest, lengthens my breath, helps me orient. When we reach the front door, we follow the white slate path around the house to the gate, then stop and face each other. A last check-in.

Kris raises her eyebrows. *Ready?*

I force my shoulders up into a shrug. *Not really.*

But I lift the heavy metal latch anyway and swing open the wide gate.

My body tenses. I've always hated walking into parties—that moment before you know exactly who's there, how drunk they are, whether they're staring at each other or dancing. Except for the times I'd walk in with Jolene, because to her they weren't parties. They were movie sets, magic acts, epic quests. The skater in the corner was a stalker. The cheerleader by the fireplace grew fangs at night and hunted to kill. The jock by the keg could break chains and escape underwater cages.

I was a queen.

And Jolene? She was God, of course. She created us all.

Tonight there are no shape-shifters or illusionists, just circles of smokers scattered across the sloping lawn, small groups laughing on lounge chairs, and couples claiming the hidden steps that lead to the upper deck. A few of them lift their heads when we walk in, then look away when they see us. We're not the friends they're expecting.

Kris and I walk past the pool. It's one of those inset, stone deals that look like a freshwater pond someone found in the woods. Like it was here first, and everything else—the exotic plants rooted between the rocks, the tiny spotlights, the house, the party—sprang up around it. Which is exactly what Bella's mom was going for. We heard her tell the landscaper she wanted her backyard to look like a magical forest, and Bella's been calling it that ever since.

"Looks like you were right about the bathing suits." Kris tilts her head forward, toward the opposite side of the yard, and I follow the path of her eyes through the hanging vines to the hot tub. You've got to be kidding me. There really *are* people sitting in there, drinks in hand. I burrow deeper into my jacket.

"I really hope they're wasted. Or freshmen," I say, trying not to stare.

"The only two acceptable explanations," Kris agrees, peering into a floater on the table next to us. She rubs her hands together, then folds her arms across her chest. It's near freezing, and we're still standing in the backyard.

"You think Bella's dad still has the man cave?" I ask. The man cave is a dark wood den carved into the corner of the basement. It has darts, vintage video games, and a smallish pool table; and it's exactly the type of place I always tried to find at a big party—when I used to go to them, that is. Someplace far from crowds and soaring spaces. Someplace on the fringe. Which is how I ended up on a small couch off Cal's living room a year and a half ago, talking to Hudson. He liked those places too.

"If he's still a man, he does," Kris says. "Want to play some pool?" She's already weaving around the patio furniture.

"Want to lose?" I'm close behind.

Kris is the first one in the house. I watch her. She's good at this—blending in. She's already at the keg, standing next to a couple of guys from our class, holding out two red cups, making some kind of small talk. As if she's actually enjoying this instead of counting the minutes until she can leave for college and cut everyone loose. Everyone except me. Obviously.

When foam finally flows over the edge of the second cup, she holds it out to me. I grab it and follow her past the black granite island, around some guys from the lacrosse team doing a group chug, through the open kitchen, and onto the thick, white living-room carpet.

I don't see Jolene at first. I'm too busy trying to follow Kris, who slips easily between arms and behind backs while I stumble and shove to keep up without spilling too much beer. We're snaking along a wall covered with two huge, white canvases when I catch a flash of Jolene's honey-colored skin on the opposite side of the room. She's sitting sideways in a corner of the oversize ivory sectional. A corner that used to fit me, Bella, and Kris too. Now it only seems big enough for Jolene, who tucks her shoeless feet beneath her, props her elbow on the back of the couch, and trips and trails her fingertips along the leather. A small audience of second-tier friends and underclassmen squeezes onto the surrounding cushions, gasping and giggling every time she speaks.

I quit fighting to move forward. Kris gets swallowed by sweaters, button-downs, and sequined tops. I stop. Someone crashes into me, spills, curses. The circle of girls behind me keeps laughing and expanding until my thighs are pressed up against the glass coffee table separating me from Jolene. I'm getting pushed, squeezed. I feel like I can't breathe.

Her hand over my mouth. Her fingers pinching my nose.

On the couch, Jolene smiles, sweeps her dark hair back to show the hint of auburn underneath and the slide of her cream-colored shirt off her bare shoulder. She throws back her head and laughs.

I kicked her under the blanket. She pressed her hand harder against my lips and laughed.

Someone knocks into me from behind, and my knees, which have gone soft, give way. I drop my cup and slap my palms against the glass table to stop myself from crashing into it. I keep my head down, not wanting to see all those eyes on me; but when I remember to breathe—when I finally sneak a peek up—the only eyes I see are Jolene's. They're glassy. She's staring at me.

The gash on my palm hadn't healed by our next sleepover. It was the fall of freshman year. We spilled our wishes. Kris and Bella fell asleep, zipped in bags on the floor. Jolene and I pulled the covers over our heads—she'd scored us the bed again—and traded lines of our story.

"Your turn," Jolene said. Our mingled breath made the small cave under the comforter hot and wet. Jolene turned to me, expectant.

I shifted under the sheets and smoothed the tiny braids tugging at my scalp. Jolene had woven them for me. "Two little girls all alone in the world, who woke from their beds and decided to live."

Jolene grabbed my hand and squeezed. I flinched when my scab cracked.

Her turn. "Two little girls all alone in the world, who dove in so deep, they grew gills to breathe."

"Ew," I whisper-hissed. "Gills?"

"Just two little slits," she said, tracing a line under my jaw.

"One here"—she lifted her finger to the other side, pressed it into the soft skin—"and one here." She paused, leaving her finger on my neck for an extra second. When she took it away, she traced the same lines on herself. "We'd have to hold our breath at first," she said, "for a long time. And then, there they'd be." Her voice trailed off.

I propped up the covers, which had come to rest on our foreheads. Usually when Jolene went into her own world like this, I let her go. We fell asleep, and the night ended. This time she turned to me, wide-eyed and energized.

"Bet I can hold my breath longer than you." A sly smile crept across her lips, which glistened, even in the darkness.

From outside our cover cave: a cough, the soft scritch of sleeping bags shifting.

"Bet you can't," I said. Jolene only played games she could win, but this time she didn't have all the information. Before she'd moved to town, I'd taken a lifeguarding prep course at the Y. I had experience. "You say when."

I pressed my cheek to the pillow. We lay face-to-face. My heart thumped.

She smiled and narrowed her eyes. "One, two." She took a deep breath. I felt her chest push out, moving the sheets between us as she sucked in a slow, steady stream of air. Jolene let the last word out quick—"Three"—and pressed her lips together.

We stared at each other. The first few seconds were easy. She smiled at me. I smiled back. I couldn't laugh or I'd lose all my breath. I had to concentrate. Soon I felt a dull pressure in my chest, but I was still okay. A few seconds more. My fingers and feet tingled. Jolene blinked, her eyes watered. She was going to take a breath first, I knew it. I was going to win this time. But somehow she kept her mouth shut, her body still. The pressure in my chest got worse. I heard my heart in my head. My lips fought me, but I knit them together. And just as I saw Jolene's mouth begin to open, just as I was about to celebrate my victory, her hands shot toward my face—one over my mouth, the other pinching my nose.

I pulled at her hands. She tightened the fingers pinching my nose and pressed her palm to my mouth. I felt the rough bump of her scab against my lips.

My chest was pain, my head a dull beat, my lungs fighting for the air they needed. The only thing I had left was my feet. I kicked her under the blanket. She pressed her hand harder against my lips and laughed.

CHAPTER 4

A VISE GRIP on my arm pulls me up and back, into the stream of people on their way from the kitchen to the basement.

"You okay?" Kris shouts. The music has gotten louder somehow, and the people packed even tighter. Someone's sweat-soaked shirt slides across my arm, an errant elbow knocks me into a group of giggling junior girls.

"Yeah," I say, steadying myself with Kris's help. It's not only arms and backs and chests closing in around me. It's memories. I'm letting them get to me.

I take a deep breath and run through the blueprint of Bella's house in my head. The third-floor den and adjoining guest rooms. The second-floor sitting area, square and backed by an oval window. The corridor of white pile carpet, opening to bedrooms and an office, spilling down the stairs to where I am. The living room. I let out my breath and look around.

Everyone's holding a cup, swaying a little too much, singing off-key, wearing that drunk sheen. It's a party. Everyone's buzzed and having fun. Except me.

Kris leans in, her lips against my ear so I can hear: "What?"

"Nothing!" I shout, picking up my cup and tugging her forward. But I'm not quick enough. Kris looks past me, sees Jolene. She clenches her jaw for a second, then, just as fast, relaxes it.

Even when we first met, when we were all friends, there was always something between Kris and Jolene: Their conversations carried a certain type of weight. They sat at opposite ends of the room or the table, like opposing magnets. It was as if they'd known each other before. Or as if Kris could see, from our intermediate school view, what it would be like in high school: the two of us dropping away as Jolene ran, fast and light, toward senior year, armed and ready to storm it like a castle.

"Really?" Kris asks, raising her eyebrows and flicking her chin in Jolene's direction. "We just got here."

"I thought you didn't even want to come," I tease.

"Right. I didn't want to come. But now we're here. Might as well enjoy it." Kris holds up her cup.

"Exactly what I was thinking," I say, glancing back at Jolene. I press my cheek against Kris's: "Let's go!"

We link arms and dive back into the thick mix of people. This time I'm not struggling to keep up.

Kris and I slip through a door that looks more like a crack in the wall and stop at the top of the stairs to take in the cool, stale basement air. Anything is better than the stink of the packed party. It's only after a minute or so, when we finally shake the scent of sweat and beer and breath, that we catch a whiff of it. It's faint, but it's definitely there. The earthy, sweet, smoky reek of weed.

"Smells like the man cave is in working order," Kris says.

"Indeed it does."

"Well, you're the addict. Take the lead."

"Please," I say, stepping in front of her, "no one's *addicted* to pot." Kris is constantly giving me shit for my "pot addiction," which, roughly translated into reality, means I've tried it a few times—enough to know I like it better than beer.

Being high makes me superaware of where I end and everything else begins—what separates things. Drawn lines. Soft skin. It's like being inside one of my maps. Everything is contained in its rightful place. Safe.

Being drunk messes with my edges. The one time I drank a fifth of clear liquor at a party freshman year, I sat on a ratty couch in some senior's basement trying to stop spinning. I pictured the map above my bed, which usually helps, but the borders morphed and the lots bled together, pepto pink mixing with puke green. I felt like I might spill all over everybody. Or they might spill all over me. Until Jolene curled up next to me and spun stories that made everything sparkly.

I force my feet down the floating stairs—another one of Bella's mom's custom designs—and into the light of the long, open basement. It's not empty down here, but it's obvious that only a few people know how to find the vanishing door. I keep my eyes straight ahead and stride quickly across the cream carpet.

Two little girls who decided to live.

"Wow. You're really jonesing," Kris says when she catches up.

"Stop being all condescending, Miss Pack-a-Day," I say. Kris hip-checks me. "Anyway, it's not like I'm actually going to smoke with these people. I just want to sit down, and the man cave is probably our best shot."

"You can admit you're trying to find Hudson, you know."

"Okay. I'm trying to find Hudson." But is he trying to find me? Or is he still angry? Either way, if he's here, he'll be in the cave. Hudson likes tucked-away places.

The closer we get, the louder my heart hammers in my chest. But this time, instead of taking deep breaths, reciting street names, or running layouts in my head to lower the volume, I let it crash. (Bang. Smash.)

We're almost through the exercise room, only a few steps away from the cave, when Bella busts through the doorway, smoke streaming behind her. We slam into each other. I spill what's left of my beer on her chest, and it immediately drips into the deep V of her shirt. But it doesn't faze her. Nothing does.

"So that's the kind of party it's going to be?" Bella asks, looking down her own cleavage. "Okay then! Guess you guys *do* have some catching up to do." She winks, swipes a finger across her chest, then touches her finger to her tongue. "You guys are drinking from the keg? You should ditch that crap and get something from in there." She motions behind her. "You know where, right? Just don't spend too long with the riffraff. They're like zombies, you know? They bite you once and you're toast. And you guys are not allowed to be toast! I want both of you upstairs for late night. I've got to work the party for a little— you know how it is." *Not really.* "But you better stay for after hours, okay? You promised!" She blows us a kiss and shuffles off toward the stairs.

"Late night?" I ask.

"After hours?" Kris replies.

"Doubtful," we say together. A few hours from now, when this house has been properly trashed by the entire senior class, and Bella and Jolene are having their postparty recap in the kitchen and clinking glasses to how popular and fabulous they both are, we'll be long gone. And not just because we have to make curfew.

Coming to Bella's party is one thing. Sticking around to rehash old memories is another. I don't need to remember what I confessed when Jolene asked me what I wanted to be. I've never forgotten.

I push open the door to the cave, which has been leaking smoke and music since Bella's exit.

"Beware the zombies," I say.

"Will do." Kris follows me into the haze.

Between the dimmed lights and the clouds of smoke, it's hard to see anything at first, but after a few seconds I get used to it. I find the pool table in the center of the room and the jukebox on the far wall. It's filled with Led Zeppelin and the Who and a bunch of other music that Bella's dad listens to. Cal's behind the wet bar, talking everybody up, as usual, and the rest of the cave dwellers look like they're sunk and stuck in the brown leather couches that line the other two walls. Every once in a while the wrought-iron door in the corner opens and a cold breeze from the backyard blows in, carrying tobacco smoke with it. Because even though you can smoke up in here, you can't smoke cigs, which is this rule everyone has always seemed to agree on but that never made any sense to me.

Since there's a game on the pool table, Kris and I stand on the side and wait for winners. A few minutes later she's shifting from foot to foot, checking her cell, and sighing. Kris might be a natural with the crowded-keg-dance-party set, but she gets antsy in closed spaces like the cave.

"Why don't you grab a cue?" I motion to the stacked rack behind her.

She flips her cell in her hand and shakes her head. "Way too close to a weapon. Especially when your best *non*friend is sitting within striking distance."

My nonfriend. Hudson. He must be on the couch behind me, the one near the bar. I want to see him. But I also want to ignore him. For all the times he walked by me in the hall like I wasn't there. For all the days he never gave me a chance to explain.

Kris checks her phone. This time it's glowing.

"'Bout time," she says, tapping her thumbs against the small, bright screen. "Jim's here. He's meeting me in the garden." Kris sends the text, glances over my right shoulder, where I imagine Hudson must be, then turns her attention back to me. "You want to come with?"

Kris doesn't really want me to join her and Jim, but she doesn't want to leave me with Hudson, either. Not after what she watched me go through last year, when he hooked up with Jolene and stopped talking to me. Kris's phone buzzes. Her eyes flash back to the screen.

"It's cool," I say. "Go."

Kris hands me her beer, then slides a smoke from her soft pack into the V of her fingers and lifts it to her lips. But I can still see her frowning.

"Okay," she says, stepping past the pool table. "If you insist. Meet me in forty-five minutes. I might even make it home on time." She sounds like she doesn't care, but she does. Her parents are cool, but they're hard-core about curfew. Not that she's ever given them any reason to be worried. They just have this constant fear that Kris is going to turn into her Phish-following, drugged-out, hippie older sister. Even though Kris doesn't do any drugs. Not even weed, which barely counts.

"Forty-five it is," I say, slipping Kris's cup into my empty one.

Kris gives me a last look and a half smile before she pushes through the wrought-iron door.

Then I'm alone. At a party. With a beer in my hand. I should feel naked and nervous. But I don't. I feel a twinge instead, behind my heart, where the fear should be. A twinge that lets me know it's gone. For now. So I do what everyone else is doing. I bring the cup to my lips for a sip, but since I don't realize how full Kris's cup is, warm beer splashes over the rim and onto my nose. I lean over, wipe the beer from my face, and laugh. And while my hand is over my open mouth, I see him.

Hudson is sitting on the far couch, staring at me. His mouth is set in a grim line. His fingers spread, clutching the knee of his jeans. I still don't know whether he's happy or pissed or what direction he wants this night to go in, but I've come this far. I'm not going to stop now. My hand tightens around the cup. It crackles as I cross the room.

When I'm a step away, Hudson breaks our gaze. He looks toward the bar and, with a quick nod, curls a dark hair behind his ear.

I look, too, and catch the last trace of concern fade from Cal's face as he turns back to his crowd with a cocked eyebrow, a brown bottle, and a joke.

"Can I sit?"

Hudson motions to the empty space next to him.

The seat is a few inches lower than I think, so when I finally sink into it, I fall a bit, spilling even more of my beer. I wipe at the drops on my jeans.

Hudson doesn't notice. He's rolling the loose white thread at the knee of his jeans and stealing glances at Cal, who's setting up the shot glasses at the bar in some kind of pyramid. Cal's always been a showman. Between him and Bella, this party basically has professional entertainment.

"You and Cal are still close," I say, figuring it's a safe place to start. But I know I'm wrong as soon as I see the deep crease form between Hudson's eyes.

"Some people stick around," he says. The beer turns sour in my mouth. He's still angry.

This was a mistake.

I'm about to get up when I feel a tap on my shoulder.

I jump in my seat, until I realize it's just the guy to my left, offering me a hit.

"I'm cool," I tell him as I take the pipe and pass it to Hudson. He passes it to the girl on his right, who nods yes, takes a huge hit, then proceeds to have a hacking fit, the kind where you cough and cough and cough and can't catch your breath. She shakes her head and, still coughing, passes it to the next person. When the music changes, Hudson and I speak at the same time.

Me: "I'll leave you alo—"

Hudson: "Want to get out of here?"

It's what we always said to escape from parties. Neither of us liked being around so many people. But why would he say it now when, obviously, he's mad at me? Why would he ask me to talk when he's been ignoring me for more than a year?

When I don't answer immediately, Hudson wipes his palm

on the knee of his jeans. "I mean, it's cool if you don't want to." He brushes another stray curl from his face and tucks it behind his ear.

I'm still having trouble speaking, but now it's not because I don't know what to say. It's because the words rise up in me too quickly—the explanation I never got to give; the things I wanted to scream the day I saw him walk into school with Jolene, wait at her locker, hold her hand, and pretend his fingers hadn't run through my hair a week before. I waited, day after day, but I never got a chance to say them. Now they're as familiar to me as my jeans, and just as worn. But here he is. Right in front of me. And I'm angry, too. I could do it. I could tell him he doesn't matter to me, that he barely exists, that when I see him, I see nothing at all.

But I'd be lying.

"There's a guest room on the other side of the basement," I say, standing up. "Follow me."

CHAPTER 5

HUDSON FOLLOWS ME out of the cave, past the flip-cup game, the Ping-Pong table, the couches, and the flat screen. I don't look over when people scream and throw their hands up in victory or turn when they laugh at something on TV. I just stare straight ahead at the door on the far end of the basement and picture what's behind it: two bedrooms on the left, both small and blue and traditional, and one on the right, enormous, with lavender walls and an attached bathroom. It's hard to forget the bathroom. It has shell-shaped soap, shell-patterned hand towels, and a glass-door shower with shell etchings. Or, at least, it used to.

I push open the door and step into the dark hallway. Hudson follows me, shutting out the sound and light from the rest of the basement with a soft click. I flatten my palm against the side of the wall and slide it around, searching for the switch. It should be right here, but for some reason I can't find it. The farther I reach, the faster I breathe. Hudson must hear me, because by the time I finally find the switch, so does he. Our fingers meet. I feel high—dizzy, disoriented, like I'm spinning. And it's not from the secondhand smoke or the warm beer. It's him. In the dark. On the fringe. It's how we've always been.

The first time Hudson held my hand was on a Saturday night, sophomore spring. Cal's parents were out, so he threw a party at his duplex. And since Cal was friends with pretty much everyone, the place was packed. Kris was with Jim. Bella was dancing. Cal was bartending. Jolene was off with her latest plaything—each boy fell hard, then fell away. Jolene always came back to me. But she wasn't finished yet, so I did what I'd always done at parties: I searched for a corner, a place away from all the noise and voices, to wait for her. I found it in a small den off the living room, lit blue by a finished movie. That's where I found Hudson, too.

He was sitting on the couch, running his thumb over the ink he'd penned on the rubber strip that lined the side of his sneaker, like he was by himself instead of at a party. I sat down next to him. We didn't talk at first. It wasn't what either of us had gone in there for. But after a little while he looked at me (steadily, studiously) for so long, it started to feel like he was the only person in the world who'd ever *seen* me. I'd caught him looking at me before, a few times in the hall, but it had never felt like this.

When Hudson finally spoke (his thumb never leaving the side of his sneaker), he asked me about loyalty, whether or not I thought it existed. I took my time answering, the way I imagined he did, choosing each word, and each person who heard it, only after careful scrutiny. I said I hoped loyalty did exist. He said he hoped so, too, but that it was hard to believe in when your mom—the person who is supposed to be there no matter what, the one who's supposed to keep promises—just up and leaves, and all that's left of her is boxes. What does that do to loyalty, he wanted to know. Promises?

I shook my head, said I didn't know. He said he didn't know, either. Then he kept working on his sneaker. And I kept sitting with him. And the sitting was a kind of speaking, too. Just being together. We sat as music swelled and glasses spilled and words slurred in the other room, as kisses finished and doors opened and girls went in search of their best friends. We sat until the party began to feel far, foreign, a forgotten star. We sat until Hudson wasn't the distant one anymore; they were. Then I felt his fingers run lightly across my knuckles, draw circles on the inside of my palm, thread between mine, and settle into the grooves, like they'd always been there.

We flip the switch and blink.

"Sorry," I say.

"No worries." He takes his hand off mine. He's still looking at me, though, waiting. And it takes me one, two, three counts of staring back at him until I realize I'm leading. He doesn't know where he's going.

"It's this way," I say. I close my fingers over my thumbs and fight the memory as I walk down the hall and swing open the door to the lavender room.

"Interesting," Hudson says, pausing in front of the enormous bed.

I forgot about the bed.

Hudson shifts his weight and brushes a nonexistent hair behind his ear.

I bypass the lavender canopy and decorative pillows on my

way to the reading chair in the corner.

"What?" I ask, in a lame attempt to make light of the massive mattress. "Your room's not like this?" I try for a smile, but the corners of my mouth sink as soon as I lift them. Hudson and I never made it to his room. We met on stoops and sidewalks and driveways. We talked about family and fear. Loyalty. For a few months we shared things that felt more intimate than kissing (which we did) and more sacred than sex (which we didn't).

And for fifteen months we haven't talked at all.

I slip off my shoes, sit down, and fold my legs under me, as if by making myself small somehow I can shrink the room and transform the bed into the couch off Cal's living room, where it was small and dark enough for us to be honest.

"Not quite." Hudson runs his finger along the metal bed frame as he walks across the room. He sits down on the wide, white cushioned chair opposite me.

We listen to the tread of feet above us, a smattering of dull thumps on the ceiling. Soon my heart joins in, thudding for each second I don't say the words swelling in my chest and screaming in my head. But after nearly a year and a half of being ignored by him, and ignoring almost everyone myself, I'm good at holding my tongue.

Hudson stares at the loose laces of his Vans, runs his fingers inside the loops. I sink farther into my chair. Voices drift in from the hallway. A high giggle. A deep murmur.

A door shuts.

The longer we sit, the more I get used to it.

The silence stretches, tethers us together. And as I sit here, with the hum of the bass above me, in Hudson's company, the more my anger wears away. Being with him stops feeling strange.

"Why are you here?" Hudson asks finally.

I sit up in the chair. "You asked if I wanted to get out of there."

"No, not in this room. Why are you here? Tonight?" Hudson slings his sneaker over the worn knee of his jeans and leans the full weight of his gaze on me. As if the blue of his eyes, or the way they crinkle at the sides, will act like some sort of truth serum.

"The bonfire," I tell him. "Didn't want to miss it."

"You didn't want to miss a bunch of people you don't like, doing something you'd rather ditch?" Hudson drops his eyes and starts tracing the hand-drawn letters scrawled across his sneaker. My heart pangs at the familiar pose.

"Unlikely," he concludes.

"Why do *you* think I'm here?" I ask him.

"Don't know." He shrugs. "Why are you here tonight? Why weren't you there last year? I've stopped trying to figure you out."

Guilt seeps, thick and viscous, through my chest. It was slow, getting to know Hudson. Every word was earned. Each confidence a gift. But losing him, that was easy.

Quick.

"Kris needed me."

Hudson's hand hovers over his sneaker.

"*I* needed you." Each word is quiet, clipped. The same way he sounded the night of the manhunt game. *Meet me,* he'd said, mouth pressed close to the phone. *Promise.*

But I wasn't there.

I clutch the arms of my chair and think about Jolene, bare shouldered and buzzed on the couch upstairs, waiting for him.

"Seems like Jolene was a decent stand-in."

Hudson sinks back in his seat and stares at a point in midair, as if Jolene's sitting here, between us.

I look in the same direction.

"She was there." He casts a quick glance my way, drops his crossed leg to the floor, and runs his hands up and down the thighs of his jeans. "She got what I was going through."

The back of my throat burns. Jolene didn't *get* him. I *gave* him to her. She drew him out of me on so many June afternoons. Word by word. Story by story. I told her how he hated to talk on the phone. How his hand felt in the dark and his skin smelled up close. How his mom had left and his dad was drinking, picking fights with him. How he was shy, then bold, closed, but opening. I talked and talked and talked, and she ingested everything I said until it was hers, and so was he.

"At least she did back then," he says.

"And now?" I ask tentatively.

"Now? I don't know." Hudson tenses at some memory, like it physically pains him. I don't know what he's thinking, but I don't have to. I know Jolene. I've got plenty of my own scars itching to open up and bleed.

"I shouldn't have mentioned her," I say. "Sorry."

"No, it's okay," he says, and sighs, resigned. "That's why I broke up with her."

"No shit," I exclaim. The idea of Hudson, or anyone, willfully disobeying Jolene seems completely impossible to me.

"Shit," he confirms, rolling a stray strip of sneaker rubber between his fingers.

And then everything about tonight falls into place. Why Hudson was hanging back in the shadows at the bonfire. Why he told me I was blowing his cover. It wasn't just about him keeping the usual distance from everything. It was because he didn't want Jolene to see him.

"Don't act so surprised," he continues. "It's not like I'm the first person to walk away from her."

I lower my eyebrows. He raises his.

"Really?" he asks. I shake my head. I don't know what he means.

Hudson props his elbows on his knees and leans his whole body toward me. "You didn't just leave me that night. You left her, too."

I left *her*.

Technically, he's right. I walked away from Jolene. Twice. But it didn't feel like leaving. It felt like being bent. Like breaking.

"Hey," he says, his voice closer to me now, so close I can smell his breath—the mix of mint and beer. "Are you okay?"

My hands are shaking. Hudson takes them in his and tightens his grip until they're still.

"Thanks," I say, staring at his hands, how they cover mine completely.

"It's cool," he says. And for a second I worry he's going to take his hands away, but he doesn't. Instead he runs his thumbs up and down the insides of my wrists.

Now that my hands are still, the rest of me trembles.

Until heavy thuds beat down on us, shaking the ceiling and swaying the chandelier. The dance party must have started. Either that or a stampede—people running from the police. I stiffen again. Hudson's grip tightens. I can feel the curve of his silver ring on my wrist.

We look up. Listen. The heavy thuds settle into a rhythm. So it's dancing then, not a signal to escape. We're safe. I relax my hands into his.

"I still can't believe you left," he says under his breath.

Something plummets in the pit of my stomach. Even here, with my hands in his, even now that I've told him Kris needed me—he's still angry.

"Look, I know I didn't show up for you, and that I stopped speaking to Jolene that night, too, and that you guys probably bonded over how much you hated me; but whatever Jolene told you, whatever she said, it isn't—"

The burn from my throat has climbed to my eyes. I blink.

Hudson squeezes my hands. When I look up at him, his eyes are clear—blue water, sparkling. "Jolene told me you left. Nothing else." Of course. She didn't have to say anything else. Breaking my promise to Hudson, not showing up for him right after his mom left, would have been enough, and she knew it. "I was pissed," he says with a quick breath and a small nod to himself. "But now I get it."

"Get what?" I still haven't told him *why* Kris and I left. But before I get a chance, Hudson lowers his head to our hands and takes a breath, then blows it out through the tight circle of his lips. It warms our fingers.

"You left with Kris."

"Yes, and—"

"You stuck with her."

"Yeah."

He lifts his lips from our hands, but not enough for me to

see his face; only that he's nodding again.

"I would have done the same thing. For Cal, I mean. If he needed me. That's loyalty." Hudson looks up, finally. I can see the brown specks in his eyes, like markers on a map I have memorized. "And the rest," he says. The rest. There is so much more. Hudson still doesn't know what Jolene did. "—how you guys unplugged from everything. No parties, no posting. You two didn't join in, and you didn't give a shit. That was hard-core," he says solemnly. "Brilliant, really."

My thoughts of Jolene and Kris get cut off.

Hudson thinks I'm brilliant. And even though I know he's wrong, that he's making history into fiction, I don't stop him. Because I like his version so much better than reality. I want to hear more about the me that he sees.

"Really?" I ask.

"Yeah."

In the few seconds that follow, there is only the sound of our breaths, the feel of his hands, the dig of his ring. Hudson studies me: cheeks, nose, neck, and eyes in quick succession.

"I'm not her," I say, chin up, back straight. *See me,* I think. *Choose me.* I wait, and so do the dull thuds above us. It's like time is suspended, until he leans into me and whispers:

"That's the point."

Hudson runs his thumb along my cheek, above my chin, across the length of my bottom lip, and pauses. I dip my head into the curve of his neck and brush my lips against his skin. Not quite a kiss. More like a memory. It was my favorite place on him. And it's there, burrowed in the familiar winter scent of him—as Hudson runs his hands up my neck and through my hair, as he sifts his fingers through the strands and tugs on them just enough to lift my head until we're facing—that I lose my sense of time and place.

Then my phone rings.

Kris. *Shit.*

I freeze. Hudson and I are tense and tangled, holding each other tight; but with each ring, the room comes back to me: the metal headboard, the crystal chandelier, the lavender walls, the glass end tables. My phone, still ringing. I should be reaching for it. I have to reach for it. But I've crossed a line, and I'm not sure how to get back. I want to talk to Kris, but I don't want her to tell me this is a mistake. I'm still trying to decide what to do—take my hand off Hudson's neck or put it farther into his hair—when the ringing stops.

I exhale.

Hudson untangles himself, but his eyes never leave me. Instead he drops his chin and lowers his forehead until it's resting lightly against mine. A stray strand of his hair falls against my face. I can't feel anything but the one spot where we're touching. I can't think anything but *It's not enough.* For over a year I've waited, stepped aside like a swinging door, while Jolene walked down the halls with him—with everything we could have been. And all that time, this is what I was missing. This is what she took from me.

Now I'm taking it back.

"Stay with me," he says. And I do.

CHAPTER 6

AFTER SAYING GOOD-BYE to Hudson behind Bella's house, I can still feel his imprint on my collarbone, cheek, and chin, like bruises. Not because he kissed me—we never made it past almost—but from the way he held me. (Head on my shoulder. Nose to my neck. Palms pressed flat to my back.) The spots where our skin met are tender, cold when the air blows over them. Pieces of my hair whip across my face. I sweep them out of my eyes and look down the long, winding driveway.

No sign of Kris. She's probably superpissed, and she has every right to be. I didn't answer the phone. I can't believe I didn't answer the phone. And now she's not answering hers. My stomach twists. I have to find her. I have to tell her.

I have to tell her about him.

And that's where I get stuck. Because I should want to tell her. She's my secret keeper, my mind reader. I should want to tell her everything. But I don't. For the same reason I didn't pick up the phone—because it was this perfect moment, and she would have ruined it. Which seems impossible. Kris makes everything better. But I can already see the steely way she'll look at me when I mention Hudson. She'll say she warned me. She'll be disappointed. And that's not how I want to feel. I want to be happy.

I turn back toward the house. It looks deserted from down here. Dark. Quiet. I'm about to start back up the steps when I see a flicker of white in the window above me. I stop, look again, but there's nothing. Then the window flashes pink, then green, then blue. A dozen hands pump the air. Great. I'm going to have to walk through a late-night dance party to find Kris. Can't wait.

Just then a few senior guys stumble by—the flip-cup players—shirt collars ringed with beer and sweat, fleeces unzipped, hats low over their faces. A girl in hot-pink heels follows, slipping on the final step. She catches herself at the last second, puts her arm out to steady herself, then pulls at her miniskirt. The guys don't turn around. "Hey, wait up!" she calls, running after them. Her heels hit the pavement hard: *click, click, click, click.*

Eventually the sound of heels disappears, but my heart picks up the beat. If Kris did stay to wait for me, it means she'll miss curfew. I look at my watch. She's got ten minutes. If she's even a second late, her parents will totally lose it—take her phone, computer, maybe even her car. Because of me.

I look up at the house. The dark window, the pumping arms, the flashing lights. Then I push off my right foot and take the steps two at a time.

I don't pause at the kitchen. I don't worry about how I look leaning up against the cup-covered counter or care that my sneakers squeak and stick to the floor. I scan the faces as quickly as I can—a few junior guys from drama and some sophomore girls spilling liquor and loud cackles. Kris isn't here. I walk past the tapped keg, through the living room, to the dance floor. The dining room is all lights and music. A disco strobe hangs from the chandelier. Pop music pumps from the wall-mounted surround sound. Everyone jumps to the beat. I squint into the pulsing light.

Pink. Black. Green. Black. Blue. Black.

No red curls.

I shoulder my way off the dance floor, cross back through the living room, and slip through the vanishing door. My blood pumps as I skip down the stairs as quickly as I can without slipping. I search the basement, the cave, even the spare bedroom Hudson and I were in; but everywhere I look, people are smoking, slurring, hooking up. I shove past them, across the cave again, out through the iron gate, and into the secret garden, as if somehow Kris will be waiting for me in the exact place I left her. As if time hasn't moved forward. As if I never brought Hudson into that room. But when the iron door clangs shut behind me, Kris isn't there, either, and the couple smoking next to the trellis, talking in hushed tones now that I'm here, is proof that time didn't stop. It passed. It's still passing.

I find the door to the ivy-covered gate surrounding the secret garden but miss the handle and end up slamming into sculpted metal. I ignore the pain in my face, chest, knee as I turn the handle and push through the door properly this time.

"Who was that?" the smoking guy asks as the gate swings shut behind me.

"You don't remember her?" the girl asks, voice dripping with disbelief. "Last year she—"

I shove the words away and climb the steep slope to the main yard. Then I skip up the wood steps to the deck, but it's empty. So is the hot tub. There are bubbles in it, but not because the jets are on. There's an open bottle of gin, a pair of boxers, and a blow-up crocodile drifting in the water, which has a green tint. I head back down the steps, around the pool, and across the lawn. The grass is hard and stiff. It crunches beneath my sneakers as I pick my way past shadowed groups of people and peer behind bushes.

"What the fuck?"

"Sorry," I say, "looking for somebody."

After a few more of those episodes, I reach the back of the yard. I'm ready to give up and call my mom for a ride—not cool, but not a death sentence, either, since she's told me to do exactly this if everybody's drunk and I need a lift—until I hear a group of guys behind the last row of bushes wondering out loud what they can do to some poor girl.

"You see that G-string? Fuck-me red, man. She wants it." The voice is slick, low, boasting. But even through a row of bushes I can tell it's not entirely confident. I step closer, try to peek through the needles; but the bush is wide, thick. I can see only baggy jeans, cargo pants, and between them a set of long, honey-colored legs.

"Try a girl who's conscious first, freak. You wouldn't even know what to do with her." This guy's smiling; I can tell without seeing him. He's the leader, or at least a step above the first kid. I inch closer, push a branch aside.

"Screw you," the first guy says, sullen.

"That's not just any girl right there, though," says a third voice, smooth, easy. Someone who doesn't care, not enough to stop the first two, anyway.

"No it isn't," the second voice says, slow, like he's tasting each word, and enjoying it.

I push my face forward, into the needles. That's when I see her: mouth open, eyes closed, cream-colored shirt slipping off her bony shoulder; brown hair spread out on the lawn chair, like her legs; three juniors circling her like vultures.

"That's Jolene," he continues. "Senior meat. The sweetest. And pretty much untouchable. Well, most of the time."

I shove the branches aside and push myself through the sharp twigs and prickly needles. For a second I'm inside the bush, and then I'm out again. The junior guys aren't staring at Jolene anymore; they're looking at me, which makes sense, I guess. This is probably the only way I could win a contest between the two of us. She's passed out, and I just walked out of a tree.

I brush a few needles from my face and push my hair behind my ears.

"Am I interrupting something?" I ask, hip to the side, glare in my eyes.

"Who the hell are you?" guy #2 says. He's all cocky confidence. He steps toward me, to let me know how tall he is, how popular. Like I care. I don't have anything left to lose in that area. I gave it all up a long time ago, but he doesn't know that. He doesn't remember me. But I remember him. He's on the soccer team. I've seen him with Hudson and Cal in the hallways and practicing at the park.

"You don't need to know who I am," I say. "Cal's looking for you." The lie is easy enough. I keep my eyes fixed and still, tilt my head, raise my eyebrows. Cal is the cocaptain of the soccer team and Hudson's best friend. He wouldn't be pleased with this scene. And #2 knows it.

"Yeah, well," he says, looking me up and down, the trail of his eyes sticky and thick like an oil slick. I let him look, just like Jolene would. I smile at him until he pushes past me. "We were just leaving anyway."

The other two follow him. When I can't hear them laughing anymore, I drop the act. My hands shake. So does my breath. I stare at Jolene, who's still sprawled across the lawn chair. If I hadn't been here . . . But I haven't been here for over a year. Has this happened before? I swallow back the taste of bile in my mouth and bury the thought. If something that bad had happened—to Jolene, of all people—I would have heard about it. That's the kind of story that flattens the forest.

I lift Jolene's arm and lay it next to her on the chair, clearing a space so I can sit down and get my shit together. I can't leave her back here. The same thing could happen again. And no matter what she's done, I can't let it.

I scoot down until I'm near her waist and push her legs together. She moves. I jump back, startled, like she just woke from the dead. She murmurs, rolls onto her side, lays her legs on top of each other, and curls up in a ball like she's home in her bed.

I look at Jolene. Really look. Since I spend most of my time avoiding her these days, it feels strange. So I start with the most familiar parts, her landmarks: the small scar on her neck from her half of the cracked necklace; the dimple in her ear from that third earring hole she always hoped would close up but stayed there instead, as if her body refuses to let her forget, as if it's just as stubborn as she is.

Then my eyes travel down, to the hem of her skirt and the length of her legs. Even her feet are pretty, fit into ridiculous shoes for this weather. The fact that she's wearing a skirt is bad enough, but sandals?

She must be freezing. I have to get her up.

I press my palms to her cheeks. "Jolene," I say, shaking her face. When she doesn't respond, I shake her harder. "Jolene!" I say again, louder now. "Wake up!"

Her eyelids flutter. She tries to lift her head, but it falls back against the hand I've slid beneath it.

"Hudson," Jolene mumbles, and my body goes numb. She knows what I did, that I was with him. "It's me," she insists. "Don't leave." She thrashes her arms in the air. Her right hand smacks me in the chest. When it connects, her eyes fly open. The whites are pink and watery, but the hazel part glistens. "You." She grips my shoulder hard.

I hold my breath. A reflex. From all the times she held me tight: hands under blankets, fingers pinching my nose, palm covering my mouth, glass through my skin. One touch from Jolene and I'm back in that smothering, comforting darkness again, where gills exist and anything is possible.

"I knew it," she says, slurring the words. She's trying to focus on me, but her eyes fight it. They move side to side, in circles, roll back, then down to me again. "I knew you'd come," she says with a sigh as her head falls to the side a final time. Her hand loosens its grip on my shoulder, slides—deadweight—down to my hand, where it slips right in.

Jolene doesn't know about Hudson. She thinks I came for her. And the thing is, no matter how many of her texts I've ignored or months I've put between us, no matter how many times I've told myself I hate her, packed our history away deep inside me, pretended that she'd disappeared; no matter what I told Kris about why we should come out tonight (we couldn't miss our senior bonfire) or what I told myself (we had to do *something* before we graduated and there was nothing left), I can't deny it.

I knew Jolene would be there with her smothering possibilities and tightfisted wishes. This is the night we'd all agreed to meet.

I came for her.

I did.

"Where are your keys?" I ask. She squeezes my hand, pulls it into her stomach, and curls up into a ball again. "Jolene," I say, insistent, "your keys!"

She doesn't move at first, but after a few seconds she drags my fingers across her waist and over her hip, to her back pocket. She presses my hand against her ass. I yank it away before I realize she was showing me her keys. I reach in and tug them out of the tiny pocket.

"Can you walk?" I ask.

"Mmmm," she says, rolling onto her back. Her eyelids are heavy, her smile wide and sloppy. "You."

"Yeah, me," I repeat, whoever that is. I lean down, lift her arm over my shoulder, and hoist her up. Her head falls on my cheek, her hair fans across my chest and back. It still smells like cinnamon, even through the faint scent of vomit. I start walking, but each step over the cold grass is slow. After a few paces I stop for a break, and her right arm, which was slung over my shoulder, bends at the elbow. Her hand lands on my chest.

Jolene took her cut palm off my mouth and pressed it against my chest. I gasped and coughed, gulping air. She laughed again.

"A total rush, right?" she asked.

"No." I rolled away from her in Bella's bed, placing one hand on my breastbone, where Jolene's had been, and the other on my throat, where she'd drawn gills. My blood beat fast in both places.

"Shut up," she said, chin to my shoulder, cheek to my cheek. "You liked it."

"No," I lied. "I like breathing."

Jolene tugged me back around until our noses touched.

"Hey. I'm sorry. You're the one who said you wanted to be something new."

"New, not dead. That was dangerous." I tried to sound angry, but my words lost their edge. I had said it.

What do *you* want to be, Mattie? *Jolene had asked over the sleeping bags. Bella wanted to be on Broadway; Kris wanted to be anywhere but here. I wanted to be something new. Bella had laughed and asked,* Shiny too? *Kris had thrown a pillow at me. Jolene had taken me seriously.*

My body softened next to hers in the bed.

"Anything new feels a little dangerous." Jolene gathered my hand in hers and traced the scab on my palm with her fingertips. "Seriously. It's not like I'd ever actually hurt you." She pulled the blanket back over our heads. "Then who would save me if I tried it for real and my gills didn't come in?" Her words floated in the dark; our hot breath filled the rest of the small space.

"Don't say stuff like that," I said.

"Why? You would save me. Right?" Jolene shifted her hips, sliding her thigh so close to mine, I could feel the curled hem of her cotton boy shorts. "You're probably the only one."

Jolene's parents checked out when she got to high school. Not that they'd ever checked in. Not since I'd known her, anyway. They were always out with friends or away on business. And when they were home, they had their eyes glued to their phones.

"Of course."

She gave my hand a quick pulse. We lay like that—under the covers, breathing each other's breath—for so long that I started to drift off again. And then, just as the real world spun away from me, words, whispered: "I know you will."

I heave her up again and drag her across the neighbor's lawn so no one will see us leave, because she's Jolene, and I'm me, and here we are again: two little girls all alone in the world.

LOT 1
MB:46-665
MB:51-103
60' R/W
YOUNGBLOO

COS.
MB:46-665
MB:51-103
60' R/W
YOUNSBLO

EX. CB

CHAPTER 7

BEFORE OPENING MY eyes the morning after Bella's party, I unstick my tongue from the roof of my mouth and swallow a few times to slick my sore throat. A stuffy darkness swims around me. The insides of my eyelids are a murky midnight blue instead of the orangey-red I usually get from the sunlight streaking in through the blinds. I must have pulled the comforter over my head.

I'm not hungover—at least not from the beer—but I definitely feel a little slow. I lie still for a second, to see if I can drift back into my dream, but then the memory of last night crashes through me, lifting my eyelids and leaving my scalp tingling.

I'm awake. I am so awake.

I pull the covers off my face and blink into the brightness, then roll over and throw my head onto a pillow. Even though the scent of chicken soup and sweet potatoes seeps through the house, I can still smell the night on my hair: Kris's cigs, the burn of the bonfire, the stink of the weed. It would be a deadly combo if not for the hint of Jolene's shampoo and the whiff of pine that clung to Hudson's shirt and skin.

Hudson.

I close my eyes, wishing I could relive the part of the night that starred him, but it's impossible. The sky is bright and clear, I'm alone, and it's Thanksgiving. I can tell from the *ting tang* of silverware being laid out in the dining room—my dad's holiday job—the swing and knock of cabinets opening and closing, and the crash of platters being piled on top of one another.

My mom goes all out at the holidays, even when it's only the three of us. Especially when it's only the three of us. My brother, Jake, is a first-year at his law firm, and he's already warned us he'll be at the office today, and maybe even tonight. Ever since my brother started working in New York City at Clarence and Biddle, he's only made brief appearances at home. So today won't really be different from any other day in this house, except we'll be eating a huge turkey on flowery china with polished silverware and drinking from heavy crystal glasses, all of which have to be washed by hand. And my mom will spend all day cooking and prepping so that she can barely eat with us before she has to get up again and start cleaning.

I sit up and pull my hair into a ponytail, then slide across the sheet and grab my cell from the nightstand. Nothing. I drop back into bed and look up at the poster on my ceiling. My parents got it for me in second grade, the first time I offered them a shortcut across town. It's a cartoon version of Westfield, full of brightly colored, bulbous buildings and that terrible font that's supposed to look like handwriting. I used to stare at it each night—walk the streets, visit the stores, find our house and picture an upside-down version of myself staring back at me.

I've been meaning to take it down for years. Now that I have a real collection, it's easy to see this map is for kids—it doesn't have a legend or a scale or a compass rose; it's not weathered or worn; it doesn't have any original folds. It doesn't color us into a neat, moss-green rectangle and label us Division 14, Block 493. But there it is, above my bed. And here I am, finding our house on Cherokee Court, scanning the streets, tracing my way to Hudson's.

It's too early to hear from him, but I expected something from Jolene, considering she's been texting me once or twice a week for almost a year and a half, despite the fact that I've never replied. I scroll through her messages. A list of one-word locations: *alone, home, lawn, woods*. Pictures of places: a half-open window, a dead-end street, a fish, the cliff. Phrases: *cut myself on our necklace, found something new for my treasure box, know you're reading this.*

I turn off my cell and throw it across the bed. I don't know why I kept those messages. I don't know why Jolene sent them when she had Hudson to share her bed and star in her stories. I should have erased every single one.

If I'm lucky, Jolene won't remember anything about last night: my hands in her hair as she heaved on the street, my arms around her waist to buckle the seat belt, the pillow I slid under her head before slipping off her heels and tucking her in. She'll have blacked it all out, and I can pretend it never happened. Because it shouldn't have. Jolene should have been with Bella, at the party. I should have stayed home, with Kris.

I roll across my bed and pick up my phone again. Still nothing from Kris, which means today is actually different. But not in the happy-smiley-family-togetherness way. This is the longest

Kris and I have gone without talking (or texting or messaging) since the manhunt game.

I really hope she got grounded. I know that's a terrible thing to say, but the alternative is so much worse—that she's so mad she can't bring herself to speak to me. All I have to do is think it, and a hole opens up inside me, hungry and bottomless. It sucks in everything about last night except for this: Kris's call, and me ignoring it. I'm about to text her when I hear the creak of the stairs, followed by the slap of bare feet on the wood floor. The sound stops outside my door, which inches open. My mom peers inside.

"Out late, huh?" She's already digging for information, and I'm not even out of bed.

"Not that late."

"Actually, it *was* pretty late. One, maybe two?" she asks, plucking a shirt from the pile on the floor and starting to fold it. "I was still up watching TV. You know I can't sleep before a holiday."

"Mom, just leave that stuff alone. I can deal with it."

"Well, it's going to get creased, which means I'll have to iron it, so—"

"Just put it down!" She drops it on the floor, pulls in her lips, and straightens her back. And I think she's going to leave, but instead she sits down on my bed, smoothing out the blanket next to me.

"So, what did you guys do last night?" she says, leaning toward me. When she gets close, she wrinkles her nose. "Ugh. I know Kris smokes, but don't you think it smells disgusting?" She flips over my ponytail and starts to separate the strands of my straight hair. I slide my elastic out, and she spreads my hair into pieces on the pillow, then runs her fingers through them, top to bottom, one by one, easing gently through each catch and tangle. I love it when she plays with my hair. I turn toward the window so I'm facing away from her and all my hair is free for her hands, then I press my cheek into the pillow. I curl up, close my eyes, and take a deep breath. There it is again. Winter.

"Yeah," I say softly as she starts a small braid above my right ear. "We went to the bonfire."

"You?"

"Don't sound so shocked."

"I'm just"—her hands freeze in midair around my hair, tugging at a tiny piece of my scalp—"I'm just, you know . . . well, how was it?" Her hands start moving again, and the smooth section drops, finished, to my neck. She collects another strip of hair and starts dividing it.

"It was a huge fire. It was hot," I say, since I've already given up enough. It's not like I'm going to tell her what actually happened. Even though she'd totally die of happiness if I did. For a year she's been crushed that I fell off the rising social track. My mom was a popular girl, back in the day. And she never lets me forget it. Not like I could. She's still got this superfabulous thick, wavy hair that always looks great, even in the morning, and the kind of cheekbones that cut across her face like she's just been airbrushed for the cover of *Cosmo*.

I sit up and take my hair back into my own hands, gathering all the loose pieces and shoving them back inside the elastic. My mom puts her hands in her lap.

"Well, I'm proud of you for going. Good for you," she says, patting the bed by my side.

Proud of me? It's not like I'm such a freak that I can't show my face at some stupid school bonfire. My mom still doesn't get it—that I haven't been to a party in the last year on purpose. That I gave up being popular for a reason. A person.

I bring my knees to my chest, pull my huge sweatshirt over my legs, and hug them tight. She lifts her head and gets this faraway look in her eyes, so I know what's coming next. "I guess it is just a big fire when you get down to it, but it's so exciting too, isn't it? I'll never forget the time all us girls brought a huge cooler full of marshmallows and . . ." Here it is, another amazing story from the high school days.

"I know, I know, you had the best time and the most fun and everybody loved you. I get it, Mom."

"That's not what I said, Maitreya." Now I'm getting the full-name treatment. Great. Next she'll tell me about her honeymoon in Asia, and the Buddha with my name who embodies loving-kindness, so I can see just how far I've strayed from enlightenment.

"Whatever."

My mom takes a deep breath and looks at me hard, like she's going to launch into one of her long, serious explanations of life, when three bright beeps come from the oven timer in the kitchen. Her ear lifts toward the door, then her eyes look back at me, and her forehead creases. I can tell she wants to stay and keep talking, but then her all-important holiday meal might not make it to the table on time, now, would it?

"I've got to put the turkey in, but this conversation isn't over. Let's not forget you broke curfew."

"Which you didn't seem to care about until just this second."

"Oh, I care about it," she says, stepping over mounds of sweaters and scattered papers on her way to the door. She stops with her fingers on the handle. "I just thought if you had an explanation, I might not care about it so much. But since you have yet to give me one, then I most certainly do care." My mom's about to close the door, but at the last second she reaches across my dresser and curls her fingers around the handle of the hot chocolate mug I brought up last night.

"Mom. Leave it!"

"Okay, okay!" she says, her hands in the air, her shoulders hunched. "Come down when you're hungry."

When she's gone, I check my phone again. Still nothing from Kris. If she keeps up the radio silence, I'll have to break it to my parents that she won't be joining us for dessert like she does every year. I can already picture their faces: Mom's down-turned lips, her tilted head, and her tweezed eyebrows angling up to meet each other; Dad's gee-whiz-tough-luck-kiddo look, the one where his lips disappear into the puffed-out skin around them and the dimple on his right cheek pops.

We've got this holiday ritual, Kris and I. We've been doing it since intermediate school. We call it the Holiday Fair Trade Agreement (HaFTA for short). I get to spend the early part of the day at her house—snacking at the buffet table, playing with her never-ending stream of cousins, and chatting with her aunts and uncles—and she gets to finish the day sitting at a civilized table in a quiet house, hanging out with me and my parents.

The thing is, nobody will notice if I don't make it to Kris's. They can barely keep track of each other with so many people and so many rooms. But my parents will definitely notice if Kris doesn't make it here. Especially if Jake isn't around to distract them with stories of how lame high school is (for me), how he's working his ass off to impress some partner at the best law firm in the city (for my parents), and how kick-ass he is in general (for himself). If my parents find out Kris isn't coming, they'll want to know why. They'll want to know what happened. And there's no way I'm telling them. I've already got this gaping hole of guilt in my gut. I don't need any extra from them, thanks.

I pick up my phone. I'm sending Kris one last text. She may be grounded for life, and she's probably pissed, but I still can't believe she'd totally ditch me on Thanksgiving. I put my cell back on the nightstand and stare at it for a second, in case she replies right away, but it doesn't buzz.

So I walk over to my desk and roll open the lower drawer. It's filled to the brim with paper ranging in age and shades, from brightest white to muddy yellow—my maps. At least the ones that aren't framed already or mounted on acid-free paper and tacked to my walls. I've been collecting and creating them since second grade, when we took a class trip to the Miller-Cory House, which is one of those museums where people dressed in colonial costumes show you how to churn butter. On our way out that day, a woman in a cape and a bonnet handed me a pamphlet that mapped the West Fields of 1740, which, at the time, wasn't much more than a midpoint between New York and Philadelphia. I still have that one, actually. The paper used to be smooth and slick. Now it's a soft memory, shiny from finger oil, feathered and peeling at the white folds, sitting at the bottom of my drawer.

After washing last night's smoke and dirt from my fingers, I gingerly lift the top layers of stained paper from the stack and set aside the acid-free buffers that separate them. These maps aren't originals, of course—those are preserved—but I still have to be careful. They were printed in 1901, the same year as the originals, and on the same type of wood-pulp paper. It's the paper that gives them that smell: a mix of must and leather, with a hint of grass and something acidic when you put your nose to it.

I found them last summer, during my daily eBay estate-sale search. As soon as I saw the crisp lines, block letters, pastel shading, and numeric labels, I knew they were Sanborns. But instead of showing the whole town, like the 1921 map hanging above my bed, these sheets divide Westfield into sections.

I lay them out in order: sheets one, two, three, four, five. I'm still looking for the sixth. I know it exists. I've seen it online at the Library of Congress site and the Rutgers Cartography Libraries, where the Sanborn Map Company's archives have been digitized.

The maps are so damaged from sitting in the seller's damp attic, I try not to touch them any more than I have to. But sometimes I can't help it. My fingers linger, skim their thin paper-skin. Truth is, I actually like the stains and folds and bleeds of ink from the things that were pressed against them. Not just because it's the only way I could have afforded them, but because you can see and feel the years they've lived. Their history is visible. Until I restack the maps and buffers, set them gently on top of the rest of my collection, and roll the drawer closed.

I cast another glance at my nightstand, but my cell hasn't buzzed or rung or played the whistling theme song Kris thumbed in when I got it a year ago. It's just sitting there, still and useless. So I do the only thing that's left. I clean my room.

But a few hours later, after I've cleared the floor, folded the shirts, and shut the drawers; after I've cleaned my desk and rotated my hanging maps and made my bed; after I've reorganized the books on my shelf, not by title or author or subject, but in which order I read them, I still don't feel better. Everything is organized, but nothing feels neat. And that's because no matter what I do to this room, it won't change anything. Color coding my shirts won't make Kris call. Changing the map placement on my walls won't make Hudson pick up the phone. I can't put everything back in order.

I check my cell one more time, just to make absolutely sure I didn't miss a text, then slip it into the pocket of my sweatshirt and head downstairs, where the air is thick with garlic, green beans, chicken soup, and stuffing. No need to tell my parents about Kris. No need to tell them anything just yet.

CHAPTER 8

TWO COURSES, THREE kinds of potatoes, four side dishes, and one twenty-pound turkey later, we're all silent and stuffed. I mean, seriously, we're only three people. My brother called right before we sat down to tell us that he wasn't going to make it for dinner, but he'd try for dessert. He said he absolutely had to stay because the partner wanted him there, and it was the kind of opportunity you just couldn't pass up. My dad's chin got so tight and narrow that it pushed up his bottom lip until he let out a loud sigh and shrugged his shoulders, like *What are you gonna do?* And my mom's gray eyes looked stormy and sad, until she snapped out of it and announced, "At least Jake'll be here for the best part of the meal!" Because she believed him. Even though he's not going to show up. He never does.

I mean, I get it—why my parents want Jake home. I can't tell hilarious stories about pranks I've pulled and games I've won. But I'm here, aren't I? And he's not. I don't know why my mom can't just accept it and get on with her life.

After carrying some dishes to the sink, I duck into the bathroom and slip my phone out of my jeans. Still nothing from Hudson. I suck it up and send him a text. I write something simple. Short. Casual. It takes me so long to come up with that perfect tone, my parents have completely cleared the table by the time I'm finished. I read over the message as my phone attempts to send it:

Am so over Thanksgiving. Brainstorming covert missions to make it through dessert. You?

It's okay. Not great, but not terrible, either.

My mom calls me to help in the kitchen before the message sends.

By the time we set the table for dessert, it's late—we waited an extra hour for Jake, who—surprise, surprise—didn't show up. We're tired, and the hushed roar of football is the only noise in the house. This is when Kris usually walks in, telling some crazy Thanksgiving tale, like the one about her cousins who wrestled each other into the kitchen and knocked the cranberry sauce onto the dog. And from then on it's all jokes and stories and laughing so hard, our ice cream dribbles off our spoons and onto our chins. But tonight she's not here, either.

And somehow my mom was so busy cooking and my dad was so busy snoring in front of the TV that they didn't even realize I sat in my room all day, drafting my own version of the missing sheet from the 1901 map. That I never went over to Kris's place. That I never went anywhere. So after my mom lays out the fruit platter, the pumpkin pie, a Thanksgiving-themed Jell-O mold, and two kinds of ice cream, she looks over to the fourth plate, then she looks at me. And I know what she's going to say.

"Where's Kris?" she asks, resting her hand on the back of the dining-room chair. Since she doesn't sit, neither do we. All three of us stand around a table full of desserts and softening ice cream.

"Oh, she's not coming," I say. "That pie really looks delicious, Mom. What flavor is the ice cream?"

"Thanks, honey. I bought vanilla bean for you. She's not coming?"

"Nope."

"Did you two have a fight?"

"Nope." Technically, that's true. No fight. No nothing. I'm just a terrible friend. I tap my fingers on the back of the chair. "Can we sit down?"

"Of course we can," my father says. "Diane, come on. Sit. You've been on your feet all day. What have we got here, vanilla bean and Swiss almond? My favorite," he says, scooping his own spoon right into the Swiss almond pint. "Mmmmm." He scrapes the floor with his chair, then sort of falls down into it and serves himself a huge bowl of ice cream. Now that he's down, I sit too, even though my mom's still standing, looking my way.

"You sure you're okay?" my mom says, pulling at her necklace. "Nothing you want to talk about?"

"Nope. Can you pass the fruit?"

"Sure," she says. But she doesn't pass it. She walks around the table to where I'm sitting and stops behind me, setting a hand on my shoulder. Then she places the bowl next to my plate. I dig out the strawberries and blueberries with the huge serving spoon. She's still standing behind me when we hear an engine and see two beams of light swipe across the dark backyard. Jake. He actually made it.

The weight lifts from my shoulder, and my mom begins flitting around the kitchen like a fly to get him a piece of turkey, a spoon of stuffing, a scoop of potatoes—bits of the dinner he missed. By the time the door cracks, she's got her arm outstretched and her cheek in the air for a kiss. Jake shakes off the cold and shucks his black overcoat, laying it over Mom's arm as Dad claps him solidly on the back. While he passes out kisses and apologies, I check my phone under the table. I have a fail message. The text to Hudson never went through. I resend it, but it fails again. So I try his old email address. It bounces back. What the hell?

"What's wrong with you?" Jake's at the table now. His stubbled cheek is rosy from the cold and rounded over a bite of turkey. "Did you get weird while I was gone?" He points his fork at me.

"I'm not weird." I lay my phone in my lap and push the fruit around on my plate. Could Hudson have changed his number? The one I used is from last year.

"Well, you're not acting normal," he says. Jake is eight years older than I am. His normal used to be fixing my Easy-Bake oven and building me pillow forts. Then he started high school, and it switched to soccer and the same party every weekend, where everyone adored him. Now it's working his way up at the best law firm in New York by putting in long hours and telling all the stories in his arsenal, which are endless and always nab laughs.

Not exactly my kind of normal.

I narrow my eyes at him. He opens his wide.

"Okay, okay." Mom cuts us off. "Jake," she says, with a tip of her head and a saccharine edge, "tell us what's going on!"

"Yeah. How are things at the firm?" my dad asks, leaning over the table to cut himself a piece of pie. "They still working you to the bone?"

That's all Jake needs. He launches into some story. And just this once, I appreciate Jake's ability to dominate dessert, or anything at all for that matter.

I lean back in my chair and sneak glances at my lap, where I left my phone.

Just when I've given up on hearing from Kris—it's been over twenty-four hours since we spoke, which is like a year in me-and-Kris time—my cell buzzes.

```
As my last sanctioned electronic communication
for an entire week, I'm texting you, even though
I'm still officially pissed. What happened last
night? Everything cool? Tell me Monday morning,
when I get released for school.
```

Monday morning. That seems like years away. Kris and I usually see each other every day, especially over break. But it's okay, as long as she doesn't hate me. At least not yet. She still doesn't know what happened. . . .

"So, everything's okay with you and Kris?" My mom leans forward, arm outstretched, and stabs one of my strawberries.

"I said it was, didn't I?" I slide my plate away from her. "Anyway, it's not even about her. I have more than one friend, Mom."

"Good," she says, setting down her fork on her napkin. Drops of red juice spot the white linen. "You should. I mean, you know I love Kris, but being friends with her doesn't mean you can't be friends with anyone else."

Actually, that's exactly what it means. But I don't bother correcting her.

She spears another one of my strawberries, then stands up and stacks the dirty plates as Jake and my dad start getting into it about the long haul to law firm partnership and whether or not it's worth it. They've had this conversation before. My dad used to work at a firm, too, before he went in-house for a software company. I push my chair away from the table. It scrapes the floor, but that doesn't interrupt them. Jake keeps talking, my dad keeps listening, and I make my way to my room while my mom's still chewing on my strawberry.

"Hey," Jake says, pushing open my bedroom door a few hours later.

"Knock much?" I ask. He's still in his suit. It looks weird to me, even though I know he wears it every day. In my head, he's always in a concert tee and jeans.

"Talk much?" He leans against the doorframe but doesn't come in.

"No one talks as much as you," I say, putting my phone down next to me on the bed.

"No one else has as much to say." He crosses his arms and smiles.

I roll my eyes. "Are you staying?" Even though Jake is totally full of himself, it wouldn't suck to have him around for a few days. When he got all popular in high school, he'd still stay home with me sometimes. We'd watch movies, listen to music. Last year when he came home from law school, we even smoked together. But I didn't get high, since it was my first time. Jake said it usually took a few tries.

"Nope," he says, standing up straight again. "Gotta go. But I'll be back Saturday for the game."

"What game?" I ask him.

Jake shakes his head. "Seriously, little sister, you need to get out more." He checks his watch. It's thick and gold. We used to have identical diving watches until he started working. "The soccer game. Alumni versus varsity. Saturday after Thanksgiving, every year. I'm not playing—wouldn't want to hurt anyone or anything—but people will be there. I'm guessing you won't?"

"I've got better things to do than watch you chug beer," I say, wishing it were true.

"Your loss," he says as he walks down the hall. "Take a shower, by the way. You reek."

"Leave!" I call out to him. And he does.

Later that night I lie in bed, listening to the rush of water from the kitchen sink downstairs, the careful *clink* and *zip* of china being packed away in special storage bags, and the never-ending sound of whistles and fouls and football fans cheering. I lie perfectly still in my perfectly clean room with my messy thoughts. There's a string inside me, a teensy-tiny string, and I'm pulling on it. I know I shouldn't. But. Hudson. He told me I was hard-core. Brilliant. He made me believe in something I thought was long gone: him and me. I pull the string a little more. I'm back there again, weak with wanting. And where is he? He hasn't texted or called, and I'm unraveling. I close my eyes. Try to ignore the string. But his hands in my hair. His eyes. Why do I let him do this to me? Why, after all his talk of loyalty, did I expect him to ditch Jolene? Why, after all this time, did I expect a different ending?

I roll onto my side and stare at the hand-drawn map I made in sixth grade. It *is* Thanksgiving. Maybe he's with his family. Maybe he'll call tomorrow.

But Friday comes and goes and I still haven't heard anything. Not from Jolene, whose car I drove. Whose front door I opened, slowly at first, then quickly, so it wouldn't creak when I carried her through it, even though her parents weren't there and wouldn't be back until some small hour of the morning, long after I'd walked home and opened my own front door.

Not from Kris, who's grounded.

Not from Hudson, who held me.

By Friday night I can't fight it. I pull the string and paw through every jealous memory I have of Hudson and Jolene: her upturned smiles; his downcast eyes; the way he kissed her in the hall, like no one else existed. I force my eyes open, make them see—Jolene didn't take Hudson. Hudson chose Jolene. He's chosen her every day since the manhunt game.

That's loyalty.

I flip over and bury my face in my pillow. I blink into the black, breathe the cotton in and out until the exhales don't ache and the inhales are smooth.

If Hudson thinks I'll take what I can get and disappear into the walls again, he's wrong. It's been almost a year and a half. I will not be that girl again.

I am not that girl.

When Hudson said good-bye to me at Bella's, he said he'd find me. Instead I'll find him. Tomorrow's Saturday—the soccer game. Hudson's on varsity. I told Jake I wasn't going, but

I will. And for once I won't control myself. I won't stand back and watch quietly while the words claw at my throat, fight my lips to get free. I'll let them come ripping out. I'll tell him he doesn't mean a thing to me. That I don't think about him. That I never did. That he can go back to her, because I'm done with him. It's over. It never existed in the first place.

And maybe, when the words are up and out of me, I'll believe them.

CHAPTER 9

I HAVEN'T BEEN to Tamaques Park in years. I half expect to drive into a swath of egg-yolk-yellow paper labeled Division 41, Block 522—but as I turn the first curve, it's obvious that everything's exactly where I left it. The tennis courts and playgrounds on my left, the basketball courts on my right. The baseball diamond, paved walking paths, and patches of open grass inside the largest part of the loop. I lean forward in my seat and look out across the open field in front of me. I spot a couple of boys kicking a ball, setting up makeshift nets and flags on the flat grass in the outfield. But Hudson isn't one of them. So I keep driving, up the tiny hill and into the small parking lot near the pond. I park my car—Jake's old one, actually—and stare out at the field.

I can almost see us—Cal, Hudson, Kris, and me (Jolene was away with her family)—that summer night after sophomore year when we walked to the park, lay down in that field, and made up our own constellations. At least Kris and Cal did. I was quiet, trying to find the real ones I knew from the poster in Jake's room: Orion, the Hunter; Perseus, the Hero; Cassiopeia, the Queen.

Hudson was quiet too. Then again, he didn't really talk if he didn't have to. But after a particularly disgusting creation from Cal involving a farm animal and the name of a sexual position, we all burst out laughing. Kris and I clutched our stomachs. When we finished giggling, I put my hand back on the ground. That's when Hudson slid his fingers into mine and left them there, between blades of grass. It was the second time we'd held hands, and it was a step up. Last time in a dark room, this time under the night sky. I curled my fingers, closing the open spaces, until we were skin to skin, and even though his hands were hotter than the July air, I felt cool and clear. As I traced patterns in the stars, I imagined how he looked, lying next to me: face angled up at the sky, skin lit by the moon. And when I gave in and turned my head to see the real thing, I nearly jumped off the grass. He wasn't staring at the stars. He was staring at me. I opened my mouth in surprise, and the long grass tickled my lips and stuck to my tongue. I spit it out, and he laughed at me while Kris and Cal fought over the best constellation name: Cal's Starfreaker versus Kris's Hard to Star. Later that night, when we walked up to the street corner to say our good-byes, Hudson picked a piece of grass out of my hair. Two months later, he threaded his fingers between Jolene's, right where I could see him. He wasn't mine anymore, if he ever had been.

A whistle blows. A bunch of alumni walk onto the grass and start warming up next to the varsity players. The whole team is here now, Hudson included.

I get out of my car and unzip my coat. The air is crisp, and the sun has hold of the whole sky. Red and yellow leaves rustle in the trees. When Jake still lived at home, and everything was loud and busy, I used to get on my bike and ride here when I needed to scream or daydream, when I wanted to be lost. Alone. But today the park is crowded.

People stream down the cracked paved path—small clusters of scarved alumni, a massive pack from the senior class, scattered groups of juniors—talking and laughing on their way to the aluminum bleachers. I find a tree a few yards away and watch as they file in, squishing together and squinting into the winter sun.

Then the extra balls are bagged, the players are in position, and a coin is flipping in the air. When it hits the grass, Cal leans over, calls, "Heads it is, chumps!" and every pair of feet on the field starts jumping and shuffling, waiting for that first pass. Hudson places his right cleat on top of the ball, looks downfield, then passes to Cal and sprints forward. His arms pump inside his long-sleeved shirt, which folds and flaps against the wind. His cleats dig down into the grass, kicking up dirt onto his bare calves.

I end up shivering in the shade. So I step out onto the path and shield my eyes from the sun. I spot Jake and his crew at the top of the bleachers. They're the loud ones. I take a quick look around for Jolene but don't see her. This is her kind of thing. Normally she'd be in the first bleacher, collecting looks and catcalls, doling out lidded eyes and half smiles to select admirers. A couple of years ago we'd be with her. Jolene at the core, me, Bella, and Kris clustered around her—the original four.

A whistle blows, bringing me back to the game. Cal's carrying the ball over for a corner kick, trash-talking the whole way.

He gets smiles, shouts, and cracks back from each guy on the field. Each guy except for Hudson, that is. He's in position in front of the goal, running up and back, trying to lose his man. He keeps his eyes on the corner and his feet moving.

I cross my arms against the cold and repeat the words I'm going to say over and over again.

Cal finally takes the kick, sending the ball soaring in a perfect arc toward the far post. The goalie launches his body up in the air and spreads his fingers wide; but before he can get his gloved hands around the ball, Hudson heads it past him, into the upper right corner of the net, for the goal. The varsity team explodes in shouts and slaps. They rush the corner, form a tight circle, shout out a chant, and do some sort of dance. But Hudson doesn't join them. He just jogs slowly back to midfield, ready for the next play.

Bella's voice booms from the sideline. I don't know how I missed her before. She's doing her cheerleader thing: elbows bent and tight to her body, hands pausing between hard claps, legs kicking up above her waist as she spells Cal's name. He turns toward her from midfield and bends his body forward in a deep bow. She replies with a few more claps and some wild "Wooo-hooos" before rubbing her lips together and smiling her self-proclaimed see-you-later-for-something-yummy smile. They must be hooking up again. They've had an on-and-off thing going for most of high school.

I search the inside of my jacket pocket as Bella cheers, sifting through spare coins, slips of paper, a tube of ChapStick. Jolene's lighter. I still haven't seen Jolene. I look out over the stands again, but all I see are hoods and hats. Jolene never covers her hair.

I stand on my tiptoes and search the short, brown grass surrounding the bleachers before shaking off the anxiety with a
quick, cold breath. I did my part—I got her home. She'll be
fine. Always is.

The whistle blows for another free kick. Hudson turns and
runs toward the other goal, away from me.

An hour later the boys are silent and sweaty. The score is 2
all. The game is in extra time. Next goal wins. The sun's light
is softer, and the wind is picking up. The crowd has thinned.
Jake and all the guys he used to play with left ten minutes ago.
My feet are near freezing, but I can't leave. I can't keep these
words inside me. I have to tell him, to say it to his face. I watch
Hudson's chest heave in and out, and match my breath to his.
Then I repeat the refrain in my head again and again, until the
words are all I can hear and think.

A few plays later Cal scores off a perfect cross, and the two
tired teams line up to trade slaps and insults. When they're done
with that, they collect the flags, gather the balls, greet whoever's
left on the bleachers, and break up into car-sized groups before
walking to the parking lot. The sky fights for some last bits of
light, until the sun finally gives up and sinks behind the tall
trees, leaving nothing but a gray sheen.

Hudson's the only guy left on the grass now, but it's like he
has no idea. Either that or he doesn't care. He's only paying
attention to one thing: the ball he's juggling. Right knee, left
knee, right knee. Left foot, right knee, head. Even when Bella
and Cal walk over to him, Hudson's concentration doesn't fade.
He finishes a series on his right foot, boots the ball into his left
hand, says something to them—only a few words—and walks
away.

He's halfway across the big field when I start following him. My blood pumps, my muscles loosen up, the sound of my breath surrounds me. Soon I'm jogging after him, desperate he'll blend into the charcoal night and disappear and I won't get to say it.

"Hudson!" I call out. "Wait!"

He stops between two large rocks that mark the old park boundary, where the blocks once divided, and turns around. As I get closer, his features come into focus. Wavy brown hair, wet with sweat. Dark eyebrows, drawn together in question. The right corner of his lips turning up the tiniest bit. I slow to a walk, but I'm still panting when I reach him at the rocks.

"You're here." Hudson pulls a hand through his hair, scratches his head.

"Yeah." I grit my teeth as the words rise in my throat, like bile. I swallow, catch my breath, steel myself. "Listen, I—"

"That's cool," he says.

What?

He presses his lips together, hitches the ball up against his waist. "I wanted to see you."

I search his face in the low light, looking for the half smile, the mischievous squint of his eyes that'll tell me this is a game to him, that I'm the sure thing in his back pocket, something to play with in between stints with Jolene. That I'm second place, always have been. But there's no longer a smile on his face, no upturned lips. Not even a hint. Instead his look is searching, intense. It's pulling me in. I look away, before I'm lost in him and I forget how to say all the things I need to, starting with:

"You didn't call."

"I know." Hudson steps toward me.

"You didn't text."

"I know." He comes closer. I can see beads of sweat running down his neck.

"You said—"

"I said I'd find you. But I guess you beat me to it." He's right in front of me now, so close I can smell him. Sweat and wood and pine. He smells more like winter than the trees on either side of us.

I turn toward the tall spruces to give myself a minute. All those angry words are stuck in my throat, choking me. My chest, so tight with rage a second before, has changed its consistency. I look for the hard place inside me that hates him for what he did; but it's soft now, as if being near him, sharing space with him, has melted it. I hate what he does to me. But I keep coming back. Because he keeps saying things like that. I stand there, staring. I don't know what to do. But Hudson does.

He takes my hand. I can feel the folds of skin between his fingers, the warmth of his palm. I fall into step next to him, and we follow the path around the pond, across the old dividing line, into Division 18. At first we walk in silence. This is how our conversations always start. But as the birds sing a series of staccato chirps above us, I start to wonder: if Hudson wanted to be with me, why didn't he text? It's not like I asked him to show up at my door on a white horse. And I know he never loved talking on the phone, but he could have gotten in touch. He could have said something.

Why do I always wait for him to speak first?

"So, tell me again why you didn't text?" I try to keep my voice light, but it rises too quickly at the end. I lower my head, study the pavement.

Hudson looks my way for a second, then squeezes my hand and keeps walking. "Couldn't," he says. "Don't have a cell."

"What?"

Hudson smiles wide. It's so rare for him, I almost trip. His hand tightens around mine.

"No email, either. Nothing digital," he says, his smile easy and big now, like I've never seen it. He looks down, laughs, like he's proud of himself.

"So, you're hiding from the FBI?" I ask.

He shrugs, looks at me again—his lips a tight smile, like he's trying to keep it from spreading, his blue eyes flashing recognition. "Sort of."

"Do tell."

"My dad works in government security," he says. I remember his dad. Good-looking for an old guy. Scary. Always serious. Always in a suit. "He thinks he can track anyone. At first I quit the grid just to piss him off. Which totally worked." Hudson lets out a soft laugh, shifts his grip on my hand. My whole body flushes hot. We're halfway around the pond now. The sky has moved through gray to flat black.

"At first?" I ask.

"Yeah." His steps slow down, his hand gets heavy. "I meant to go back on, but Jolene was so pissed."

Jolene. Just when I'd finally forgotten about her, here she is.

"Not because she couldn't talk to me," he says, sneaking a glance in my direction, "but because she couldn't talk to me online. She couldn't tag me in a picture. She couldn't update her status with a message to me if I wasn't on there to write back, or like it, or whatever. I was sick of it." He pauses. "What we did—what I do—it's not for anybody else."

We stop in front of the rock that marks the farthest edge of the park. There's nowhere left to go.

"I get it," I say, my eyes on the pond, the trees, the sky, anything that'll get the picture of them together out of my head.

"I knew you would. You always did. You're not like that."

"Nope," I say. No Instagram fan club here. My body tenses and shakes, an involuntary shiver.

"You're cold," he says. "Come here." Hudson unwinds his fingers from mine, puts the ball down at his feet, and pulls me to him. My cheek is near his neck; I can feel the heat rise off his skin, the movement of his chest through his sweatshirt. I don't want to move. But when he slides his arms down to my waist, instead of him I feel Jolene guiding my hand under her shirt, across her stomach, over her skirt. I see the lawn chair, her legs everywhere.

Hudson said he broke up with her. But is it ever really over with Jolene?

I pull away from him. He presses his lips into a line, sits down on the large rock, and steadies the ball with his cleat. I sit next to him on the hard, sloping surface, our thighs touching, our arms wedged together. Neither of us speaks. There's only the wind, the stray scratch of a dry leaf blown across the cement, and the thing I haven't told him: that I took Jolene home from Bella's party.

"Anyway," Hudson says, rolling the ball back and forth with his foot, "after being off the grid for a while, I didn't really want to go back. I liked the quiet." Hudson shrugs. "I quit social stuff first, then email. I got rid of my cell last. That part was inspired by you."

"Me?"

"The night you left your phone at the manhunt game," he says.

"Right." I dropped it in the basket at the beginning of the game; we all did. And then later, Kris and I left. We didn't go back—not for our phones, not for him. Not for anything. It's like my life cracked that night, like it split. He went in one direction. I went in the other.

"I kept it, you know," he says.

"Kept what?" I ask. I've gone back to that night so many times, wondering if I could have done something different; but each time I make the same choice. I walk away from Jolene. She ends up with him.

"Your phone," Hudson says. He stops the ball with his foot, looks at me.

"Really?" It's the one thing I didn't mind losing that night: the screen was shattered, and my parents had refused to replace it. They left me phoneless for a week before they caved and gave me a new one, along with a speech about responsibility and consequences.

I'd always thought Jolene had taken the one I left at the manhunt game. She loved collecting things. My things especially.

Hudson runs his hand down my jeans and spreads his fingers out over my knee like a starburst, like he used to. An old part of me aches.

"I kept thinking you'd call it, maybe. Until the battery died a few days later," he says. "It was stupid, I guess, waiting."

"No," I say, less a word than a sound, pushed straight up from my heart through my throat. "Not stupid." If he had any idea how long I've waited for him. How much I've hated and wanted and wished things were different. How often I've gone back in my mind to the time before him and Jolene, when it was him and me.

He waited for me.

Moonlight moves through the clouds, falls in flat shadows around us. Hudson turns toward me. We're face-to-face.

"I've been waiting," I say. "Every day." Saying the words—out loud, to him—does something to me: unties strings, seals cracks, fixes splits. There's only him and me and us and this. I never left. He never met her on the steps. It's like I can finally, truly breathe. The wind blows. It's not cold, but new and fresh on my skin.

Like his hand on my cheek. I close my eyes and lean into it. Then his hand is through my hair, circling my head, cupping my neck. I think he's going to draw me in, but instead he pauses, looks at me. My heart beats slow and heavy.

And then we kiss. Not beneath stampeding feet at some party or on a stoop with a group of friends in the distance, but alone. And we kiss like we're alone. Slow. Careful. Curious. Hudson traces the curve of my lips with his, from the corner to the small dip in the middle of my upper lip, where he pauses, his breath ragged and quick. Then he runs his mouth along my cheek before coming back for me. And when he does, his kiss is soft but urgent, his tongue searching. And I'm tugging him toward me, picturing him in my head, even though he's right in front of me, breathing him in and out like he's life, because that's what he's given me: the last fifteen months undone. But it's not enough now, never has been, really. I want the rest. The part we didn't get. I move my hand along his neck, slick with sweat, and pull him closer, tighter. He grabs my hair, kisses me hard, desperate, deep, like he's trying to find the same thing in me: all the things we thought were lost.

I lose track of time. At some point Hudson pulls his mouth away from mine, draws me in until our noses touch and our foreheads press together. His hands cradle my cheeks. Our mouths are open. Our breaths are deep. We heat the frosty air between us.

I lean back into him—just one more kiss—but before I get the chance, my phone vibrates in my pocket. I let my lips linger for an extra moment in front of his—so I can memorize it, that amazing feeling of being on the edge of him—before sliding my phone out. Because I know it's late, and I know I'm supposed to be home.

I check the screen. My mom's cell.

"I've got to go," I say, with half a voice.

"I know." He threads his fingers through my hair.

"I don't want to."

He smiles. "I know." He moves forward, a fraction of an inch, enough for our lips to touch. Then he's standing up, and I'm beside him, and we're making our way back along the path through the park in the dark. Hudson's arm brushes against mine. Our palms meet; our hands lock. We walk.

It's not until we cut between the two large rocks that the panic sets in. What if when I get in my car everything goes back to normal? What if the small part of Tamaques Park that crosses into Division 18 is the only place we can erase everything that's happened?

"I wish you'd kept your phone," I say, taking care to keep my voice steady. "This whole off-the-grid thing is really inconvenient. I can't even text you."

"You see, you're thinking about it all wrong." He lifts our

hands to his lips and blows hot breath on them. "No one can text me when I'm with you, either. No interruptions. This"—he raises our intertwined fingers—"is just for us."

"That part I like."

"That's what I thought," he says. We reach the edge of the field. Hudson's cleats click when we step onto the concrete. "You should try it."

"I don't think I could." I click my cell on and off in my pocket with my free hand and consider it. Who actually texts me? My mom. Kris, when she's not grounded. Jolene . . .

"But you've already done it. You and Kris. You guys disappeared, dropped off the popular cliff."

"That's not the same thing. We didn't cancel our email or take down our Twitter or Instagram accounts. We didn't ditch our phones."

"Nope, you just left yours for me."

"Exactly." We cross over to the small parking lot backed by woods.

"Well, if you change your mind, I've got a drawer in my room that's perfect for holding phones that don't ring. You never know. You might like it."

"Maybe." I'm standing in front of my car, but I don't want to get in. "This is me."

Hudson nods, closes his hand hard around mine one last time before loosening his grip, letting me go.

"So, I'll see you," I say, shoving my hand into my pocket.

"See you at school," Hudson says, flipping up his hood.

School. Another planet. A different dimension. I try to imagine it—Hudson and me in the halls instead of him and Jolene—but I can't, and it shows on my face.

"It's not as bad as all that," he says. "They do serve lunch."

"Are you trying to cheer me up with the cafeteria?"

"Never," he says. "Bike racks are much better. Meet me there when you're finished eating. Before the end of sixth period."

"Before the end of sixth," I agree, trying to find his eyes. But it's dark, and darker under the shadow of his hooded sweatshirt.

All I see is the half smile on his face as he takes two steps backward, lifts his chin, and turns around. I watch him walk away—his shoulders hunched, his head down, his cleats clacking over the pavement. I feel a pull, a tug toward him. My heart stretches thin, but I don't follow him. I don't tell him the truth: that no matter how far I dropped from popular, Jolene was still with me.

CHAPTER 10

BY THE TIME I pull into the driveway on Cherokee Court, it's raining and I'm late. I walk into the kitchen in the middle of dinner. My mom freezes her fork in midair and shifts her eyes to my dad, who exhales loudly and reaches across the table for more bread without acknowledging me. I sit down across from Jake's empty seat—he must have gone back to the city—and place my napkin in my lap. We eat. Glasses hit the table hard, silverware screeches on plates. My parents exchange looks while I sit—head down, chewing—trying to hide the heat prickling my cheeks, the same flush I felt as I rushed home with all the windows open.

When we're finished eating, my dad curls his fingers around his coffee mug, my mom spins her rings, and I get the lecture I was expecting. The one about curfew and coming home on time and calling when I think I might be late and being respectful and not making them worry. The one I've heard them give Jake a million times. The one they've never had any reason to give me. My dad jams his finger into the old wooden table and spits as he speaks. My mom purses her lips and nods in agreement at all the right places, while trying to steal looks at me. Because even though she doesn't like when I come home late, I know a part of her is happy. That I went out. Possibly to party. But I don't meet her eyes.

I stare out the window, where the floodlight in our backyard illuminates the tree behind our patio. I watch the leaves bob up and down under the weight of the rain, like they're taking hits. When my dad stops speaking, I nod and shrug my shoulders and say I'm sorry.

But I'm not.

I think of the past year. Me and Kris. Our Thanksgiving rituals: HaFTA, Black Friday shopping spree, Trivial Pursuit Saturday, Blue Sunday. I still feel like a shitty friend for ditching her Wednesday night, but I don't regret it. Because for the first time in fifteen months, I did something new.

What do you *want to be, Mattie?*

My dad has reached the part of his speech where he draws invisible lines on the table and reiterates the rules. I'm still looking out the window. The rain is easing up now, the leaves are done taking a beating. They're dripping.

Maybe I'm not hard-core yet. Maybe I'm not all the things that Hudson sees. But as I listen to my dad in the homestretch of his lecture, I think: *Maybe. Maybe I can be.*

When my dad's finished, he leans his big barrel chest forward and hits his elbows on the table. It slants toward him. "Do you understand?" he asks.

"Absolutely," I say, placing my palms on the arms of my chair and pushing myself up. "Are we done?"

"Guess so." He reaches back to the counter behind him for his laptop. My mom looks at him, expectant, but his eyes are fixed on the screen when I turn to leave.

I spend the rest of the night locked in my room with my physics homework, reading about how light bends and moves through lenses. It makes me wonder if people move the same way: if we bend and change, if we get redirected when we meet a curved surface. I think of Hudson's body curled around mine, and I picture myself, a ray of light, refracted, traveling in a different direction now that he's held me.

CHAPTER 11

MONDAY MORNING AFTER Thanksgiving I stand in my underwear and examine my open drawers. I flip through over-size sweaters, concert tees, long-sleeved V-necks, and faded boy's jeans, even though I know exactly what's in each drawer and in what order. They are the clothes I've worn every day and night for more than a year, but they seem like someone else's. A girl I used to be.

I lean over my top drawer, arms open wide like I'm going in for a bear hug, lift up the neatly folded stacks, and launch them onto my bed. Then I do it again and again and again, until all my drawers are clear and my room looks like it's been ransacked. Until all the cleaning I did the day after the bonfire is completely undone.

Then, still breathing deep from the effort, I sift through my things looking for new combinations of shirts and jeans. But everything is too tight, too itchy, too dull, too big.

Nothing fits.

And the blue numbers on my alarm clock stare at me: 7:10 a.m. Kris will be here soon.

My eyes drop to the drawers beneath my alarm clock. I haven't opened them in ages. I tug at the top one. Old maps and notes spring out. Most of them are from intermediate school, before I got my first cell phone. Except for the piece of folded pink paper resting near the edge. This one is from junior year, when I wouldn't answer Jolene's texts. I unfold it along the old creases. "Are you mad at me? Love you. (Still.)" It's from the first day she walked into school with Hudson, looking all lovestruck, waving to me, like *Can you believe it?* As if I was supposed to be happy for her. As if she didn't have everything she wanted already. No, she had to have him too.

I shove the note back in the drawer and slam it shut. When I do, the bottom drawer rolls open an inch. I pull it out the rest of the way. It's stuffed with tops I used to wear when I went out: a fitted green shirt, a navy-blue button-down. They're still cute. But when I slip them over my head, they don't fit right either. I might not have Jolene's cleavage, but I'm not as flat as I used to be. Plus, the shape of these shirts is all wrong now: too short, too narrow. I keep digging through the drawer. At the bottom I find my old jeans. Dark hip-huggers. Boot cut. Button fly. Jolene used to tell me they were too loose. I figured it was just because I didn't have her hips.

But when I pull them on, I realize Jolene was right. They must have been big before, because now they hug my body perfectly. I smooth my hands over them and remember Hudson's fingers spreading out into a starburst on my knee, his cold hands on my cheeks, my shoulders, my waist. Which is still naked.

I walk over to my closet and sweep aside the button-down

shirts and holiday skirts, but all I find are old dance recital costumes. Sequins and satin isn't going to cut it. I'm about to slam the door when I spot something blue in the corner: a gift bag, full of once-fluffed turquoise tissue paper. A birthday present from my mom. I completely forgot about it.

I pick up the blue bag by its hot-pink ribbons, push the tissue paper to the side, and run my fingers over the fuzzy edge of the sweater. Kris was over the first and only time I tried it on. She refused to call it a sweater, actually, on the grounds that a sweater should, by definition, keep a person warm. I poke my fingers through the loosely knit yarn and remember her suggestion—that I should layer it with a black tank. But since my favorite one is stretched out from sleeping, I pluck an old one from the pile on my bed and pull it over my head. It's tighter than I remember. Clingy. My skin spills over the curved neckline a little, like I actually have cleavage.

I thread my arms through the delicate sleeves of the sweater, tug it gently over my head, and catch a glimpse of myself in the mirror. It's like seeing a stranger. I watch the girl in the glass straighten her neck; it's long and graceful. She faces me full-on and smiles, just the tiniest bit.

This isn't one of Jolene's games. This isn't magic or a movie set. I'm meeting Hudson sixth period.

Me.

In the bathroom, I rummage through my mom's makeup bag until I find black eyeliner. My hand shakes as I slide the thick pencil along my lash line. When I'm done, I smear the jagged marks into a smoky smudge, throw the pencil back into the quilted bag, and rifle through my mom's lipsticks; but all I find is peach. Five shades of it. I'm double-checking the color of the last tube when I knock over the Vaseline. It's not perfect, but it'll do. I pop the lid, glide my finger across the gooey surface, and smooth a clear sheen onto my lips.

Then I push open the bathroom door and run into Jake. Literally.

"Watch it! Some of us are fragile in the morning." He adjusts his flannel pajama pants. His short hair is flat on one side, and he can barely open his eyes.

"Didn't you leave yesterday?" I say, trying to shove past him.

He blinks and stretches, blocking my way. "I was hungover yesterday, then working on a doc review all night. Didn't sleep. Which might explain why I'm hallucinating, because it looks like you're wearing makeup."

"Shut UP." I elbow him in the ribs.

"Ow," he whines, doubling over. But I can tell he's faking it. We used to wrestle all the time when we were younger. I slip past him and skip down the steps.

My mom pokes her head out from the kitchen. She's wiping suds off her hands and arms with a towel. When she sees me and my makeup, she raises an eyebrow.

"Something special happening at school today?"

"Nope." I tear my jacket off its hanger and throw my backpack across the floor. It hits the front door.

"Well, you look nice," she says with a smile.

"Thanks." At least I don't look hideous. But considering she's my mom and she bought this sweater, maybe I do. Not that it matters. There's no time to change. I push my arms through my jacket sleeves.

"You know," she says, cupping my chin, "I could help you fix that eyeliner. Clean it up a little bit. If you just let me get—"

I twist out of her grip. "I like it that way."

"Okay." She sighs and wipes her hands on the dish towel again, even though they're dry.

I pull on my boots. Kris is going to be here any second. I'm never this late. Usually before school I get dressed in five minutes, scan some select map sites and eBay sellers for new merchandise, then make my to-do list for the day; by the time Kris shows up, the list is folded and snug in my back pocket and I'm halfway out the door.

"You'll be home after school?" my mom asks.

"I don't know." I heave my bag onto my shoulders. My backpack rubs at the skin between my jacket and jeans. These are lower than my usual Levi's and don't have pockets big enough for folded paper.

"Are you going out with Kris?"

I face the narrow window next to our front door, willing my mom to walk away. I don't want to get into it with her, about what happened. I'm too busy trying to figure out what to tell Kris about this weekend, but nothing sounds right, because Kris isn't the person I call when I get home; she's the person I just left. I don't know how to tell Kris anything. She just knows.

"Kris is grounded. I might hang out with Hudson."

"Who's Hudson?"

"A boy."

A honk blares from the street. Kris swerves toward the curb in front of my house in her rusted red Corolla, the one she inherited when her sister got caught driving while high.

I open the front door. A cold draft rushes past me.

"Wait!" my mom says, and I do—one foot in the house, one foot out. "Have a good day." She gives me a conspiratorial smile. "But not too good. You know how Dad gets. Don't be late, okay?"

"Okay." I let go of the door and run across the lawn, as if I can outpace the rain. When I get to the car, my hair is wet and Kris is halfway through her cigarette.

"Okay. I'm the worst friend ever," I tell her as I climb into the front seat and slide my backpack between my knees.

Kris lifts her eyebrows, tilts her head, finishes her drag. Then she opens her window and taps some ash to the ground. "Don't go giving yourself any awards just yet." She tucks the cig between her lips and pulls into the street. She painted her nails over the weekend. Red. They match her hair. "It's not like you locked me in a shed," she says, glancing at me.

The shed. Kris's fists. Bursts of sound drowned out by summer screams. "Manhunt!"

(Slam. Bang. Clickclickclick.)

Sweat bursts into small beads on the back of my neck. For a second I think Kris knows, as if somehow Jolene has left traces of herself on me—the scent of her shampoo, the glint of her sparkly lotion on my fingertips—then Kris cracks a smile.

"No," I say, shaking my head. "Not in a shed. But I got you locked in your house. I suck."

"Yes," she says plainly. "You do."

"Runner-up then?"

"Runner-up," she agrees, taking the turn too fast. Our bodies slide to the right.

For the next few minutes we don't speak. I watch tiny drops of rain collect on her windshield, fading the colors of the cars and the street, softening their edges, smudging their borders until I can almost pretend we're actually passing from the moss-green rectangle of Division 14 to the cornflower blue of Division 11, which juts up against the high school. Kris doesn't turn on her wipers. She taps her fingers on the steering wheel, nods her head, ashes her cigarette. She drives us to school like it's any other day.

I rub my palms on my jeans and lean back in the seat, squinting through the watercolor windshield, looking for the piles of leaves Kris likes to drive through.

"Nice jeans, by the way." Kris doesn't look at me when she speaks.

"Thanks." I wait for her to ask where I got them, but she doesn't. "On your left," I call.

Kris spins the wheel with one hand. Gold and crimson leaves hit the windshield. When we're on the right side of the street again, she takes a long pull on her Camel and starts an old conversation, one we should have had yesterday. "Top Ten Plays." The words come out coated in smoke.

Kris and I usually commemorate the last day of Thanksgiving break by doing our homework, eating massive amounts of chips, and counting down the Top Ten Plays of the holiday. That's what Blue Sunday was supposed to be: bitching about the depressing prospect of lockers and hallways, and laughing about our fucked-up families. Not getting each other grounded or hooking up with people on our Do Not Call lists.

"You want me to go first?" I ask.

"Unless you want to hear the top ten shittiest Thanksgiving movies on cable," Kris says, exhaling through the thin slit of open window.

"Okay," I say. "Number ten," I start, then stall. I still don't know where to begin. The weekend rewinds in my mind: the cold breeze rippling the pond; Hudson's warm mouth pressed against my neck; the things he said after the soccer game, in the basement, at the bonfire—about who I am, and how I left Jolene.

Jolene, who still smells like cinnamon, even when she's throwing up; whose weight I carried across the lawn; who looked up at me, so drunk she could barely see, like she was expecting me.

And that's when I realize why I don't know where to begin. Because this started way before I ignored Kris's call. It started a few weeks after the manhunt game, when Jolene sent me a text and I didn't mention it. I didn't answer it, either, but I kept it. I kept all the texts Jolene sent, the same way she kept all those things hidden in her treasure box. I looked at them and wondered what they could be.

Kris flicks her cig to the road and spins the wheel. We slide to the left. In the paper version of things, we're in moss green. In real life, we're at school.

"Was it that good or that bad?" she asks, slowing down to search for a spot, since the lot is full. I scan the sides of the street and help her look for a Corolla-sized opening.

"Both," I say.

She nods.

"I can do that." She slams on the brakes and pulls up three inches from the parked cars on our right. I don't bother looking back. To me it always seems like we're going to hit another car, or a curb, even though Kris always parallel parks perfectly. When she's finished fitting us into the space, she smiles to herself. Then she turns off the car and faces me, a stray red curl falling in front of her wide green eyes. She doesn't move it to the side.

"Okay. Just number one then," she says, crossing her arms.

I tighten my grip on the straps of my backpack and hold her stare. Ten through two can be anything—like the time Kris's uncle squeezed her mom's ass, thinking it was her aunt's, or when Jake snorted Sprite out of his nose. Number ones are different. They're Trivial Pursuit questions that don't make any sense, late-night theories about how the school is really a reality show run by robots. Stupid stuff no one else would think is funny.

"Okay," I say as a group of sophomores walks by, dressed in variations of the same outfit. "Number one." My temples knock out a loud beat on either side of my head. "Driving Jolene home from Bella's party."

"Bullshit," Kris says, loud enough to make a few of the sophomores whip their heads around, searching for the sound.

"True shit," I say, taking a quick breath.

Kris narrows her eyes. I wait for her to be angry, pissed, surprised, shocked. Anything. But all she says is:

"Interesting." Then she reaches behind my seat and lifts her bag out of the back.

"Interesting?" I repeat as I step out onto the thin strip of grass next to the sidewalk and slip my backpack over my shoulders. "Meaning?"

The first bell rings. Kris slams her door and walks onto the lawn. I fall into step next to her, but our strides don't match.

"Meaning," she says, swinging the heavy school door open for me, "you're not the reason I missed curfew, even though I'd love to let you keep believing that."

"You're the worst," I say as I walk past her.

"Runner-up." She lets the door shut behind us. Our eyes

adjust to the fluorescent light as we walk down the hall.

"Then why'd you get grounded?" I ask. "What happened?" My hand moves to my back pocket in search of my to-do list. But the pocket is too small, and the list isn't there. I didn't make one this morning. I shove my fingers into the tight pocket anyway, so it doesn't look like I had my hand on my ass for no reason.

"More like who," Kris says, eyeing a line of giggling, lip-glossed, hand-holding freshmen headed in our direction.

"Okay, who?" I ask. The girl on the end is talking to her friend. She doesn't even see us. That's how sure of her world she is. That's how invisible we are.

"Bella," Kris says as the girl walks into her. Kris stays stiff, knocking the girl sideways, into her friends. They're startled, but like birds, they swerve back into formation.

"Bella?" I ask. The second bell rings. Kris and I walk backward, away from each other.

"Bella," Kris calls out, like it's the name of some mystical creature.

I turn my palms up to the ceiling and hold my hands out to the side in question. Then I crash into a classroom door. The first row of my Spanish class laughs. So does Kris, from the opposite end of the hall. *Later,* she mouths as she ducks inside a doorway down the hall.

I lower my head, sidestep Señora, and shuffle to my seat. She pulls her lips down into a questioning frown and shoots her brows to the ceiling. Then she brushes her hands together as if wiping them dry.

"Welcome back, *chicos,*" she announces, and shuts the door. Señora is at her desk grading papers, her thick glasses balanced on the end of her nose. I'm sitting in my assigned seat, staring into space. I should be conjugating irregular verbs. Instead I'm trying to picture Bella and Kris, and whatever strange, otherworldly event could have brought them together.

Because when Kris and I left the manhunt game, we didn't just leave Jolene. We left Bella, too. And corner tables in the cafeteria, prime seating at school assemblies, underclassmen adoration, the social ease of being the most sought-after juniors. Pretty much everything. We dropped so far from popular that we couldn't even see Jolene. And that was the point. If nobody cared about us, nobody talked about us. We were free. At least that was Kris's reasoning.

And I agreed. *I did.* That doesn't mean I don't pick up my cell every now and again and scroll to Bella's name. After Kris, Bella is my oldest friend. I've never laughed so hard as the first day I went over to Bella's house in fifth grade, and we made up fake names and a full-on choreographed dance with costumes to the latest Taylor Swift. Bella was like that, even then: she could make a party out of anything. But each time my finger hovered over her picture on my screen, I heard Jolene in my head. I imagined what she must have told Bella—the story she spun about why Kris and I left, complete with details and dialogue, wide eyes and surprise. It would have sounded real. It would have *been* real as soon as it left Jolene's lips. That's what made Jolene so convincing: she didn't tell stories, she believed them. Her steady eyes, her sure voice, and her smooth delivery left no room for doubt. And anyway, if Kris and I were going to carry out her plan to live in the sewer of social life and become untouchable, being seen with Bella—party-planning queen of our class—would have ruined it. So even though Bella had sent me a few texts right after the manhunt game, and even though I'd typed some replies, I'd never hit send.

But Kris had made a clean break. Now all of a sudden she feels compelled to risk everything—her curfew, and our carefully crafted status as nobodies—for Bella? It doesn't make sense. I try to think of something that will make it fit into the map of Kris, but I come up empty. When I think of Kris, I think of her with me.

It reminds me of that game we used to play at intermediate school dances, the one where you cross your arms at the wrists, clasp each other's hands, and spin around as fast as you can.

For over a year we've been letting the rest of the world whirl around us while we held on so tight we couldn't see anything but each other. But just because the background spun and blended and bled into streaks, it doesn't mean it disappeared.

I tap the point of my pen on the sheet of paper in front of me and look over the list of irregular verbs and their meanings. We've done this before. We do it every year. "To keep us fresh," Señora says. As if we'll start to rot if we can't remember how to say *She went, He goes, I'm going.*

Maybe she's right.

CHAPTER 12

AFTER SPANISH I hook my thumbs under the straps of my backpack and walk the usual route to homeroom: down the hall, up the stairs, stick to the side so I can exit right. My shoulder brushes along the wall. I examine some random girl's ponytail. Because this is part of the usual too: swallow, tense, breathe, don't look at Jolene.

Even though Block 241, where the high school sits, is a solid square of moss green according to Sanborn, the land is divided. The masses stay to the right. Royalty lounges on the left, at Jolene's locker, where she holds court, and Hudson's hand. Or, at least, where she used to. It's the first place I saw them together after the manhunt game: Hudson's head lowered, Jolene's neck extended, their lips meeting. I should have looked away. That's what you're supposed to do when you see people kiss. But I couldn't believe it. His hand on her hip. Her head tipped so they would fit. Not in a dark room or a secluded spot under the stars, but under the fluorescent lights for everyone to see. I stood there watching them, willing Hudson to pull away. And for the briefest second I thought he might. His spine straightened, his hand seemed to push back instead of pull in. But his eyes didn't fly open to find me. Jolene's did. Deep in a fresh kiss, she stared at me, like she knew exactly where I'd be.

I hadn't known until that moment that I'd really do it—leave Jolene and Hudson. Everyone. That I was done. Sure, that's what I'd told Kris. And yeah, I hadn't spoken to Jolene since the manhunt game. But it had only been a few flat, end-of-summer days. I'd still felt her with me: her voice reciting *the two little girls* before I fell asleep, her breath on my neck. I'd wondered how long she'd stay mad at me.

I'd wondered about Hudson, too—why he hadn't returned my calls. I'd convinced myself he was dealing with his dad's drinking, his mom's leaving. That he was gaming with Cal or tired from tryouts. That everything would be fine the first day back at school, easier when I could see him, and he could see me, and he could smile, and we could laugh like that night in the grass.

But when I finally saw Hudson, he was with Jolene. They were kissing. I looked then, but never again.

Until now.

I turn my head. I can't see at first. There are too many people. Backpacks, shoulders, mouths, sweaters, and heads block my view. I move from side to side and squint my eyes. My stomach gets tight and my breath jagged, as if when the crowd clears, it'll be last year again and I'll see them. But as the crowd thins, the scene looks nothing like it once did. Hudson isn't there. Neither is Jolene.

She isn't talking to Bella outside history, either. Or leaving the gym when I walk in.

I don't have to walk the long way to psychology. I don't have to fix my gaze and stare off into the distance. I don't have to count my steps in my head to know how close I am to the next assigned seat. At first it's weird, not having to avoid Jolene. I feel like I'm floating. Not in a weightless, amazed way. More like a drifting-into-the-ether kind of thing. Like I've been disconnected from something essential, something that belongs to me. My shadow, or my reflection.

By the middle of the day I start to wonder if she's sick, even though the thought is ridiculous. Jolene's never sick. Even when she's sick she's not sick. She shows up at school. She doesn't like to miss anything, unless she has a reason.

"You walk through the hall like nobody's here."

I stop halfway into physics and turn around. Someone slams into me, curses. I step to the side and let the stream of people rush past me into class.

Hudson's back is up against the locker, his headphones down around his neck. A tiny, tinny version of a song surrounds him. Maybe that's why he seems a world apart from this: the lockers; the classes; the kids doing double takes, shooting us surprised eyes and singing their own, hushed song as they pass by *(Is that* Mattie *with him?).*

Or maybe it's because when I look at him, he takes me away from it.

"Maybe they're not," I say, lowering my chin, looking up at him through my lashes. I've never done it before, but I've seen it. Jolene used to look at him like this.

Maybe we're both not here, Jolene said, my stomach to her back, our bodies curved together in her bed.

Maybe I wished you gone and you disappeared, I think.

The idea startles me.

"Maybe not for you," Hudson says, lifting his hand a few inches in the air. Mine rises to meet it. Our fingers twine. "But the rest of us do have to deal with them sometimes."

"Too bad," I say, leaning into him the way she did.

"Yeah." He ducks his head toward me, and for a second I think he's going to kiss me right here in the emptying hallway; instead he pauses, his mouth near my ear. "Meet me at the bike racks, on the north side, before the end of lunch." Then he stands up and loosens his grip on my hand. It slips slowly from underneath the unbuttoned cuff of his flannel.

"Okay," I say.

Hudson nods, brings his hands to his headphones and flips them over his head. He takes a breath, like he's been holding it all this time, and shoves his hands into his pockets. Then he gives me the start of a real smile, but turns before I can see the rest, leaving me alone when the bell rings. I slide inside the closing classroom door. I can already see the diagram of lenses on the board.

I stuff a sad-looking fry in my mouth and round my back as I lean over the cafeteria table toward Kris. I checked my phone again on the way to lunch, but I don't have any new messages. It's been over a week. This is the longest Jolene's ever gone without texting.

"Bella was crying on the third-floor stairs?" I ask, licking the salt off my lips.

"Crying doesn't really do it justice," Kris says, examining the outside of her burger. "It was more like keening. You know, that kind of piercing, high-pitched cry that sounds like a sick animal? It was like that." Kris takes a tiny bite, then makes a face and puts the burger down on her plate. "She was really freaking out."

"She must have been," I say, sorting through my fries for the crispy ones.

"Meaning?"

"Nothing," I mumble. But Kris has her green eyes on me. I meet her gaze, picture the cafeteria spinning behind her, around us. Then I finish chewing, swallow my food, and say, "It's just that, you know, there was a time you wouldn't be seen talking to her."

"True." She taps her nails on top of her Coke, lifts the tab, cracks it open. "But there was also a time I wouldn't be caught dead at one of her parties."

"Noted."

Kris looks over the tray of food in front of her before shoving it aside in disgust. She wraps her hands around the cold soda. Frost forms on the can in the outline of her fingers.

"So, you two just hung out in her room?" I ask.

"Pretty much."

"Romantic," I say. My eyes drift toward the clock. There's only ten minutes left in the period. "Then what?"

Kris takes a sip of soda, bends the tab on her can up and down, up and down, until it breaks off in her fingers, then she drops it into her palm and closes her hand around it. "She started talking," Kris says.

"Now that sounds like Bella." I sneak a look at my watch. I've got to go. "Did she ever stop?"

"Not for a while. At first it was hard to hear her. Because of the keening. But once I got her in her room, she calmed down." I nod. I'm trying to listen, but my mind drifts to Hudson. The headphones nestled around his neck, covering the curve of skin I almost-kissed. "Anyway, when she finally stopped to take a breath, she told me some extremely choice things about our all-time favorite, and your very own number one." Kris is grinning now, her voice getting louder. "That's right, ladies and gentle-men; I'm talking about Jolene."

Jolene.

Of course.

The same day I watched Hudson and Jolene kiss for the first time, I watched Jolene and Bella, too. From across the cafeteria, where I sat with Kris (legs crossed, trays balanced on our knees, backs cold against the windows, butts hot from the heater), I saw Jolene turn the full shine of her eyes toward Bella after she spoke, like they had a private joke. I recognized that look. I remembered how it felt: the swell in my chest, the glow of being chosen. Of belonging. I still felt knit to them, and to the table where we'd staked our claim. But after that day half the seats stayed empty. Phantom limbs. Every once in a while someone joined them—Bella's cheer friends, Jolene's groupies, boys, ath-letes, even the most ambitious underclassmen—but no one's ever been granted a permanent seat. Most days it's just the two of them. Eating. Preening. Leaning. Whispering.

What does Bella know? What has Jolene told her?

I want to hear about it, but Hudson is waiting. And I'm not going to let Jolene keep me from seeing him, even in gossip form.

"What did she say?" I'm cleaning up my tray as I ask, put-ting my napkins on top of my plate, gathering my books and my bag.

"Plenty," Kris says, dropping her elbows on the table between us. "But it doesn't look like you care." She tips her head toward my tray, like it's evidence.

"I want to know," I say, "but I forgot to switch my books before lunch, and you know Riles will flip if I show up to calc without my text."

"Mmmhhhmmm." Kris doesn't move; she doesn't start to clean up. She just watches me stand and balance my tray in one hand. "Well, don't hurt yourself or anything. It's only calc."

"I'll try my best." I turn around with my tray. "See you at the car."

"Until then." Kris raises her can to me, then chugs her Coke.

I bus my tray, push through the cafeteria doors, and when I'm sure no one can see me, I break into a light run down the empty hall.

CHAPTER 13

I SLOW DOWN when I get to the north end of the building. I can't catch my breath, and I've started to sweat. Perfect. I swipe my fingers across my forehead, wave the bottom of my shirt a few times, and keep walking. My breath evens out as I turn the last corner, into the stairwell that leads to the north exit and the bike racks. I check my phone one more time (nothing from Jolene), then flatten my palm against the cool metal, push open the door, and blink into the bright, white sky.

The rain has stopped. The clouds are thick. Wind whips loose leaves around the parking lot and sways the trees in the field. A group of senior boys push past me, unlit cigarettes pinched between their lips. They flip their lighters in their fingers as they head across the street to the armory, where they can smoke in peace.

I wrap my arms tight across my chest, tuck my chin, and start walking in the opposite direction. My hair, free from its usual ponytail, flicks across my face, sticks to my lips. I pull it back quickly with my finger, but a new gust slaps it across my mouth again, so I decide to leave it.

By the time I get to the bike racks, where Hudson's sitting—headphones up, eyes down—my cheeks feel flushed and my eyes are tearing.

I stand in front of him, my face turned into the wind. He's not wearing a jacket, but he doesn't look cold.

"You came," he says, looking up at me. He brings a thumb to my cheek and wipes away a tear. His touch feels strange on my face. Not because he hasn't touched me in softer places, but because we're outside, in the light, in front of all the filthy classroom windows, where anyone can see.

I slide his headphones down to his neck. "I said I would."

He runs his hands through his hair. His eyes are dark blue today, deep as night.

"Saying it doesn't make it true," he says.

Hudson may think I'm hard-core, but he still doesn't trust me. Not completely. And even though his doubt sears a hot streak behind my ribs, I don't flinch.

"Good point," I tell him, eyes steady, voice clear, so he can see: this time is different. I'm different. "But I'm here, right?"

"You are indeed."

He slips his middle fingers through my belt loops and pulls me to him. I close my eyes when we kiss. His lips are soft and warm. He moves his mouth along mine, leaving parts of my skin wet with him. When the wind picks up again, the wet parts go cold.

I shiver. Then I hear something snap in the distance. A twig. Or was it a squeak? The sound of a window opening?

Windows rattled in their frames.

My eyes fly open.

Want to play a game?

Jolene?

But no one's there.

I squeeze my eyes shut and kiss Hudson. I press my mouth so hard against his lips, I can almost feel his teeth. He yanks my belt loops so fast I swear they'll rip. There's no space between us anymore. No room for the wind to get in. When the next gust comes—lifting strips of my hair, lashing them against my cheeks and his—I hear the rattling sound again. But I don't open my eyes.

Jolene isn't here.

She hasn't sent me a single text since I laid her in her bed.

I run my hand from Hudson's neck, down his arm, to where his fingers grip my hips. When he feels my hand on top of his, he grabs it. I sigh. He swallows the sound and my breath, holds my hand so tight my fingers must be white.

I press my palm into his—the place where she cut me, where she got in.

This is just for us, Hudson said.

Maybe he's right.

Maybe it's over.

The first time I walked away from Jolene, it was raining. Gusts of wind smacked her bedroom windows, rattling them in their frames. I jumped at every splash and slap. Jolene looked up from the floor where we sat and narrowed her eyes at the wet, blurry world outside, like she was challenging it to crash straight through the glass and smash us.

Nothing had broken us yet.

It was September, sophomore year. The four of us had survived being freshmen. While other girls had turned rabid, ripping each other to shreds, we held sleepovers and séances, swore confidences, snagged a corner table in the cafeteria, and got invited to senior parties. We were becoming captains and chiefs and queens. Kris had journalism. Bella had a set of blue-and-white pom-poms.

I had Jolene, and she had me.

The window trembled again, glass clattering against wood. Jolene threw her Vogue on the floor between us. It landed with a thwack.

"Want to play a game?" She scooted closer to me, pulled her knees to her chest, wrapped her arms tight around them, and wound her lips into a wicked grin.

The last game we'd played, I'd nearly suffocated.

"What kind of game?" I asked, flipping the page of my Cosmo too fast—"Ten of Our Favorite Questions"—and tearing the thin print halfway off in my hand. I lined up the ripped pieces and pretended to keep reading. Unfortunately, my cheeks gave me away. I felt them flush. And even though I hung my hair over my face, it wasn't thick and dark like Jolene's. It didn't cover anything.

"Why?" Jolene asked, smirking. "You scared?"

"No," I lied.

"Good." A smile spread across her face. "Because I can't do it without you." Jolene grabbed my hand and hauled me off the floor, and I didn't fight her. Not when she led me to her parents' bedroom (they were at work—they were always at work), or dragged her dad's nylon climbing bag from the closet. Not when she coaxed a thick coil of rope from the bag and placed it in my hand, or when she tugged me back to her room and set the ropes out on the floor, doubled them, and formed them into figure eights. I didn't resist *because she couldn't do it without me. We were the two little girls.*

Jolene's fingers moved quickly, threading the rope through, pulling it taut, testing the complex knots. Her dad had given her a lesson one weekend before he went climbing. The last time she'd shown me, she'd been clumsy.

When the ropes were four small circles, Jolene stood up and smiled, impressed with herself.

"What are we playing?" I asked.

Jolene looked at her watch. Her eyes walked over the ropes, across my hands and feet, toward the duct tape (had it been there before?), then off into the distance.

She didn't answer me.

"Time to get ready." I'd barely registered her hand in the air before I felt the slap and saw black. I brought my hand to my cheek, felt for blood, but there was none. It just stung. I blinked back tears. It felt like her hand was still on my cheek. Like it always would be.

"Your turn," she said. "Hit me."

I stared at her. I didn't feel like me. It was like my center got knocked to the side with my cheek, and the rain on the windows had washed out the street, the sky, everything. Like we were off the map and inside one of Jolene's stories.

"Come on." Jolene stepped closer, her eyes locked on mine. "Do it."

So I did. Because she told me to. My hand flew through the air and hit her skin with a crack. Her head swung to the side. A spot of blood beaded on her bottom lip. She licked it and smiled.

"I knew you could do it," she said, then left the room, her long ponytail swinging behind her.

I was still staring at my hand when I heard the loud scratch from downstairs. The grunt of something heavy being forced out of position. A series of pops and clicks. The squeal of metal on metal. A loud whoosh of wind and the quick pelt of water against wood. The clear clap of a door knocker. Jolene's feet up the stairs.

When Jolene appeared again, her hair and hands were wet. The rain had come for us after all. No smashed glass required.

With dripping fingers she slid the ropes over my ankles and wrists, then cinched them. And still I didn't resist. Since the night I'd gasped for breath, I'd held my own hand over my mouth, trying to get back to that hazy place without oxygen where I could sink and spin and grow gills, where anything was possible. But it hadn't worked.

Jolene grabbed the duct tape off her desk and unrolled a section. The sticky strip snapped when she tore it apart with her teeth. She pressed it against my lips and smoothed the edges over my cheeks.

Sweat burst from every inch of my skin. My pulse pounded in my temples. I sucked deep breaths through my nose, trying to make up for the air my mouth couldn't reach, which didn't do anything except make me dizzy. I shut my eyes and tried to center myself. When I opened them again, Jolene was slipping the other set of ropes over her own wrists and ankles. She sat down behind me and went silent.

The rain still hadn't let up. It kept throwing itself against the bedroom windows.

Were we just going to sit here like this? I tested my wrists. Twisting them burned. Struggling was worse. I quit moving my arms and leaned back against Jolene in question.

What are we playing?

I heard the distinctive tooth rip of tape and then an engine's roar over the downpour. My stomach pitched.

"Oh," she said, "by the way. We're expecting someone."

The slow fade of roar into rain. The click of bootheels on wood. The suck of the shut door.

"Mattie? Jolene? Are you guys here?" Bella called. A question. Then, after she had time to take in the scene, fear. "Mattie?!" Panic. "Jolene!"

Jolene and I sat, bound, back to back, in the bedroom. Bella called our names again and again as she searched the first floor.

MattieJoleneMattieJoleneMattieJolene.

My skin expanded and contracted in time with my heart. Adrenaline radiated from the center of my body to the tips of my fingers. My chest caved and burst with each breath.

What kind of game was this? Not two little girls but three. That's not how it was supposed to be.

Bella's boots stomped up the steps. She froze in the doorway when she saw us, face pale beneath her bronzer. Mouth open. Eyes wide with fright.

I tried to call Bella's name, to tell her it was fake, but the tape. I tried to move, but the ropes. I shook my head, twisted my neck, but Jolene bucked and screamed behind me. And I must have looked just as crazy, because Bella didn't budge. She just stood there, body rigid, fists clenched. That's when I felt the crack of a skull—precise and solid and loud—on the back of my head. My chin hit my chest, and my eyes squeezed together. It could have been an accident, but I knew it wasn't. I knew in my gut. It was Jolene, and she was pissed that I wasn't playing.

I took the hit, absorbed the pain, felt the knock echo through my brain, then tried to get Bella's attention again. But no matter what I did, everything kept happening.

My whole body pulsed. My scalp tightened. My lips tired behind the tape. My shoulders ached. And Jolene kept thrashing behind *me, her flattened cries rising higher and higher like they were mea-suring the pressure in my head.*

I shut my eyes and let a scream rise from my gut to my sealed-shut lips.

Then someone laughed.

Bella. Her mouth still open. Not in the shape of shock, but the wide circle of a smile.

"Gotcha!" she sang as she reached up and ripped the sticky strip from my mouth. Which hurt like hell.

"Ow!"

"You totally believed me, right?" Bella knelt in front of me, balled up the tape, and threw it in the garbage. "Jolene told me I was the only one who could convince you it was real since I'm the best actor in the school."

An act. Bella had been acting. And for that I drove my shoulder into her. She landed flat on her ass and laughed.

"You're a star." Jolene tossed the words to Bella, who smiled, closed-lipped, at the compliment; but her eyes were on me. Her ropes lay loose on the floor. Her tape was crumpled and clutched in her fist.

We hadn't been messing with Bella. They'd been messing with me. It had all been for me. The rope burns on my wrists spread up my arms, to my neck and cheeks.

"Screw you," I said, straining against the rope, rubbing the red skin raw.

"Come on Mattie," Jolene said, her voice slow, patient. "It was just a joke. Of all people, you should get it"—she raised her eye-brows and looked me dead in the eye—"since it was your idea."

My throat went dry. The walls crept in. My voice came out hoarse. "It was your idea."

It was, wasn't it?

My memory shifted, twisted, bent like my arms did behind me.

"I don't think so," she said, kneeling down in front of me. Her voice was as pleasant as can be, but her face was strange. Downturned mouth. Crease between the eyes. It took a minute for me to process. But by the time she loosened the loops around my ankles and wrists, I'd figured it out. Jolene looked . . . hurt.

Then the crease disappeared. Her skin was smooth again.

I tore my hands away from her and scrambled to my feet, but my legs were stiff from sitting for so long. I stumbled.

A slap of rain rattled the window in its frame. A voice came from behind me: "Hey, don't leave. You're supposed to sleep over." Closer now. "Are you okay?"

"I'm fine." The colors and shapes of the room collided and burst apart again. I blinked my eyes a few times and swept my sleeve across my wet cheeks. Then I grabbed my coat and jammed my books into my bag.

"Stay." Jolene's voice, the one she used under the covers. "Please. My parents are away."

I threw off her hand, shouldered my bag, and shoved past her.

"Leave me alone," I hissed.

Which is exactly what she did.

LOT 1
MB:46—665
MB:51—103
60' R/W
YOUNGBLOO

COS
MB:46—66
MB:51—10
60' R/W
YOUNGBLO

EX. CB

CHAPTER 14

I'M STANDING UNDER a bare-branched tree crunching leaves with my sneakers when Kris finally hurries across the street, car keys in one hand, a soft pack of Camel lights in the other. She starts talking before she reaches me.

"It's T-minus"—she looks at her watch—"fifteen minutes till I'm due home, so buckle up. I'm not going to stop the story for anything but smokes." And as if to prove her point, she smacks her soft pack on the heel of her hand and grabs a cigarette with her lips. Then she unlocks the car and we both climb in.

"You're still grounded?"

"All week," she says, pushing in the car lighter and throwing her bag into the backseat, "except for journalism."

The lighter pops with a hard *click*. Kris leans forward to light her cig, exhales a sigh of smoke, and pulls out into the street. Then she tells me what happened.

"So, there she is, Bella of all people, resting her foundationed forehead on my knees, doing that mix of high-pitched singing and screaming. And even though it's her party we're ditching, I get her to her room and make sure the door is locked, that nobody comes in. After a few minutes she's running her middle fingers along her lower lashes to fix her mascara and reapplying her lipstick. At that point I'm already past curfew, so I know what's waiting for me when I get home—the parental flip-out, followed by severe punishment—so I figure, well, fuck it. I'm already screwed, right? Might as well be the amazingly supportive person I am and pay the price that good people always do. So I hand her a tube of liquid eyeliner and ask what happened." Kris takes a long drag, lifts her chin, blows the smoke out of a crack in her window, then looks at the clock in her car.

"Thirteen minutes," I say.

"But only ten with you." Kris lives on Tudor Oval, which didn't exist in 1921, at least not as anything other than a blank stretch of blue on Block 507, Division 17, three minutes southeast of Cherokee Court.

Kris grips the wheel with both hands.

"So here are the highlights: Jolene's wasted—like, falling-into-the-flip-cup-table wasted—god, I'm so sorry I missed that—and you know how Bella wants everyone to have the best time always and forever?" Kris gives me an eerily close version of Bella's best-party-ever smile before collapsing into rolled eyes and sloped shoulders. "So Bella's steering Jolene toward the stairs and throwing out these joke-slash-apologies to everyone, which she's probably totally used to doing with her mom—you remember how her mom used to get when we were over?" I nod. Bella's mom had a glass of clear liquid with two ice cubes attached to her hand, and whenever we were over, Bella had to lead her out of the room or else she'd never leave. "But also because, you know, everything's a show with Bella. But that's her mistake, right? Because since when does Jolene give up center stage? So Jolene throws Bella's hands off her shoulders and plows through the living room. But since Bella's not going to be upstaged at her own party, she shouts 'Drunk bitch coming through!' And Jolene"—Kris hits the gas, leans into a curve—"Wait, I want to get this exactly right." Kris slows down on a straighter stretch of road. She flicks her cigarette. The long end of ash falls into the tray. "Okay, so after Bella calls her a drunk in front of the entire party, Jolene spins on her heel and shouts, 'Just like Mommy! No wonder you like it when I tell you what to do. Should I give you a good-night kiss, too?'" And then Jolene kisses her. Not good-night style. Like, tongue and everything."

Jolene kissed Bella? I picture her kissing Hudson in the hallway, how her lips pouted before parting again. How her eyes shot open and found me.

"No way," I say as Kris swerves the car through a pile of brown leaves gathered on the side of Tice Place. I press my palm against the door so I won't crash into it.

"I know, right?" Kris asks, crushing what's left of her cigarette in the ashtray and shoving it closed. I roll up my window and rub my hands together between my thighs to keep them warm.

"So, for a second, Bella just stands there, lip liner smudged and everything; and Jolene laughs one of her lean-your-head-back laughs, where her wide mouth gets freakishly big. Then, even though she could barely stand up straight two seconds before, Jolene leans into Bella, all mannequin-still, and says, 'You liked it, didn't you? You want to do it again.'"

I cross my arms and lean forward in my seat. Did she?

Kris reaches toward the dashboard and cranks up the heat.

"Then Bella starts telling me how Jolene's treated her like shit before (news flash!) but that this—*this!*—calling out her mom in the middle of a party was over the line." Kris turns to me. "Here is the part where you are both impressed and surprised that I did not mention my shed moment, or your afternoon with the ropes, since *clearly* those were in no way, quote-unquote, *over the line*." Kris shakes her head, then looks back at the road and takes a deep breath. "I mean, especially yours, since Bella was part of it."

"I'm impressed you didn't mention it," I tell Kris, my voice as soft as the heat rushing from the vents.

"You should be," she says, her eyes dead ahead. "Anyway. Bella said that's when she finally snapped."

"Bella?" I ask. Bella has a million and one smiles and even more laughs. She's friends with everyone. She doesn't snap. Especially not at Jolene.

"Bella," Kris confirms, steering with her knees so she can reach up, grab a hunk of red curls in each hand, and tighten her ponytail. "Wouldn't have believed it if I didn't hear it myself."

"So what happens when Bella snaps?"

"Fantastic question!" Kris says, slapping her hands back onto the wheel with a smile. She's enjoying this, and her accelerator is feeling it. I grip the handle on the door as we round the corner. We're almost at Cherokee Court. "Apparently when Bella snaps, she gets serious and spills secrets."

"What'd she say?" I ask. I slip my hand into my pocket and smooth my thumb over the cool metal of my Zippo.

Kris parks in front of my house, unbuckles her seat belt, and turns her whole body toward me.

"Well, someone's eager to hear about the weakness of the enemy! But I can't really blame you. I was too. So, here it is. Apparently, after getting kissed by Jolene and starring in the number one fantasy of every senior guy in the room, Bella announces, in her best stage voice, 'Look, Jolene. I get it. You're desperate. Hudson just dumped you, and now you're looking for someone new. I know I'm the obvious choice, but these lips are taken. I'd tell you to go home to your mom, but she probably ditched you too. Mine might be drunk, but at least she's here.'"

"Hudson," I say. He didn't just break up with Jolene; he'd done it that night. No wonder Jolene ended up on that lawn chair with the junior vultures. No wonder she called out for him. *Don't leave.* She was slurring and furious in those seconds before she realized it was me on the chair next to her instead of him. I thought she was just drunk. But now I wonder: What was she trying to tell him? *It's me.* Who else would she be? And her eyes. Pink and watery. From being wasted? Or could she have been crying?

I flip open the Zippo in my pocket and dig my thumb into the small metal ridges of the flint wheel. Whatever happened between the two of them, I know where she ended up. Alone. And I know Jolene hated going anywhere alone. Especially home.

"Yeah." Kris pauses. "Apparently he broke up with her right before the bonfire. Figured you might know something about that." Kris doesn't mention that I neglected to tell her anything about it. Instead she drums her cigarette-free fingers on the wheel, then starts up again. "Anyway, so now Bella, who's got her entire makeup arsenal spread out on her vanity, says Jolene puts a hand on her cheek and whispers, 'Hudson couldn't keep up with me. You should really shut your mouth when you don't know what you're talking about.'

"So Bella shoots back, 'I know this is my house, and my party, and that you're going to leave. I don't need to be treated like this. I don't need you telling me what to do.' Then Jolene brings a hand up and brushes Bella's bangs to the side—and you *know* how Bella feels about people touching her hair—and says, 'Then why do you always listen?' and walks away. We all thought she left, but . . .'"

"She passed out on a lawn chair in the back. She was trashed."

"And here I thought you missed all the fun."

"I had no idea how she got there, though." I lift my thumb off the flint wheel. The skin stays indented where I pressed it into the metal. "Wow."

"I know. Kind of makes you jealous, right?" Kris asks. "Like you wish you'd said it?"

"Yeah," I lie, turning Bella's words over in my head.

I don't need to be treated like this.

The way Jolene treated me—it wasn't *nice*. It was ferocious. Protective. Enveloping.

"I've been consoling myself with the fact that it wouldn't have hurt Jolene half as much coming from one of us," Kris says, "since we're not friends with her anymore."

"True," I say.

I face away from Kris and stare at our neighbor's lawn across the street. Some patches are thick, lush, bright green. Others are brown, dead, brittle. I wonder what happened to those dry patches, when they lost their nourishment, if they died slowly or all at once.

I click the lighter shut and grab for the door handle; but my palm is sweaty and my fingers are stiff and I can't grip the slick metal. I wipe my hand on my jeans and try again. This time it gives.

I get out of the car, then turn around and stick my head through the window to say good-bye, but Kris keeps talking.

"I mean, who would have called it? Bella!" Kris tilts a fresh cigarette out of her soft pack and shifts her car back into gear. "I didn't know she had it in her."

"Me neither," I say.

But I wonder if Jolene did. If she knew exactly what Bella would do, like she knew exactly where I'd be when she needed me.

I knew you'd come.

"Time to get back to the big house," Kris says. "Those college apps aren't going to write themselves." She lifts her fingers to her forehead in a mock salute.

I do the same, then step away from the car. Kris pinches her cigarette between her lips and peels into the street.

I watch her leave. Usually she sticks her hand out the window and gives me a wave, or the finger—but today the window stays closed. I can't see anything but smoke.

CHAPTER 15

I MEAN TO go home. Really, I do—it's not like I don't have my own college apps to complete. But when I spot my mom's silhouette in the kitchen window, I change my mind. She's not mad at me like my dad, but it's only because she wants details: why I was late, who I was with. She's probably dying to comment on my change in clothes too, to tell me whether or not they flatter my body shape. But I can't do mother-daughter girl talk right now. I still have Bella's story in my head. I keep trying to make it fit with my memory of the rest of the night: Hudson's hand on my knee; Jolene's breath on my neck, sour and alcohol soaked, as I dragged her across Bella's lawn. But every time I get close, I feel the weight of Jolene again, not on my shoulders, but in my throat and behind my eyes.

So instead of going inside and locking myself in my room, I get in my car. At least in here I can move through town for real. I don't have to imagine myself on the black lines of a map, driving through divisions, following the same worn paper path over and over again.

I zigzag through the streets as they switch from moss green to pepto pink to egg-yolk yellow to cornflower blue and back again. Eventually the small, wooden houses with faded paint give way to large homes with square lawns and meticulous landscaping. Hudson's is up ahead, on Arlington Avenue. It looks exactly the same: white brick, manicured lawn, curved slate path, black front door. I stare up at his window and wonder if he'll think I'm a stalker for showing up like this. Even though it's his fault. It's not like I could send him an email or text to let him know I was coming.

Hudson's front door opens as I step out of my car. I freeze when I see him, but he doesn't look up. He shoves his hands into his pockets and bows his head. His worn, ink-sided sneakers are silent on the slate path. I want to call out to him, to hear his voice and the things he says about me. But there's something about seeing him like this, when he thinks no one's watching. It's so private.

So I don't move as he pulls his keys out of his pocket, or when he stops short of his car—a used blue Honda with faded white streaks on the bumpers. At first I think they're scratches, but then I realize they used to be stickers. Someone tried to scrape them off but couldn't get them unstuck completely.

I lean back, thinking I should go—he looks so comfortable and sure, so happy to be alone—but my car door isn't completely closed, and when my full weight falls against it, it lets out a loud *click*. Hudson's head turns toward the sound. His face rearranges when he sees me—his eyes ease into a squint, his freckles fall into place, his chin tilts—until he's someone I know again and not the person he is by himself.

"Covert mission?" he calls out, sliding his keys back into his pocket. They clink together inside his cargo pants as he walks across the street.

"Wouldn't really be covert if I told you," I say.

"You've got people to protect; I get it," he says, nodding. He leans in and lifts his eyes to me like someone might be listening. "We better get out of here." He holds out his hand.

"Good thinking." I take it. It's warm and strong. He leads me to his car.

"Ignore the dirt on the floor. And the notebooks. And the old cleats and empty water bottles," he says, pushing his hair back from his face. "Actually, ignore pretty much everything."

"Except the company," I say.

"Right," Hudson says with a comma-shaped smile. He shuts the door for me and takes his time walking around to the driver's side. In front of the car, he lifts his eyes to the sky and considers the cloud-covered sun, which is already sinking. When he's finished, he gets in and revs the engine. "You have anywhere to be?" He slings his arm over my seat and reverses out of the driveway.

I check my watch. "Not until dinner."

"Good," Hudson says, taking his arm back. He doesn't tell me where we're going, and I don't ask. My mind races at first—rolling out routes, running through blocks and divisions, reorienting with each turn—but I force myself to stop. I can't possibly guess. I don't want to. I settle into my seat.

"Didn't *you* have somewhere to be?" I ask. Hudson doesn't have a cell. He can't call or text if his plans change. He could have practice, something for the team. Someone could be waiting. Cal. Jolene. I wonder if he knows where she is. If she's been in touch with him.

"Yeah," Hudson says, putting his fingers on my knee and spreading them out into a starburst, "but then you came."

Hudson flips down his visor. Attached to the back is a sleeve of silver discs tucked in black vinyl pockets.

"You've really got a thing for CDs," I say.

Hudson runs his fingers along the curved, shiny edges and shrugs. "Small price to pay for a little privacy."

"Right," I say, remembering Hudson's ban on all things digital and why he stuck to it: *What we did . . . it's not for anybody else.*

What they did. Jolene and Hudson. In this car, probably. I lean forward, so my back isn't touching the seat.

Hudson slips out a disc and guides it into the player without taking his eyes off the road. "Tell me what you think of this," he says as the first track spins, then begins. I open my mouth, and he laughs. "Once you've heard it."

"Right." I shut my eyes—so I can't peek at street signs—and listen.

The speakers thrum with a deep, slow bass, mixed with soft chords from a piano, then a drum kicks in with a light cymbal, marking the rhythm. I keep waiting for words, but none come. The longer I listen, though, the more the instruments sound like people. The saxophone especially, soaring and sliding like it's crying. It makes me feel like an open-ended question. Unwritten. Ready to spin out in any direction. I grip my seat and open my eyes.

"You like it," he says.

"I like it," I tell him.

"Cool," he says, fighting back a smile. "Thought you would."

"Why's that?" I ask.

But I must have said the wrong thing. Hudson's smile fades. The muscles around his mouth tense. He tightens his hold on the steering wheel. And I don't ask him anything else. I might not know what the problem is, but I know this: Hudson will talk when he's ready.

I look out the window. The bright white clouds from earlier this afternoon have gone gray. Front porches are lit. Streetlights, cut lawns, and closed-curtained houses go by. The song ends, and a new one begins. It's different from the last. A deep, somber voice croons over an acoustic guitar.

"My mom made me this CD." Hudson's jaw clenches the second he says it, like his mouth is a trap and the words weren't supposed to get out.

"Oh," I say. The last time we talked about his mom, on that short call before the manhunt game, Hudson was pained, pleading. I inch my hand over the middle console and slide it onto the gearshift, under his.

"I used to think she was weak. I used to hate her," he says, swallowing. "I used to think she hated me."

"No," I say, squeezing his hand. But he sits up, pulls his hand away. I put mine back in my lap.

"It was the only thing I could come up with. Why else would she leave?" he asks, turning to me. "Why else would you?"

I freeze.

But Hudson continues.

"Then she got into all these things." He shakes his head. "They were stupid, right? Book clubs. Charities. Traveling. She was busy half the time and gone the other. At first I thought"— he pauses here, blinks a few times, grits his teeth—"I thought she liked being away from me. It made sense. She spent more time traveling than she did in her house across town. But after a while she seemed, I don't know. Happy. Way happier than she ever seemed with my dad." Hudson hits his turn signal, and we make a sharp right off Lawrence Avenue and onto Route 22. We head away from Westfield. And in the green glow of neon lights advertising chain restaurants and car sales, Hudson looks at me. His eyes move over my face the way they did in Bella's basement.

"She left because she needed to. My dad's a jackass, right? So she stopped taking his bullshit. She left. Just like you."

His words hit me square in the chest. "Hudson—"

"That's why I like you," he says, taking a hand off the wheel and running it along my jaw. "You did the same thing. You left because you needed to. You did what you wanted and didn't care what people would think. You don't give a shit."

I let out a hard breath as his fingers meet my mouth. It reminds me of the park, the blades of grass, the way he laughed. I lower my head until my lips graze his skin, let out my breath along the length of his hand, the inside of his wrist. Kiss it.

The car goes over a small hill, a rise and fall that plunge my stomach in a way that feels familiar, and when I look around I realize why. Hudson took a U-turn off 22, onto a pitch-dark street.

We're at the reservation.

Trees climb on either side of us, bending over the road like a canopy. Hudson takes back his hand and jerks the wheel to the right. The Honda shakes and vibrates underneath my feet. I lean forward to look out the window.

The sign says Hangman's Hill. I didn't think this section

of it actually existed. It's marked on only one of my maps, so I always assumed it was a trap street—something the mapmaker put in to catch plagiarists.

"Sit back," Hudson says. Before I can ask why, the street drops out from under us, and for a second the car is suspended, then the front tires hit the ground. Other than a little bit of bouncing, we're fine. I turn to Hudson, my eyes wide. "Told you," he says, smirking.

After that I stick myself to the seat. Each time the street bucks beneath us, I hold my breath until the tires hit the ground again.

"There are thirteen," Hudson says when we reach the intersection at the bottom.

"Guess this isn't your first time," I say, my heart still racing.

"First time with someone else in the car," he says.

He never did this with Jolene. "I'll take it," I say, facing away from him. It's dark enough now that I can see my reflection in the window. I forgot I had my hair down. I let it fall over my eye. The girl in the window stares at me.

Hudson rolls the car to a stop at the foot of the cliffs. After the rush of the thirteen bumps, stopping here feels like sinking.

Hudson kills the engine, cutting off a drum solo on the stereo, and we get out. Gravel crunches beneath our sneakers. We're on a piece of land that overlooks the town. It's mostly dirt and rocks—the same place Bella, Kris, Jolene, and I used to park our bikes before heading up the trails. I always assumed it belonged to the house next to it.

"Are we allowed to be here?" I ask, stepping closer to the edge. Hudson stands next to me, the arm of his jacket touching mine.

"It's just land," he says. "Why not?"

"I wasn't sure if it was private." I tip my head in the direction of the house. The light goes on in the window. A woman walks into the kitchen.

"Maybe. Maybe not," he says. "Why, you scared?"

The wind whistles around us. Dry leaves rustle in the trees, bending and breaking off in the breeze. Then the wind dies and there's silence. And it's strange and empty, and suddenly that's how I am too. And I'm afraid that if I don't move—if I don't do something soon—the empty feeling will grow and grow and grow until it takes me over.

So I grab Hudson's hand and run. I don't look down as my feet hit the narrow path that winds around the house and up into the forest. Hudson runs behind me, clutching my hand tight. I think he's saying something, but his words get caught in the wind. I can't hear him. I can't hear anything but the air in my ears. I can't feel anything but the rocks under my sneakers. I can't see anything but the end of the path. When we get there, I laugh with all the breath I have left. A strange, happy howl.

Hudson is breathing easy, but he has an odd look on his face. Like he can't believe what I just did.

I smile. It feels wider than usual.

Then a quick buzz comes from behind us, and with a crackle and click we're caught in a flood of light. The back door squeaks open, and a voice shouts. Hudson takes my hand, and we run across the front lawn toward the car, our laughter trailing us. Nobody catches us, but it feels like we escaped something when we're safe in the car and the drum solo is back on the stereo, beating in time with my heart.

We drive deeper into the reservation. It's completely dark

now, the night pulled close and tight around us. No late-afternoon glow streaming through the leaves, no short blast of brightness from behind the clouds, just the ripple of moonlight across the water and the thrill of all the things that happen when the sun is down.

Hudson parks across from Lake Surprise, on a small hill I know only as a few curved elevation lines on my map. I've never seen it in person, and now I know why. Long, low branches and oversize leaves hang between the car and the road.

We're hidden.

This is what I've always wanted: him and me. Us.

So why does it feel like it's not enough?

Hudson cracks the window the slightest bit. For a second I go cold, until he leans toward me and I feel the heat coming from his body. "Out there on the cliff. Your laugh," he says. I bring my hand to my mouth, remembering the strange sound. He noticed. "You laugh the same."

"The same as who?" I ask.

"As you," he says, fighting back a smile. "You laugh just like you used to."

"I do?" I ask, because I don't feel like I used to. I feel like an abandoned shell. Hollow. Ready to house new claws.

I drop my hand from my lips. Hudson's thumb replaces it.

A car comes around the curve. Light rushes across Hudson's face, showing the cluster of freckles on his forehead, the length of his dark eyelashes, the corners of his lip as it curls, comes closer. Then it's dark again, and difficult to see. But I can smell his breath—that particular brand of mint—his woodsy deodorant, and, right before we kiss, the thing that doesn't smell like anything else, except him.

I press my lips against his. I taste the dark corners of his kiss. But it's not enough to fill the emptiness. It's just a dent. A tiny speck. So I tilt my head, snake my hand around the back of his neck, and pull him into me.

I kiss him hard, hungry, like I don't give a shit.

"Wait," he whispers, lips still so close, almost touching.

"What?" I ask, worried I've done something wrong. That he can see right through, to the real me. The wind picks up outside. Branches scrape the car windows. I wait for him to say it. That I'm a fraud. A fake. That I'm pretending.

"Just"—Hudson swallows, licks his lips—"slow down." He runs his hands along my arms and slides his fingers between mine. Then he curls and closes them—locking us together.

The song switches. First comes the rough strum of a guitar, then the voice: not so much singing as talking to me. Smooth, sincere, deep—so deep and dense it fills the space between my lungs and heart until I shake, like I'm the one singing, like the sound is moving through me.

"Okay," I whisper, shifting my hold on his hand. The inside of my finger hits something hard. I unclasp our hands and place mine under his, propping it up so I can get a better look at the thick silver ring.

"A gift," he says.

"From Jolene," I guess.

"I wasn't going to bring her up"—Hudson glances at our hands, then back up at me—"but yeah." He balls his hand into a fist. "I don't know why I still wear it. Sorry."

"It's okay." I don't know if it's the music, or the hard-core girl Hudson thinks I am, or the heady smell of him mixed with the smoky scent of early evening, or if we've actually altered history—gone back to a time before she lived within me and redrew the boundaries—but I don't care that we're talking about Jolene.

I run my thumb over the ring, then place my fingers on either side and tug. At first it doesn't budge, but on my second try it gives a little. Hudson spreads his fingers, pulls hard in the opposite direction. When it's off, he flexes his hand, holds it up, and turns it back and forth in the line of moonlight through the windshield. I set the ring on the dashboard and trace the pale strip of skin circling his finger. I can't take my eyes off it, this soft, pristine piece of him. I can't stop thinking about how it's been there all this time, trapped underneath the ring. "We can talk about her if you want."

She's here anyway. In the scar on my palm, the line on his skin. We're both branded.

"No," Hudson says with a brusque shake of his head. "I don't."

Hudson presses his palm to my cheek. He leans close, then closer; and when he's closest, his freckles blend together in a blur. Strands of his hair fall across my cheek and tickle my eyelids as he kisses me. His hands find my waist. The bottom of my sweater. They pause.

I lean across the console. It digs into my hip bone, but I want more of his lips and hands and the breath he takes every few seconds, like he has to come up for air. I slide my hand under his thermal and up onto the waist of his jeans. I touch my thumb to his skin. He jumps. My hands are cold. He pauses for a second, but I keep going. I've never done this before, but it's like something inside me knows what to do, and it's taking over.

I slant my head, move slowly at first, then faster. He follows my lead. I dip my shoulder, expose my neck. His mouth moves over it. I lift my chin. He unzips my jacket. But it's still not enough. So I lean farther over the console, twisting my torso, pushing the sides of my feet against the floor until I'm almost off the seat. Hudson pushes back against me. Lips, chest, cheeks, breath. His fingertips brush my shoulder. The touch is so warm, I lose my footing and sink back into my seat.

And something sinks into me, piercing through my jeans and puncturing the skin on my hip. I flinch. Hudson pulls away immediately, balls his hands into fists, and looks away from me.

"Sorry," he says.

"No." I run my hand along the side of my jeans and the length of the seat. "Something just . . ." My thumb hits metal, sharp and straight. I pluck it from the dark. "Here." I hold it up to him. "This."

It's an earring.

I turn it around in the dim streaks of moonlight to get a better look, even though it feels familiar in my fingers. The three small, interlocking loops. The stones hanging inside each one: emerald, amber, amethyst. Purple for me, green for Jolene, amber to bind us. Jolene found them in a sale basket in the back of an antique shop downtown. When the store clerk explained about the amber—how insects get trapped in the soft, sticky tree resin, then smothered as it flows and hardens around them—Jolene insisted on buying them. She wore them for weeks. The earring looks exactly the same as the day she found it. The only part that's different is the end of the post—it's slick and red where it cut me.

"That's hers, too," Hudson says, reaching for it.

"I know," I say as he takes it away.

Hudson lowers the window. The cold creeps in, and the sound of snapping twigs in the distance. When the window is halfway down, Hudson draws back his elbow and chucks the earring as far as he can. I watch it arc through the air and land in the middle of the road. "She left her shit everywhere." He shakes his head. The window rises behind him. When it closes, the car is warm again. At least it should be. I cross my arms tight across my chest, but I can't shake the chill.

"Listen, you don't have to worry. It's over with Jolene," he says.

It's over.

"No. I know." I let out my breath until there's nothing left.

Hudson taps a soft beat on his jeans, looks at me, turns up the heat. I blink my eyes. They're sticky. Dry.

"When did you know?" I ask.

"What?"

"That it was over?" The words feel like they're being unearthed, drawn out from someplace deep inside me.

Hudson's fingers fall flat against his leg. "Which time?" he asks with a flat laugh.

"What do you mean?"

"Jolene was a huge fan of the breakup. Big fight. Silent treatment. And then the whole 'I need you. I don't deserve you. There's something wrong with me. Please. I love you.' Rinse. Repeat. You know what I mean?"

I did.

"Right. But when was it real?"

Hudson's eyes rise to the windshield, search for something beyond it. He parts his lips and takes a measured breath, like he's testing the air, or himself.

"When she stopped meaning it." He loops a loose thread around his finger and rips it from his jeans with a sharp jerk of his hand. "Or maybe when I stopped needing to hear it."

He rolls the white string between his fingers. "She used to do this thing when we were out drinking. It was pretty impressive, actually. She'd match me shot for shot. The first time I thought it was an act, you know? There she was in front of me with the glass in her hand and everybody watching, and this thing in her eyes, like she had to prove it. And I figured, 'This isn't going to end well.' But most of the time she handled it like a pro. Until this one night. I mean, even *I* was having a tough time. There's only so many shots of Jäger a guy can hold down. So I take care of it, right? I know it's gross, sorry. Anyway, when I come back, she's a mess. Bella brings her over to me, and at first I think she's just drunk since she can barely stand up; but she was . . ."

Hudson pauses.

"What?"

He shakes the thread off his hands and takes a tired breath. "You have to understand; Jolene wasn't the hot chick or the popular bitch with me. When we first got together, she was quiet. Goofy. Sad. We were both going through stuff at home. But a few months ago she got clingy. Vicious. I thought she was just dealing, you know? We'd both been through shit before. But this time she was taking it out on me. And that night when she said she needed me—she was yelling. She was angry. That's when I knew, I think. That she didn't need me, she needed somebody. And I was sick of trying to prove it was me."

She needed somebody.

"She pulled the same shit before the bonfire." Hudson stops, shifts his eyes away, then back to me.

I nod to let him know it's okay. I know he was with Jolene before me the night of the bonfire. Even though he still doesn't know I took her home.

She needed me.

Hudson looks down at the dash. "Anyway," he says, "sorry. But you asked."

Jolene needed me that night, but she doesn't now.

I'm not hers anymore. And she's not mine.

I take Hudson's hand and slide it up my thigh. Then I close my eyes. Somewhere outside, the sound of an engine cuts the night. The insides of my eyelids flash red, then go black again.

And as Hudson's fingers skim the top of my jeans, I imagine Jolene's earring on the street, smashed to bits, all the trapped things inside the amber set free, their dead bodies tumbling into a new century.

LOT 1
MB:46—665
MB:51—103
60' R/W
YOUNGBLOO.

COS
MB:46—66
MB:51—103
60' R/W
YOUNGBLO'

EX. CB

CHAPTER 16

I WAKE UP the next morning before my alarm. The sun is pale, and my parents are still asleep. I swing my legs out of bed and head for my desk. Getting up this early sucks, except for the fact that I won't have to face my dad peering at me over his computer or my mom's questions. I managed to avoid them last night by eating as fast as I could and claiming I had a ton of homework and college-application stuff to get through. I even laid out my books on my desk, flipped open my notebook, and fired up my computer. But I couldn't bring myself to open my Excel spreadsheet or take a colored pencil from the cup in front of me. Since I hadn't made my list that morning, I couldn't decide what to do first, so I didn't do anything. Instead I scanned the usual antique sites and sellers on eBay.

An 1860 Kitchell map I'd been watching—not because I liked topographical stuff, but because it had a late date for hand painting—had sold for somewhere around five thousand dollars. I did a search for "Westfield, NJ, original maps, 1901," but nothing new came up. Until I scrolled to the bottom and found a seller named happyelizabeth. Her entry (full of exclamation marks and bold, brightly colored block letters) shouted:

> **Found these boxes in my grandma's attic! Have to sell her entire estate and don't have time to sort! Boxes are labeled by year, pick one and I'll send! Could contain antique artwork, drawings, maps, etc! Originals! She was a collector! Find a treasure!**

The pictures showed beat-up cardboard boxes full of paper. Even if there was something valuable in there, she definitely wasn't taking care of it. The whole thing screamed scam, except for the price. Each box was up for fifty dollars. Not bad for a long shot. Since the auction didn't end until December 26th, and there were no other offers, I bid fifteen dollars on the 1901 box and went to bed.

I settle into my desk chair and refresh my email to see if there's any action at happyelizabeth, but the browser freezes, so I force quit. And while I wait for the computer to fake sleep and wake up functioning, I do my weekly rotation. I lift my Sanborn map from the nail behind my bed and lay it flat on my comforter, put the 1929 panoramic from Jake in its place, center the 1868 Colton original my parents gave me for my Bat Mitzvah above my dresser, and rehang the Sanborn above my desk. If I wasn't worried about sun-bleached spots, I'd keep the Sanborn above my bed. It's the only one I bought myself. Not that the Colton map isn't nice, but my parents don't get it. My mom probably picked the Colton because it has ornate borders and decorative lettering. Jake probably chose the panoramic because it has a cool point of view. And it does. No doubt. But that's sort of the problem with both of them. All these mapmakers—Colton, even Kitchell—they all had an agenda. Colton was a New York publisher who used fancy metal plates for his engravings because he wanted to build a good reputation. Kitchell fought the government to finish his map because he wanted to document New Jersey's topography. But the Sanborn maps, they're transparent. Stark lines for streets. Unadorned boxes for buildings. Crisp block lettering, bare as bone on the white sheet. Nothing pretty. No agenda. Nothing but the real thing.

Which is why I want to find that missing sheet of the 1901 map so badly. Because even though Westfield Township was formed in 1794, it didn't finish forming for another hundred years or so. Garwood took some land from here, and Cranford from there. Same with Plainfield, Clark, Scotch Plains, and Fanwood. Westfield was pushed and plucked and starved and prodded until 1903, when it finally pushed back. The town charter was signed, and the borders have barely shifted since. If I could just find that missing sheet, I'd have a near-perfect version of the earliest town outline.

My computer is taking forever to reboot, so I head down the hall to the bathroom, shove the shower handle all the way to the left, and step in, hoping to rinse away the restlessness—the itch under my skin that came alive on the cliff last night.

The first splash of scalding water hurts, but after a minute my muscles relax and my shoulders slump. I slide soap over my arms and across my collarbone, down my stomach, over the rise and dip of my ribs, and around my hips—the places where Hudson touched me. His skin was callused and tough, rougher than I'd expected.

I turn around. The burning water beats my back, plasters my hair along my cheeks. My skin is red from it. I work the shampoo into my hair, then extend my neck and dip my head into the stream. I feel the push of Hudson's lips, the press of his jeans against me. I wrap my hair in my hands and wring it out. I hear his voice in my head—it was rough too, out of breath—see his lips still glistening with our kiss when he said, "We should stop."

I bet he never stopped with Jolene. I bet he couldn't resist her.

I turn back around, let the hot water hit my face and reach for the tender spot on my hip where Jolene's earring pierced me. The cut is small but deep. The scab on top is ridged and thick. Hard. Like Hudson's hands, his voice. Like him. The way I want to be. Not soft and pulpy like cheap paper or open like the inside of a tree—rings exposed for everyone to see—but closed, hard, covered. Like bark.

If Jolene's done with me, then I'll be done with her, too.

Just when I'm starting to feel weak from the heat, there's a hard knock on the door. I shut off the water.

"Maitreya, it's getting late," my mom calls. How long have I been in here?

"I know what time it is!" I shout. "I'll be down in five."

After I get dressed, I run down the stairs, swing myself around the bottom of the banister, pull my jacket from its hanger, and grab a bagel from the kitchen.

"Is that Jake's shirt?" my mom asks, trailing me in her cotton pajamas and fuzzy slippers.

"Yeah," I say, shoving my arms into my jacket and shouldering my backpack. I push through the door into a sharp morning. "So what?"

"Won't you be cold?" she calls. She's holding the door open with one arm and wrapping the other around her waist. The collar of her pajama shirt flaps in the wind.

"I'm fine," I shout over my shoulder as I throw my bag into the car.

"And you'll be home for dinner?" she asks.

"That's the deal, right?" I ask, sliding behind the wheel. It's my day to pick up Kris.

"Right," she says.

"Then I'll see you for dinner." I turn the key in the ignition.

She steps back and lets the storm door swing shut in front of her, but she doesn't leave. She folds her arms across her chest and watches me, squinting, like it's hard to see, even though the glass is perfectly clean.

I wave. Then twist around to back out of the driveway.

It's not until I catch myself in the rearview mirror that I realize I never checked my reflection this morning. My hair falls in wisps around my face. My cheeks burn red from the cold. My mouth seems wider, my eyes darker. And the neck of Jake's shirt—the cotton jagged where I cut it—slants across my collarbone, hinting at the bare shoulder under my jacket.

I look like someone else.

She smiles.

I follow Kris into the journalism room before first period, shrug off my jacket, and throw it on the heater by the window. If she notices Jake's shirt or the way it hangs off my shoulder, she doesn't mention it. She's too busy analyzing the whiteboard in the corner of the room, making sure this week's issue has enough article assignments. Our high school has one of the few weekly independent papers in the nation, and Kris takes it seriously. Not just because it's an approved venue for criticizing Westfield, but also because she thinks it's her ticket out of here. Editor-in-chief of a nationally award-winning newspaper isn't the worst thing for your college application. Plus, being a staff member has its perks: passes to leave campus during school hours; keys to the room, so you can come and go as you please.

The week after I walked out of Jolene's room with rope burns on my wrists, Kris made me a set. I'd told Jolene to leave me alone. She'd done one better. She'd stopped talking to me, and so had every other girl in our class except for Kris. It was like Jolene had cast a spell over them, or rearranged the facts until I was a stranger. So instead of growing gills at sleepovers, I built up my map collection and hung out with my mom on the weekends. At school I was stone—no stares, shouts, or shoves could penetrate me. At night I was wet cement, pouring myself out drip by drip to reset and harden again by morning.

That was the year we studied symbiosis in biology. We learned about the shrimp and the goby fish. How each has its strengths and weaknesses. The shrimp digs killer burrows but is basically blind; the goby has excellent eyesight but nowhere to hide. So when they get together, the shrimp provides the protection and the goby acts as lookout. Without each other, they can't survive. That hit home. But it was the gutless marine worm that really got to me—the one that needs bacteria to substitute for its missing stomach. Because that was Jolene—the bacteria that crept under my skin and found a place to live. She was my guts, and without her I felt like I couldn't eat, breathe, or sleep. Like I might not make it. Like I was dying a little, from the inside, just from being me again, in my small box of a world. But if that were true, wouldn't Jolene be dying a little too?

I watched her in the hall one afternoon, laughing with Bella. She seemed fine without me.

So a week later, after lots of convincing from Kris, I started hanging out with the journalism kids. I didn't know most of them at the beginning, but the longer I hung out with them, the less they seemed like the staff of the paper and the more they seemed like potential friends. I even started doing some work with them. Turned out my lifelong map habit was good for something—during those endless hours spent staring at lines and fonts and colors, I'd developed an eye for design. I suggested a few changes to the front page one night, and pretty soon I was laying out the whole paper. It was only four pages—six for a special edition—but it was mine. Eventually Kris gave me the honorary title of Design Editor, even though it didn't mean anything—it wasn't on the masthead. I wasn't even taking journalism yet. But I was starting to feel better. Like less of a gutless worm and more of a human.

I pass between the round tables, find a seat at one of the large monitors, wake up the computer, and open the file for the current issue. So far the only finished articles are Kris's op-ed on the New Jersey school rankings system and Jim's cover story on insufficient funding for the independent study program. Usually this is my favorite time to play around with the layout: reset the text boxes, thin the lines above and below the pull quotes, make sure that the fonts match and the pages pop, but today I can't seem to take it all in. For some reason, I can't immediately see what's off about it, what needs to be changed in order to make it flow and fall into alignment. It just looks empty: blank columns gaping like wide eyes and open mouths.

"By the way," Kris says. I swivel in my chair and find the

back of her fuzzy, chunky cardigan. Her red ringlets are held up by two pencils. Her blue, dry-erase marker squeaks against the whiteboard as she writes. "You're giving Bella a lift home."

"I am?"

"Yup. She doesn't want to ride with Jolene after what happened at the party." Kris caps her pen and grabs her bag.

"Jolene's not here."

"She wasn't here yesterday," Kris corrects. "She's back today. According to Bella."

My eyes dart to the door, but all I see is the bland, tan tile of the hallway and the banner that shouts Be Your Best Selves!

"So you invited her to come with us?" I get up from the computer and swipe my jacket off the heater. It's hot where it covered the vent and stings my arm for a second before the heat releases. "You sure that won't ruin your untouchable status as a Nobody?"

The bell rings. Kris holds the door open for me. "Bella told off Jolene at her own party. The social hostesses of the senior class aren't speaking. I'm pretty sure nobody's status is untouchable at this point."

CHAPTER 17

HAVE YOU SEEN *Jolene?*

The whispers begin by second period. Behind cupped hands and locker doors, her name snakes its way from mouths to ears.

She looks pale. Sick. She has the flu? No, mono. No, Lyme disease. No, she tried to kill herself. Pills. She can barely move. She's back in school, but only for a few periods. She doesn't have the strength for a full day. Trust me. We're friends. I sat with her once at lunch. She liked my bangs. And I'm telling you. She's not okay. Yeah, she was beautiful. But now. Ask anyone. They'll tell you too. I saw her near the wall, crawling into class on all fours. It's so, so sad. How does that happen? I mean, for so long she was everything and then—well, Bella was the one with all the friends, I guess. Like I said, I sat with her once. I could do it again. But if she's going to hit on me, forget it. I heard what happened at that party. No wonder Hudson dumped her for that new girl. Wait, you know her? Wait, I know her? Tell me!

Kris was right. Now that Bella and Jolene aren't speaking, everyone else is.

By the end of the week Jolene is in the buzz of the fluorescent lights, the scrape of metal against linoleum, the scratch of chalk across boards, and the hissing, bitter wind that follows me out the door and back in again. And even though I held her hair back and tucked her in after Bella's party, I start to wonder: What really happened that night? What did it do to her? Where has she been? Where is she

when Hudson presses me against the wall before physics, tips up my chin, and makes my lips wet with his—

when I give Bella a ride home from school. When she sits with me and Kris in the cafeteria—

when I leave lunch early—

when I spend afternoons in Hudson's room, familiar now, with the feel of his hands on my jeans, the sight of my shirt on his floor, the temperature of his sheets (how they're cool when I get there and warm when I leave)—

when I abandon all other routes to trace the space between his freckles and the straight stretch of his collarbone—

when I ditch my phone in a pine-scented drawer, where I can't check it for texts—

when I grow new skin where she's been—

when I harden?

Has she seen me?

CHAPTER 18

I'M IN FIRST-PERIOD Spanish rearranging the desks for *¡Charlemos, Chicos!*, aka Talk Tuesday—the day we play out these little skits. According to Señora, it's the only way we can truly *experience español*. I lean over and push a metal desk across the room with both hands. It resists with groans and squeaks. On the final shove my shirt shifts, exposing my shoulder. Hudson's shirt, actually. I grabbed it from his floor one afternoon. He told me to keep it. I didn't ask before I slit its neck. I blow my hair out of my eyes and stand up, leaving my shirt where it is.

Señora's long skirt blooms behind her as she walks with purposeful strides around the room, pointing to a corner there, straightening a desk here, examining the scene with puckered lips, squinted eyes, her hands on her hips. She's always extra-energetic on Talk Tuesdays. It's almost like she's as bored with conjugating verbs as we are.

"*¡Vamos chicos!*" Señora says, surveying the room with a satisfied grin. "*¡Hablemos!*"

So far this year we've been to the market, made breakfast, introduced ourselves at a party, dumped our boyfriends and girlfriends, and ordered food in a restaurant.

Today we're doing directions.

I spend half the period telling two girls in matching sweater vests to make a left and go straight to get to the bus station, then we switch places. The script says to introduce myself, explain I'm lost, and ask for help finding the nearest transportation.

I'm about to tell them I don't know where I am when I feel it—a slight shift in the air. I stop midsentence. My eyes find the door. I see a flash of dark hair, chestnut on top, auburn underneath.

"*¿Necesitas ayuda?*" asks one of the sweater vests. *Do you need help?* I turn back to them. They look sideways at each other, then toward me. I adjust my shirt and smooth my hair.

I thought I heard the sharp crack of Jolene's laugh in the hall this morning, too, but when I turned, it wasn't her.

For the past week Jolene has been as slippery and scattered as the whispers. She came back to school, but it's like she's not here. She doesn't eat lunch in the cafeteria anymore or linger by her locker. She's not on my long or short routes to psychology. And she's obviously not talking to Bella outside history, since she and Bella aren't talking at all.

"*Sí,*" I say. "*Estoy perdida.*" *I'm lost,* I tell them. As the words leave my lips, I feel it again. I jerk my head up, and there she is: her dark hair hanging so straight it looks wet, her hazel eyes locked on me, her palm pressed against the square of glass, her scar darker than it should be. I blink my eyes, raise my own hand without thinking.

One of the sweater vests sighs in front of me, cocks her head.

"Are we doing this or not?" she asks. I look at her, then back to the door again. Jolene's gone.

"Or not." I cut through the conversations of stilted Spanish and wrestle my backpack from the pile on the windowsill. The strap burns when I slide it over my bare shoulder, but I don't wince. I don't give a shit. The bell rings. The sweater vests split as I walk between them.

I steel myself in the hall on the way to history. *I am not shiny and pink.* Gym. *But a scab on top of new skin.* Psychology. *I am sealed.* Physics. *She can't get in.*

I don't see Jolene.

By the time I'm walking to lunch, I feel okay again—solid all the way through to my center.

Hard-core.

I toss my hair and hitch up my backpack, feel my shirt rise, showing an inch of skin along my stomach. I know it's pale next to Hudson's black T-shirt, not because I'm looking, but because they are; every backpack-carrying, book-switching, makeup-fixing kid in the hall pauses when I pass. Their stares blaze. But after a year of invisibility, it's a warm, welcome weight. I wear it down the center of the hall and throw open the door to the cafeteria.

The air is heavy with meat and grease, burned bread and sweat, but today there's something sweet mixed in.

"Mats!" Bella calls over the crowd, giving me the beauty queen treatment: tight-lipped smile, rotating wave. She's spun halfway around in her seat, talking to a junior from the football team, arching her back, laughing. Across from Bella, bent over a messy pile of loose-leaf paper, her dark-red curls spilling onto the table and down the back of a fitted, striped sweater I don't recognize, is Kris, in her old seat. I drop my backpack on the floor and sit down next to her, in mine.

"Hey." We're not phantom limbs anymore but the real thing, back in our original places, at our original table. Well, almost. One seat is empty.

As Bella air-kisses the junior good-bye, Kris looks me over—Hudson's cut shirt, my low-rise jeans, the stretch of exposed shoulder where my split ends hit my collarbone—and raises her eyebrows.

I lift my chin in response.

Neither of us speaks. But that's how it's been lately. First because Kris was grounded and then because when her week-long sentence ended, my afternoons with Hudson didn't. And with Bella joining us in the car and the cafeteria, the only time we have left alone is a few free minutes in the journalism room before the bell each morning, but for the past week I've been using that to finish homework. She doesn't even know I gave up my phone, that I dropped it in the drawer Hudson offered and haven't checked it in days.

Kris curls her hands around her Coke and turns back to Bella.

"I'd totally make up with Jolene," Bella says, dragging her enormous studded purse onto the table and diving in with both hands and half her head. Tucks and folds of leather and gold expand and contract as she rummages through it and, finally, emerges with a compact. She clicks it open. ". . . if she'd just apologize. Hell, I'd probably even kiss her if she said pretty please."

"Might not want to tell Cal that," Kris says.

"Whatever," Bella says from behind the compact. "We're just

hooking up. And anyway, he loves it."

Bella and Kris banter like I'm not even here. It's amazing to me how quickly they fell back into the old rhythm—Bella's singsong laugh, Kris's cutting commentary—and how quickly Jolene fell out of it. But then, that's the answer, isn't it: now Kris and Bella share a common enemy.

"I think you need to practice some anger encouragement," Kris says to Bella. "Like, some people need anger management. And you need the opposite."

"I hate fighting." Bella blinks her eyes, blows herself a kiss, snaps her compact, and shoves it back inside her bag. "What's the point? My mom's angry enough for the whole world when she's sober. Which Jolene totally knows. Which is exactly why I need the apology."

"Which is why you need to get the hell out of here as much as I do."

I let their voices recede into the banged plates, shouts, and shoved trays around us until it's all a solid piece of sound. My eyes drift toward the door. The square of glass, just like the one in Spanish class. I see her hand again—our scar—pressed flat against the pane. I run my thumb over the raised line on my palm before folding my hand into a fist.

"How's *your* list coming, Mattie?" Kris asks. I pry my eyes away from the door and toward her voice.

"What list?" I ask.

Kris pulls a yellow pencil out of the curls coming loose on top of her head and taps it against a sheet of blank paper.

"I mean, I don't see what the big deal is," Bella says, filling in the crack in the conversation. "My parents both went to Ivy League colleges, and look where it got them. They don't even talk to each other. Make me a list of schools ranked by fun and then *maybe* I'll consider one."

Kris sketches something as Bella runs through the endless list of qualities she's considering in a college: fraternities and sororities, parties, holiday celebrations (*Hello! Halloween!*), Division I sports teams (for cheering purposes), location (spring break opportunities) . . . Kris lifts her pencil and spins the piece of paper into the middle of the table. Bella twists her torso to look.

"You just did this?" Bella asks Kris. "It's, like, an actual list of schools for partying you just pulled from memory?"

"Makes sense, since Kris picked a college in fifth grade," I say.

"True." Kris sticks the pencil back through her curls. "But I'm still considering all my options." She pushes the paper all the way across the table. "Here. It's yours."

"Really?" Bella scans the page with her pointer finger, moving her freshly lined lips as she silently reads Kris's notes, which are printed neatly across rows and down columns.

Kris presses her stomach into the table and seesaws toward Bella so she can glide her finger across the upside-down grid.

"I circled the safe schools, squared the average, and starred the reach." Kris swings back until she's sitting on her seat again.

"You really think I could get into Rutgers?" Bella asks.

"Why not?" Kris shrugs. "You're captain of the cheer squad, and you won some of the drama competitions at the Paper Mill Playhouse last year, didn't you? And even though you don't try in school, you did decent on your SATs. Anyway, even if you didn't have all those things, it's a reach. Someone's got to get in."

"I'm totally someone!" Bella jokes.

Kris raises her Coke like she's toasting.

My eyes drift toward the cafeteria door again.

"Which applications have *you* finished?" Kris asks. It takes me a second to realize she's speaking to me—that Bella's back behind her compact with her entire stock of eye makeup laid out on the table in front of her.

"None," I tell her.

"Deadline's coming up."

"You've said." For as long as I can remember, Kris has been waiting for this—December, our senior year—the month she can finally send in her applications and start disengaging for real.

Kris finishes the last sip of her Coke and sets down the can with a hard *click*.

"Is it him?" Kris asks, her voice barely audible over the layered conversations in the cafeteria. If I didn't know it so well, I might not have heard it. But I do. And I did.

I lean over the table, lower my voice to match Kris's. "Is *what* him?"

"Is Hudson the reason you're wearing those clothes, ignoring your phone, and talking as much as a first-year foreign exchange student?"

"No."

"Because he's not worth it."

"And Jim is?"

"I didn't change anything for him," Kris says, tapping her empty can on the table.

"Maybe that's the problem."

"Jim and I don't have a problem. He knows it's over when we graduate."

"Do you think that changes the fact that he's in love with you? Or do you just not care?"

Kris looks over her shoulder, then back at me. Her lips move like she wants to say something, but instead she sits up and sighs. It's a rare victory, to leave Kris speechless, but it doesn't feel like a win.

"Just—don't tell me what Hudson's worth, okay? You don't know him."

"Fine. I don't know him. But I know that no guy is worth it."

I don't argue with her. On this we agree. We always have. That's why it's so disappointing that she can't, for a second, believe me.

"I told you. It's not about him." Kris has been friends with Bella again for a week, and she's telling her she can get into Rutgers. She's been mine since grade school, but she can't imagine me reaching for anything. Being different. Better.

"Weird timing then." Kris shrugs.

I grab my backpack from the floor before she can say anything else. "See you at the car," I say, with a quick wave. Bella blows me a kiss from behind her compact, but Kris keeps quiet as I head for the doors and what I know is beyond them: brisk wind, warm sun, red cheeks, dark hair, deep breaths. Someone who believes there's more to me.

CHAPTER 19

I TAKE QUICK steps across the gray pavement toward Hudson. He's in loose jeans, soft at the knees, and a flannel shirt, cuffs unbuttoned, collar flapping. Dead leaves spin at his feet, lift up into the field, and flatten against the surrounding trees, whose branches blow into impossible curves before snapping back against the strength of the coming storm.

He's looking down when I push his headphones off his ears and press myself against him with a hard kiss. He pulls away at first, surprised. But I keep my hand on his neck, my eyes closed, and my mouth open, until his stiff lips soften and his head tilts. I kiss him until the only thing I can hear is my heart and his breath and the music—something acoustic—floating up from his headphones. And when I'm finished—when our noses touch and we're taking fast white breaths—I try to kiss him again, but he closes his hands around my shoulders and holds me where I am, his expression as dark and tight-knit as the cloud cover above us.

"What?" I ask. It's not the first time he's stopped me, or himself.

His grip tightens before he lets go of me completely and leans back against the bike racks. I shove my hands into my pockets, find my lighter, and form a fist around it.

He shakes his head. And as he does, the wind kicks up. Whistling. Whispering.

Jolene.

I wonder if he's heard it too—the two syllables, so familiar, springing from people's lips like a hiss, a hush, a secret. Or if his headphones block that out as well.

"Tell me," I say, my voice pushing back since my hands and lips can't.

"Nothing. You just . . ." He pauses. His shoulders rise and sink, like he's made a decision. "Just nothing," he says, and starts walking toward the building. I rush to catch up. The bell rings as I follow him between parked cars.

"Hudson." I grab his hand at the top of the steps. He stops and faces me, his fingers rigid, his expression solemn. "Is this about what everyone's saying?" I ask.

Is it about her?

"Yeah."

"Oh."

Hudson shakes his head. "I mean, no. It's about everyone, but I don't give a shit what they're saying."

"Right," I say. "Me neither." I lift my eyes to his. I try to make them hard, to be the girl he sees when he looks at me. The one he's certain of. But Hudson's not looking at me. He's not really looking at anything. He's thinking. And no matter what he says, I've got to believe it's about Jolene. He was certain of her once, too. He's got to be wondering how she is, where she's been.

There's a bang behind the door. It shakes, like something's trying to escape.

Hudson sets his deep-sea eyes on mine. Behind him, a cloud shifts, shadowing his face, darkening the sky. "Later, okay? Not here," he says. "Come over."

"Come over," Jolene said, her voice thin, shaking.

I nod.

The second bell rings. We go in.

"Jolene?" My voice came out thick and slow, heavy with sleep. I took my phone away from my cheek and squinted at the time: 12:30 a.m. Then I shut my eyes again and pressed the phone to my ear.

"Sneak out. You can walk to my house." I could hear her breath, quick and close to the phone.

"Now?" Lying in the dark, listening to Jolene's voice, was confusing. It had been a month since the ropes, since we'd spoken.

"Leave your parents a note, tell them you went for an early walk. I know they sleep in. They'd never notice. Just—come over."

I blinked myself awake. It might have been a month, but I hadn't forgotten what Jolene sounded like when she needed me.

"Okay."

"I'm in my room," she said. Then she must have hung up, because the call ended.

I got up, threw on clothes, splashed water on my face, and hit the road.

Outside, the streets were the way I'd always imagined them: clear, cold, open. The road unfolded before me. I crossed blocks and divisions, walked over numbers and through colors, toward the center of Sanborn's 1921, where Jolene's street sat, dressed in cardboard brown and adorned in hand-drawn letters. It wasn't until the tip of my nose started to sting ten minutes in that reality set in. I wasn't walking a map in my head. I was outside, and it was freezing.

A dog barked down the street. I whipped around to see a dark figure dragging it along on a leash, moving toward me. I sped up and rounded the last corner onto Carleton Road.

All the lights were off in Jolene's house, except for the one in her room. I walked past the front door, toward the right window on the first floor, and ran my hand along the top of the frame, sending the spare key clattering to the cement porch. The noise startled me—not because I was worried about waking her parents; they were always out—but because it had been so tinkly and bright, so different from the sounds of the night.

I inched open the door and climbed the rug-covered steps in my boots. I listened to my heart, its thudding pulse in my neck, my chest, all the way down to my toes, like I was in some Edgar Allan Poe story. Beat, beat, beat, beneath my feet. When I got to Jolene's bedroom, I peered beneath the door. The light was solid, no shadows of movement. I pushed it open.

"You scared the shit out of me!" Jolene stood against the wall, her eyes wide, her hands clutching a baseball bat. She threw the bat to the ground and dragged me onto the bed. I kicked off my boots. She drew the covers up and over us.

"You told me to come over," I said in my defense.

"And you did," she said, reaching under the blanket, squeezing my hand.

"What's going on?"

"Nothing," she said, looking away from me, our hands locked

and hot, her toes curling and uncurling next to mine. "I just hate being here alone."

"Now you're not."

Jolene smiled at me then. Not the smile she gives everybody— the wide one where she dips her chin to the side, narrows her eyes, and flashes her teeth—the real one: lips pressed together, corners of her mouth curved up, eyebrows high, like she's surprised herself that it happened at all.

It was the smile that made me say it. "Two little girls all alone in the world, who woke from their beds and decided to live."

Jolene looked at me, her eyes wet for a second, before she said, "Two little girls who walked out of this world, peeled off their skin, and let magic seep in."

"You win," I said. "That was good."

Jolene rolled onto her back and stared at the ceiling. Her sheets smelled like her: Cinnamon shampoo. The lavender lotion she used before bed. And something astringent too, something she must have washed her face with.

We didn't talk for a while. Just lay there, holding hands, in the only lit room of the empty house; until she reached over, switched off the lamp on her nightstand, and leaned back in the bed next to me. The lengths of our arms touched.

"You hurt my feelings, you know." Jolene pulled my hand onto her stomach and let it rest there. "That whole thing with the ropes—" My body tensed. Jolene pulled my hand farther across her body, past her belly button. "You didn't trust me. You were always saying how bored you were, how you wanted to do something different. I was trying to do that for you."

"Then why didn't you tell me?" I asked, my voice tight.

"Wouldn't that have been boring," she said, turning her head toward me, smirking. She looked back at the ceiling, inhaled. Our hands rose and fell with her breath. "I can't believe you thought I'd do something like that to you," she said, guiding our hands up a few inches. I could feel the ridges of her rib cage. "I mean, I know I shouldn't have done what I did afterward, with everybody. But you left. You were supposed to stay, and instead you just walked away." Her voice broke a little at the end. Was Jolene crying? I'd never seen her come close. "Anyway," she said, with a sniff, "you may as well thank me. Nice friends who would turn on you like that, in a second. I was hurt. They didn't have an excuse."

"It's true." I hadn't thought of it that way. Jolene rolled over so she was facing away from me, but she took my hand with her again so that my chest was pressed against her back, my legs against her legs.

We listened to the sounds of the house. The creak of the windows. The whoosh of the heater.

"So," Jolene said as the rush of air stopped, leaving the room suddenly quiet, "now that you're something new, let's play again. What do you want to be, if you could be anything?"

. . . you're something new . . .

I tried on Jolene's words, and they were true: Right after the ropes, I'd felt isolated. Then I'd gotten used to it: walking, stone-faced, through school; spending my free periods in journalism. I'd gotten used to the sight of Hudson, too, leaning over his locker, hair hanging over his eyes. Him in his faraway place and me in mine. Until he looked up one day when I walked by as if I wasn't a stranger who stared at him in the hall, but someone he recognized.

He was the only boy who'd looked me in the eye. Other than Kris, he was the only person who saw me.

What would make him call me at midnight, I wondered? What

would make him hold me tight? What would it feel like? What would I be, if I could be anything?

"I want to be loved," I whispered.

Jolene held my hand to her chest.

"What about you?" I asked.

It was a few moments before she answered. "I want to be real," Jolene said softly. "Sometimes when my parents stay out late, I wonder if I'm even here. Do you know the last time my mom was home to see me most nights? It's when she still tucked me in and told me stories." Jolene let out a breath. "She told the best stories."

I smoothed Jolene's hair back with my hand and set my lips against the lobe of her ear.

"You're here," I said. "I'm with you."

"Maybe we're both not here." Jolene shifted her hips. I shifted too, until we fit again. "What if we're both not real?"

"We're not," I said. "We're better than real. We're the two little girls."

CHAPTER 20

AFTER MR. RILEY'S red-faced, desk-slapping lecture in calculus, the corridors seem calm. Quiet. I start to wonder if I've
imagined the whole thing—her palm against the glass in Spanish class, her name in the wind. But when I walk into the library
for study hall, I stop thinking and see. The wind never stopped;
it's just a storm whirling around me.

Jolene's sitting in my seat.

She hasn't morphed into someone else the way people said.
Her honey-colored skin still glistens. Her dark hair still shines.
The auburn streak still glows underneath, even under the hor-
rible halogen lights. She doesn't look sick. But something is
different.

"Due to some schedule changes, we've got someone new
today, as you can all see," Ms. Glick says, motioning toward
Jolene. And then, in a decidedly sharper tone: "Maitreya! Seats,
please!" For a librarian, Ms. Glick has always been loud.

She starts the roll call. I clutch my calculus text to my chest, walk past the biography section and along the decal-decorated window, and take the only open seat, which is across from Jolene. *What is she doing here?* My eyes dart down, my fingers itch for a to-do list, my mind wants its mantra of street names, color-coded blocks, neat divisions. But I don't give in. For almost a year and a half I've kept my head down. I've done my time. Now I'm the one at the corner table with Bella and Kris. I'm the one heading to Hudson's after school today. And I deserve it. Whatever's wrong with Jolene, whatever's she's doing, won't make me retreat.

I fight through the clawing, restless feeling. I still my hands, steady my breath, and lift my head. I look at her.

Jolene's slim fingers pull at the zipper on her black backpack, which sits on the table between us. Her nails are unpolished, her eyes unlined. I haven't seen her this colorless in years. Not since we had sleepovers and she came back from the bathroom, face clean, and told me stories.

We spend study hall in silence, the way we're supposed to. I stare at my calculus notes. Curves and graphs I don't understand. I try to do the homework, but instead of tangents and proofs, I end up drawing what I always do. The same thing that covers my notebooks and scrawls across my margins, hangs above my desk and lives in my head. But this time, instead of starting with a border and a compass rose, I go straight for the center of the map and work my way out, until intersecting streets take over the page and bleed off the edge.

Across the table, Jolene takes notes from one of those thick Norton Anthologies. Her hand moves smoothly along the page, script slanting slightly to the right, letters round and wide, same as always. She doesn't say anything about being outside my Spanish class this morning or why she transferred into my study hall. She doesn't say anything at all. Until the last few minutes before the bell, when everyone's shutting books and capping pens and sliding zippers. Only then do I feel her hot, strong grip under the table and the thick triangle of paper she presses into my palm.

I close my fingers over it.

I don't unfold the note during English, or when I pack up my books after class. I hold it tight in my fist as I sit shotgun next to Kris (who doesn't have a cigarette; did she finish it?) and listen to see if Jolene spoke to anyone else. But Bella's telling a joke, and Kris hasn't said a word to me since the cafeteria. So it's just me and the whispers and the note I clutch tight against the cold when Kris drops me off with a hard look and a weak salute.

It's not until I'm parked in front of Hudson's house that I cup my hands around the note—the same way Jolene did with her treasures—and pry them apart slowly, as if the paper might sprout wings and fly away.

CHAPTER 21

I GATHER THE sleeves of my jacket in my fists as I walk up the slate path to Hudson's front door and ring the bell. For a few seconds I don't hear anything. No voices, no footsteps, no movement. The wind blows under my jacket and up my shirt. I'm about to peek through the side windows when I hear the fast thud of feet down the stairs. Hudson opens the door. I've barely slipped off my boots and jacket before he takes my hand and leads me to the second floor, past the framed pictures rising in a line on the wall. Hudson as a bald baby, a little boy with a bowl cut, a skinny seventh grader kneeling next to a soccer ball, a scowling freshman in front of a washed-out blue background. His older brother at all the same ages, looking at me with the same sparkling blue eyes but from a face cut with sharper edges: square jaw, dimpled chin, angled cheekbones. A family portrait—one with their mom still in it. She's smiling. She seems happy. Even though inside she was screaming to leave.

I wonder if Hudson ever suspected who she was underneath.

I wonder if he suspects me. I look up at him, as if the answer might be in the arch of his back or the slope of his shoulders. But all I see are broken-in jeans hanging loose on his hips and the soft stretch of his thermal across his back when his arm swings forward to push open his bedroom door.

The smell envelopes me—wood and wind. Him. It's from the furniture. An ancient, stained-wood bookcase stuffed with peeling paperbacks, ruffled comics, used pads of drawing paper, pencils. A wide dresser with deep drawers (perfect for ditched phones) and bronze metal handles. A long, sprawling desk with nothing on top of it but nicks and dents. A worn wood chair to match, shoved out and angled back, like it's waiting for someone. A window above the desk, open a crack to let in the late-fall air.

I know every inch of Hudson's room by now, but it's the window that's always seemed the most familiar.

The first thing Hudson does when he closes the door behind him is tell me he's sorry. The second thing he does is kiss me—lightly on my collarbone, insistent on my lips. He doesn't hold me back or pull away like he did earlier. He leans into me until I'm up against the wall and out of breath.

"I'm sorry about today," he says again. "I should have told you." I can't help thinking Hudson knows, somehow, about the note. Or that I took Jolene home. I can't help feeling guilty, like I should be the one coming clean. But even so, I don't speak. He'd get angry. He'd see me differently. And that's something I can't risk right now. I need to be the girl he sees. I need to know she exists.

"Told me what?"

"Hold on," he says, turning away from me. "Music." He

walks toward the huge black stereo sunk into the corner of the thick carpet, reaches down into what looks like a lake of circular silver fish, and plucks a disc from the middle. He slips it into the tray and presses play. While it spins, he takes my hand—the one Jolene grabbed under the library table—and leads me to the bed. He sits down on the green flannel sheet, leans back against the wall, rests his elbows on the fraying knees of his jeans, and faces me.

Then the deep voice sings from his speakers, the one that was playing in the car at the reservation. It's so intimate—like there's another person in the room.

And then there is.

"I didn't want to talk about Jolene," he says.

So it was about her after all.

"It's okay," I say. But it's not. I've been working so hard to shut her out, and now she's here again. I feel this building pressure inside me, like my blood is trying to burst out of my skin. But it's not me who caved and said her name, I remind myself; it's Hudson.

"You keep saying that." He rips a white string from the hole in his jeans. "But it's not. I just need to say this so you don't think—so you understand why sometimes I . . . stop."

Hudson won't look at me. His eyes are glued to his fingers, the soft, twisted thread they roll back and forth. His hair hangs loose in dark waves around his face.

"It's okay," I say again. I'm not sure whether I'm saying it for him or for me, but either way, it seems like the right—the only—thing to say. Especially when my heart is thudding and my blood is buzzing. Now that Hudson's talking about Jolene, I want to know everything.

"I left her. But there are some things that won't go away."
The piece of thread drops from his fingers, drifts to the bed. He
palms the knees of his jeans. "When we were . . . together . . .
I always had to be the one to . . . start." He flicks his eyes up
to me. I nod. *It's okay.* He rests his elbows on his knees, hangs
his hands between them, and weaves his fingers together. "But
then once we were . . . into it . . . she'd get *really* into it. Once
she bit me."

I let out a quick huff of breath. Hudson presses his lips
together.

"Sorry, I'm okay. It's— I'm listening," I tell him.

Hudson readjusts his elbows on his knees, leans forward.
The bed squeaks. "So she'd get really into things, but then if I
did too, she'd freak out."

"Freak out how?"

Hudson shrugs. And I think he's going to stop telling me,
which makes the buzz inside me grow loud and big. But then
he speaks. And I'm relieved.

"She'd stop my hand, yell at me, tell me I was going too fast.
Or that just because we were together once didn't give me permission to do anything she didn't want." He blinks a few times,
licks his lips. "I mean, shit. It's not like I ever . . . At the end
she'd only touch me in public anyway. It was like— You know
what?" He looks up. "You don't need to hear this. I just wanted
to explain. Why I'm not always sure, you know, what I should
do. With you. I know you're not her. It's just . . ."

Hudson's shoulders hunch forward. He nods, but not to the
beat of the music. It's like he's in pain. But it's not his fault.
Jolene. She does this to people.

She's done it to me.

I take his hand and fit our fingers together. His skin is three shades darker than mine, even in the winter, except for the thin line circling his finger where he used to wear Jolene's ring. That pale strip matches mine exactly.

"She tied me up once," I say. Hudson's head jerks up, and his body rocks backward, like the words I've stored for so long have an actual force. "She tied my wrists and legs together and taped my mouth. And I let her. It was supposed to be a game, but—" I stop for a breath and the words stop too. Then something covers my mouth—the tape—no, his lips, strong against mine, sealing us together. He eases me onto the bed. My head hums and my blood pulses. I breathe into him, and he breathes back, until I think maybe he's breathing for me, or I'm breathing for him, or we're the same person. Then his tongue finds mine. We taste and test the new secrets between us, teasing them back and forth until they're ours. Until she's ours, instead of us being hers.

When he lifts himself up, my body feels too light. I think he'll stop, and I can't stand it. But he doesn't stop. He traces a slow circle around my wrist. His touch is so light I want to cry. When he lets go of my wrist, he takes my hand and sits me up so we're facing. He leans into me until our foreheads touch, then slips my shirt over my head. He lays me back down on the flannel sheets and unbuttons my jeans. I stare at the ceiling as he tugs them down past my knees, the same way I tugged at the note from Jolene.

She folded it into a triangle, just like we did in intermediate school. The only script on the outside was my name—not Mattie, but Lorraine—the one she gave me in her stories. Same way I'd call her Jane. We used to sign every note that way. I flipped the folded paper around in my hands, staring at the perfectly curved letters, then slipped my finger inside the tight triangle and pulled the tucked edge free.

Hudson slides my jeans over my feet. I kick them to the floor. He takes off his shirt. I press my palms to his chest. He breathes. I feel his heartbeat. It's so quick. He lowers his lips to my shoulder and kisses me along my collarbone. When he reaches my bra strap, he lifts it with his index finger and lets it fall down my arm.

I unfolded the note slowly, flattening each careful fold. I pinned it against the center of my steering wheel and ran my palm over it a few times before I let myself look.

Hudson slips his arm underneath me and unhooks my bra. I run my hands through his hair, down his neck, as I move closer to him. And we kiss, but kissing is so much more when I can feel his shoulder blades and the curve of his back, the angle of his hip and the waist of his jeans. I run my fingers along the rough denim, then slip them beneath his boxers. His breath hitches, then comes back deeper. His chest moves in and out against mine.

Written in bleeding blue script across the creased sheet were the last lines Jolene had ever spoken of our poem.

Hudson's lips brush mine before he tugs at his own jeans. Then we get rid of everything that's left between us. For a second we are still, nothing but skin and breath thrumming on the bed.

"Do you have . . . ?"

"Yeah," he answers. There is some fumbling in his nightstand drawer, then the rip of plastic. A few seconds later he's holding himself above me—arms straight and shaking. His eyes, clear as sky, open wide. His eyebrows lift. He asks if I'm okay.

I say yes.

Hudson lowers himself slowly.

Two little girls all alone in the world,
who went to sleep twins
and woke up in one skin.

CHAPTER 22

JOLENE WRITES ME notes every day after that. Instead of maps, I collect folded triangles covered in blue felt-tipped pen, addressed to Lorraine. I anticipate her hand under the table, the shape of the paper in my palm, the scent of cinnamon that lingers through English and on the drive home with Bella and Kris. They talk about Jolene like she doesn't exist, like they were friends with her long ago in a land far, far away. But they still talk about her.

Everybody does.

It's like some kind of fucked-up social physics: now that Jolene isn't physically on display in the hallway, the front lawn, the cafeteria—now that she only shows up for class (and barely that)—something needs to fill the space. The whispers have mated and multiplied and morphed from scraps of speculation into full-blown stories. But her name doesn't haunt me anymore. I don't hear it in the squeak of my sneakers or the click of a closing classroom door. Because Jolene is with me now. She's the crinkle and slide of the note unfolding, the careful curves of script detailing each memory. Everyone talks, but nobody knows about study hall. Nobody knows about us.

Not even Hudson.

I tell him other things about me and Jolene. Our history. Every day after school, in his arms, on his flannel sheets, I tell him whichever memory Jolene has revived for me. The scar on my palm, her mom's necklace, the night I came over when she called at midnight.

He tells me stories too: how Jolene took care of him when no one else did—made him food when his dad didn't come home and warmed his bed when his parents' lay tucked and untouched. How the two of them curled up on her couch as the rest of the house echoed, empty, around them. How they streaked through the rooms, raging against their parents.

He tells me how Jolene turned sour the day he started talking to his mom again. How she made him say he loved her over and over again until the words lost meaning. And how he stayed with her too long because he promised he'd take care of her, and he wanted to be the kind of person who kept his word.

Under desks, on top of beds, from clasped hands to shared breath, the past unfolds. It flows from Jolene to me to Hudson, forming a tinted lens of shared memory that colors everything and, eventually, finds its way into the present.

CHAPTER 23

I SHOW UP for study hall the Monday before Christmas break, and there's a printout taped to the door. It's supposed to say: "Study Hall in the Auditorium Today. Library Closed. Heaters Broken." Except someone has taken a black marker to it, so what's left is: "Library Hosed. Haters Broke."

I hug my thin sweater to my chest. It's the one my mom gave me, the one I wore when I went to the reservation with Hudson, and it's not warm enough.

I spin around and nearly collide with three boys talking their way into the library.

"Closed," I say as they separate to let me through. "Auditorium."

"Is that Hudson's new girl?" I hear as I walk away.

Girl. As if we're a line of interchangeable things hinged to Hudson, which replenish each season. It's gross and sexist.

And electrifying.

To be seen. To be new.

I cut back through the crowd and skip down the stairs. I haven't been to the auditorium for anything but assemblies since drama, first semester of junior year. Performing for people isn't my thing, but the idea of being someone else was appealing. Especially then, when it was just me and Kris, working our invisibility.

I shove open the heavy door with my shoulder, step onto the scuffed wood stage, and take it in. The thick rippling curtains. The racks of colored spotlights floating above them. The half-painted set pieces.

Fumes of fresh wood and paint follow me as I exit stage left and walk down three shallow steps. Ms. Glick shouts instructions: check in at the front, no assigned seats, study quietly since we're sharing the space with the cast and crew of *Pippin*, the school musical, which opens this week.

I check in and head straight for the back of the auditorium, beneath the balcony. It's dark under the eave, and I like having everyone in front of me. I watch heads slant to trade secrets, and search the silhouettes for the toss of Jolene's dark hair or the slope of her shoulder, but I don't see either. So I scoot down the bristled velvet, balance my knees on the seat back in front of me, and settle in with some calculus. But the curves blur and the seat squeaks and it's too dark to see and where is she?

I close my notebook as the drama crew takes the stage—a mix of black bodysuits and clownish costumes.

I should be relieved that Jolene isn't here.

Trading notes in study hall was safe. Assigned seats and enforced silence made it that way. But here it's different. Each chair is a choice. Every whisper takes a trip around the auditorium. Here, we could be seen.

Hudson could find out.

Kris. Even though we haven't been hanging out as much as we used to, our friendship—it's not unfixable. But if she found out about Jolene . . .

The damage would be permanent.

I should reopen my notebook, get a jump on my homework. I should ignore the doors and dark corners.

Instead I lean forward, rest my elbows on the seat back in front of me, and scan the audience one last time. When I don't find her, I give up and watch the drama crew settle into some sort of formation in the center of the stage. I can barely hear what they're saying, but I can see their faces transform from frustration to rage, their necks and elbows angle, their hands and fingers twirl as if they're performing an endless magic trick. Then the soft sound of a piano floats in, and every mouth onstage forms into a tight O. This time their combined voices reach me. They sound like ghosts.

"Hey!" A hiss from behind me. Hot breath on my neck.

"Wha—"

"No! Don't turn around. We can talk like this." I lean back in my seat. These are the first sober words Jolene's said to me since sophomore summer (everything else has been in notes and texts), but I can still tell from the lilt of her voice that she's smiling.

"Okay." I glue my eyes to the stage, sit stiff in my seat. There's a group of girls a few rows up. All they'd have to do is turn around and we'd be—

"Relax." Jolene sets her hand on my shoulder, sinks her fingertips between the wide stitches of my sweater. "It's dark back here. No one can see." Her skin is warm. Then it's gone. She sweeps her hand across my hanging hair. A soft tingle travels across my scalp, down the length of my spine. And the fear goes with it.

Jolene isn't going to give herself away. She's been halfway hidden since Thanksgiving. I'm still not sure why; but the point is, if she's here, it's not to reveal herself. She's under the balcony. She's whispering. She doesn't want to be seen.

She wants to be with me.

I sink into my seat.

"Your hair is so long," she whispers.

"I know. I let it grow," I say to the stage, which has just transformed from a bland set of black-and-white benches to lush greens, high pinks, and a random tree.

"It looks awesome," she says. I can't help smiling. "I always liked it like that." A second later my hair falls flat and something squeaks. It must be her seat. I sink farther into mine and wait for a story, a memory, whatever she would have written in her note today. But she doesn't say anything. I wait a little longer. And just when I'm about to tell a story of my own, I hear her voice again from behind me, but this time it's farther away. "Does he love it?"

My body goes rigid. We've never talked about Hudson. We've never talked about anything. Not since I saw them kiss at her locker. I feel like I'm cheating, but I'm not even sure who I'm cheating on. Hudson or Jolene? Obviously Hudson wouldn't want me here with Jolene, but I doubt Jolene wants me with Hudson, either. And I haven't told her what Hudson's been saying about her. The stories. Especially not the one that won't leave me, the one I've started hearing in her voice instead of his: Jolene begging over and over again, *Tell me you love me.*

I sit up and stare straight ahead. All the set pieces have been cleared. The stage is naked. Three girls in black bodysuits—smiles plastic, elbows bent—emerge from behind the right curtain in a triangle formation. They inch toward center stage like injured figure skaters: one foot swerving left and right, while the other drags behind them.

"He doesn't hate it," I say, brushing my hair back, taking care to keep my voice casual. Vague. Neutral.

Neither of us says anything for a few minutes. The sounds of the auditorium bounce around us—dares and protests and laughs and lines and songs—but none of it compares to the thick air between me and Jolene, the thing that's been between us all along.

Hudson.

"He always wanted me to cut mine," she says finally. "But I can see why he'd like yours this way."

I shut my eyes tight. *What does that mean?*

Another part of me laughs, answers: *You know exactly what it means.*

"Then again, Hudson wanted me to do a lot of things," she says, her fingers in my hair again. I imagine the things Hudson wanted her to do. Then I try to unimagine them. He's with me, I remind myself. Not Jolene.

She sweeps my hair up off my neck and twists it into a bun. The tension tugs at my temples. "And I'm glad I didn't change for him. He said he loved me, but obviously he didn't. *He* didn't take me home from Bella's party."

My throat feels as tight as my scalp. Hudson might be with me, but he's never said he loves me. Then again, he said he loved

Jolene, and he left her to fend for herself when she was dead drunk at Bella's.

Jolene pats her fingertips down my neck, the way we used to give the chills in intermediate school, then leans so far forward in her seat that our cheeks meet and whispers, "You're too good for him, you know."

My hair falls loose against my neck. My cheek goes cold. She's not touching me anymore, but her words swirl and swell in my chest.

I still think the label "best friend" is empty, but when Jolene says stuff like that, I remember why I used to call her mine.

I turn around—forgetting for a second who might see us—but before I can twist completely in my seat, I'm blinded. I shield my eyes with my hand. My arm is hit with high heat. Hot pink. I blink. By then the spotlights have spun to other parts of the auditorium, coloring them pink and green. A voice yells, "Cut the gels!" and it's dark again. I blink a few more times, and when I can finally see something other than a faintly flashing disk, I twist around to find Jolene; but all I see is a bouncing, squeaking seat. The only trace of her is a smudge of clear lip gloss on my cheek.

I face forward again. The strange dancers are gone, but the stage is full of actors costumed in carnival colors. They bow, beckon, smile, lick their lips. A couple of them drag something. A set piece. Large. Dark. It's not until they stop at center stage, behind a lone boy dressed in drab rags, that I get a good look at it. The set piece stands taller than the boy. It's black. Curtained, like an upright coffin. It's presented to the boy with twirled wrists and upturned palms. The cast whispers. Smiles. Hisses. Or maybe that's the sound of something burning? It smells like smoke, but nobody seems to notice. Especially not the boy. He touches the black wood, tests the box, as the chorus coos behind him. They want him to go in. They want it so badly. And he wants to go too, I think. But instead he turns to the audience and starts to sing. His voice sounds fragile at first, like it might break. But it doesn't.

LOT 1
MB:46—66
MB:51—103
60' R/W
YOUNGBLO

COS.
MB:46—66
MB:51—10
60' R/W
YOUNGBLO

EX. CB

CHAPTER 24

THAT AFTERNOON IN his room, Hudson rolls out from under the flannel sheets, grabs his boxers from the floor, slides them up to his narrow hips, and runs a hand through his hair. I prop myself up on my elbow and scoot over to his side of the twin bed. I trace the curve of his spine with my eyes, the rise and fall of his sharp shoulder blades, the muscles in his arms as he reaches for and discards another disc that isn't worthy. I pull the sheet up to my shoulders, then change my mind, let it slip down a little so when he turns around, he'll be surprised.

The thing about sex is, people always talk about having it. Like it's something you can pick up and hold and hug to your chest, or stow away in a drawer for safekeeping. Like it's something you can own. But it's actually the opposite. Because when it's over, you don't have anything to take home.

Hudson slips his middle finger through the inner circle of a disc and places it in the tray. He doesn't turn around. I pull the sheet back up and cover myself.

"You're going to like this," he says, grabbing a thermal from the floor and tugging it over his head. I watch his stomach disappear. He's dressed, and I'm still naked. I sit up and scan the floor for my blue bra and the bed for my delicate sweater, which Hudson threw aside undelicately. I find my black tank top first and reach for it without releasing the sheet.

"And if I don't?" I say as I slip the thin material over my head and rake my fingers across the flannel near my feet in an attempt to find my underwear.

"You will," he says.

I wriggle into my clothes underneath the sheet, then walk across the room, careful not to step on anything round and silver. I stand in front of the window, stick my hand through the opening, feel for flakes. It's supposed to snow tonight, but so far it's just cold.

I find my bra on the floor and turn around so I can shimmy it up under my tank top without Hudson seeing. Then I walk over to the mirror to fix my hair. I pull my fingers through it, trying to untangle the knots, but there are too many, so I give up and gather it into a ponytail. Jolene was right; it hasn't been this long since intermediate school.

Hudson snakes his arms around me and kisses my neck. I watch us in the mirror: his eyes closed, his hand across the strap of my tank top, his mouth moving slowly up my neck; my head tilting to the side, my eyes wide, my hair the darkest it's been all winter. Almost as dark as Jolene's.

"Do you think I should cut my hair?" I ask.

"Definitely not," he says into my neck.

"You don't think it would look good short?"

Hudson stops, cocks his head, considers my reflection.

"Nope. Looks good like this." His arms tighten around my waist. His lips are back on my neck.

"The last time I had it this long, Jolene used to braid it for me."

Hudson lifts, midkiss, from my skin. The crease in his brow deepens, folding his freckles together for a split second before they flatten again. "Really?"

"What?" I let my hair fall to my shoulders and turn around to face him. Hudson drops his arms, steps back, shakes his head.

"Jolene." Her name. An accusation.

"You say her name like it's a dirty word."

He raises his ear to the air like he isn't sure he heard me correctly. "Isn't it?"

A lone instrument pierces the silence, some kind of horn blowing a high note, clear and strong. Then the rest of the band picks up again, and the bold sound blends into the background.

I lean against the dresser, even though the handle pokes the skin right above my jeans. "But you dated her for a year. You loved her."

I wait for him to deny it. Instead he sinks down on the edge of his bed and digs the heels of his hands into his eyes. Then he looks at the floor and flexes his jaw.

"Love doesn't just go away," I say. There must be traces of Jolene inside him. Some internal mark to mirror the pale strip on his finger. He can't be rid of her completely.

"Look." His eyes rise. I step toward the bed. Hudson grips my hips, gathers me in. "I did love her." My breath catches, holds, coats the two words stuck in my throat: *Love me.* Hudson scoops a hair behind his ear, works his jaw again. "At least I tried to. But Jolene, she didn't love me. Or maybe she tried, too. All I know is, it didn't work."

Hudson pulls me down to the bed beside him. "It's bad enough I talked about her so much. That I made you do it too. But I'm done now. For real. You know why I did what I did, and I know about whatever happened between you two. And now it's over. Right?"

"Right," I say, because his voice is casual, but his eyes are hard. Because I know it's what he needs to hear, even if it's not the truth.

Hudson brings his fingers to my knee and spreads them out like a starburst, but the warmth doesn't shoot through me like it used to. It stops at the ends of his fingers, leaves when he lifts his hand.

He ducks his head in front of me, forces me to look at him. He smiles. His eyes crinkle at the sides. I don't tell him those stories about me and Jolene weren't for him. I don't tell him about the notes. But when he kisses me, I can't help but see her words in my head.

Remember when we used to end each note with "Love you"?
Still do.
J

CHAPTER 25

IT'S A FEW days before Hanukkah and my mom's feeling it. Each night, dinner isn't so much a time to eat as a catalog of possible presents. Luckily, I don't really have to participate since my mom is pretty good at handling the conversation all by herself. But every once in a while, after she has piled the table with food, filled our plates, forgotten the napkins, fetched my dad a drink, and finally grabbed something for herself—but never a full serving—she'll turn to me.

"Do you think Jake would like that? A new coat?"

I lean over the table to grab a roll. My mom's hand shoots across my stomach to keep my shirt from draping into the gravy. I grab my shirt myself and sit back down. She clears her throat, picks up a single green bean from the serving dish, and crunches it between her front teeth.

"I don't know, Mom. I'm not him."

"Don't be fresh," my dad says, surveying what's left on the table. We haven't spoken much since The Talk. Though I've been home for dinner on time, so I guess there isn't much more to say. "How are those applications coming?" he asks.

"Great," I lie.

"Good," he says, spooning some gravy over the rice on his plate. "You should have Jake take a look at them."

Jake used to help me with my homework. He was more patient than my parents, and better at explaining things. But that pretty much stopped when he went to college. And anyway, he can't look at applications I haven't written. No need to bother my father with that small detail, though.

I push my plate away and uncross my legs, but before my feet touch the floor, my mom asks, "Is Kris coming for the holiday? We missed her at Thanksgiving."

My mom thinks I've been with Kris every afternoon for the past few weeks. I'd told her the paper had a special issue and that I had to put in some overtime with Kris in journalism. It's not a total lie. The holiday edition is always a double issue, so usually I do help Kris out with it. At least I have in the past. This year she hasn't asked, and I haven't volunteered.

I stand up, clear my plate. "She's been here every other year, right?" I ask, as if that's an answer. As if the past is this immutable thing that will always keep happening.

Later that night I'm stomach down on my bed, surrounded by Spanish handouts, brain deep in the conditional tense, when I hear the slap of bare feet down the hall. They pause on the wood floor outside my door. I should have known my mom wouldn't let the Kris thing go. I drop my pen, balance my chin on my fists, and count five breaths before the door creaks open.

"Hi," my mom says, peeking in. She's changed since

dinner—exchanged jeans and a blouse for plaid pajama pants and a sweatshirt.

"Hey," I say.

My mom sidesteps into the room and looks around, taking in my maps, which have been hanging in the same spots for weeks; the clothes on the floor; the book on my bed; and the sheet of loose leaf in front of me.

"You're still doing homework?" Her eyes skip to the digital clock above my drawers. Since I started high school, I've timed my nights to the minute. My mom knows this. She doesn't knock on my door until 10 p.m. That's when I finish my homework.

It's 11:15 p.m.

"I was."

"Oh. Sorry." She takes a half step back. "Should I go?"

"No—" I don't feel like talking to her about Kris, but I know she's just going to keep asking. Might as well get it over with. "It's fine."

"Okay." She sits down on the side of the bed, reaches behind my neck, and flips my tag inside my shirt. I shrug her off. She folds her hands in her lap.

"So," she says, inclining her head in my direction. She's smiling.

I was expecting questions. Some concern. A nostalgic story about one of her many high school friendships.

But a smile? One she can barely contain?

This is not what I expected. This is not good.

I flip over my homework and start drawing—skipping the compass rose again in favor of straight lines, intersections, and streets reaching toward the corners of the lined sheet.

"So," I respond.

"Sooooo. How's Hudson?" She rocks toward me as she says his name, tilting the bed in her direction. My pen skids off the page, dashing a diagonal line across three streets.

So this is an interrogation after all. It's just not about Kris.

"He's fine." I keep my eyes on the paper and my answers short. I know what she wants—I'm pretty sure she's been waiting to talk boyfriends with me since freshman year—but I don't understand why I should give it to her. She had tons of boyfriends before my dad. I only have this one. He's mine, and I don't want to share him.

But my mom—she's looking at me with this expectant, excited expression. I can't remember the last time she looked at me like that.

And I have to admit, it would be nice to talk about Hudson with someone who doesn't hate him, or never dated him. I tick my eyes toward my mom. She's still smiling.

I smile back.

"He's good, I guess."

"Yeah?"

I shrug. The curve in my cheeks deepens.

"So," she says, moving toward me on the bed, "what's he like?"

"I don't know. Quiet, I guess. Different." *He was hers,* I want to say, *and now he's mine.* "He likes music."

"He plays music?"

"No. He *likes* it." I sit up and scoot back on the bed so there's a long stretch of comforter between us. "He plays soccer."

"An athlete." She nods. But that's not who he is either.

"No." I shake my head. "Forget it."

"Well, he must be different if he's got you wearing this." She picks up a cut T-shirt from the floor.

I yank it out of her hands. "I'm wearing this because I like it."

"Okay." She gives me that silver stare of hers, the one that makes me feel like she can see inside my head.

I drag my map onto my lap and try to salvage that stray mark.

My mom sighs. "Look, I came up here because I know Dad's been giving you a hard time, but give him a break, okay? He doesn't know how to deal with all this. You've never had a boyfriend."

"Thanks for the reminder."

"What I mean is, we think it's good, what you're doing. It's what you should be doing. Making friends. Going out with boys."

Friends, she says. *Boys.* Like there are so many.

I draw the same curve of road over and over again, digging in my pen, darkening the line.

"Okay, I get it. You don't want to talk about it. Fine. Just remember to call if you're going to be late."

"I will."

"And be careful."

"Mom."

"You know. If things get serious. Use protection."

"Mom!"

"Okay!" she says, getting off the bed. "Finish your homework. But don't stay up too late."

CHAPTER 26

WHEN I CLIMB into Kris's car on Thursday, with the morning's first flakes melting into my hair, the backseat is empty. "Where's Bella?" I ask, dropping my backpack between my knees.

Kris checks her mirror. "Doctor's appointment."

We don't speak as Kris passes two piles of brown and yellow leaves. They are pristine. Perfect. Dusted with a light coating of snow and begging to be flattened. Kris eyes them as we go by, but she doesn't swerve. Up ahead at the next intersection, I see a third. The wind lifts a few leaves from the top, twirls them in a dance, tosses them aside.

Kris taps her fingers on the wheel, tightens her ponytail, taps the wheel again. She doesn't have a cigarette. I'm starting to think she quit. After all the shit I've given her, I wonder what finally did it. I open my mouth to ask and clap it shut again. I should know the answer to something so obvious about Kris. And if I don't, is it really mine to know? Has she asked me about Hudson lately? College applications? Jolene? She doesn't even know I lost my virginity.

Melted snow forms dark circles on my jeans. I stare straight ahead, trying to see each individual flake that dive-bombs the windshield. It's only as the specks of white fly by me that I realize I haven't marked the colored divisions in my head as we drove through them. Not for at least a week. And now they're all getting whitewashed.

"My mom asked about the holidays," I say. "She missed you at Thanksgiving."

"Of course she did." Kris turns on the wipers. "I'm the only one who eats her themed Jell-O mold."

I laugh. Kris smiles. The moment fades, and there's silence again, the soft sound of snow buckling beneath the tires. I should ask her about Hanukkah, but the idea that it's not a sure thing, that it isn't just assumed she's coming, makes me hesitate.

"How's the holiday issue?" I ask instead. If Kris and I can't be sleepovers and fortune-tellers anymore, surely we can be something else. . . . I swallow back the artificial taste of the word itself: *friends*.

A label. Doesn't mean anything.

"It's at the printer," she says, opening the window to its usual slit. This must be it. I wait for the slip of the pack from her pocket, the slap of her hand on the bottom as she steers the Corolla with her knees. I reach for the lighter in my jacket—Jolene's—but Kris doesn't need it. She dangles her fingers out the window. There's nothing between them but wind and wet flakes.

"Nice."

"A deadline's a deadline," she says, like it's no big thing.

"Even when we don't have help." She doesn't look at me. She doesn't have to. The words do what she knew they would. Guilt burns red streaks across my cheeks. "We could use some help handing them out, though. You know how it is before break."

"Yeah," I say, "sure. Everybody disappears. I remember."

"Cool," she says, bringing her fingers back through the window for our final turn toward school. Their tips are red from the cold. "I'll find you later." As she says it, the tires spin free for a second and we glide across the intersection over a slick mix of ice and snow. I can barely register the fact that we're out of control before we hit a gritty, salted section of street and the Corolla's rubber tires grip the ground again.

Neither Kris nor I mention it as we pull up to school.

Kids swarm the white lawn and gather by the doors. They lift their heads and hands to the sky with delighted smiles. They look young. I feel old watching them.

Kris parallel parks in one of her trademark spaces: a corner spot so small nobody else even slows down to consider it. It's not worth it to them: the attempt; the possibility they won't be able to make it, especially near the front lawn before school, with everybody watching. But for Kris it's no problem. Once the Corolla is snug in its spot, she shuts the window and kills the ignition. Neither of us reaches for the door. We watch as white flakes stick to the windshield, blotting out arms, houses, hats, jackets. Soon we won't be able to see anything. I take off my seat belt. The *click* sounds loud in the silence.

"It's not him?" she asks.

"No."

"Then what is it?"

"What's what?"

"What's *this*?" She looks me up and down, raises her eyebrows, shrugs her shoulders. *Explain,* the motion says. *Explain yourself.*

"Maybe I've changed."

"Maybe," she says, drumming her fingers on the wheel. "But I don't think so."

"What about you?" I free my hands from the straps of my backpack. They're stiff and shaking. "You quit smoking."

My voice sounds strange, like when you hear yourself on a recording and don't recognize it, because that's not the way you sound inside your own head.

"My mom caught me, and I promised to quit a habit that's killing me. It's not the same thing." Kris sucks in a deep breath, blows it out slow, and I imagine smoke. "So, this is who you are now?"

"What if it is?" I ask, my voice tight and rising. This voice I recognize. This is me with a full throat and wet eyes. It's me about to cry. "Is that so terrible? If I'm different?"

"No. Different is fine. Different is cool." Kris grabs two hunks of hair in her hands and fixes her ponytail. "But you don't seem different. You seem like someone else. I mean— Shit, Mattie. If I didn't know you better, I'd say you seemed like Jolene." She says the last part with a huff and a half laugh, like the thought itself is ridiculous. That I could be anything like Jolene.

"Just because we're not together every second doesn't mean I've turned into someone else. Just because it's so impossible for you to believe I could change—" I blink back a budding tear, take a ragged breath, and reset. "Doesn't it ever get to you? That it's been me and you—just me and you—for so long?"

I turn away from Kris and try to focus on something else. Something other than the end of us. But nothing else exists. The window is caked with white flakes.

"No. It doesn't," Kris says, quick and cold as the mounting snow. "Because that's what I wanted. It's what you wanted, too."

I turn back to her. As soon as she sees my face, her expression changes. She's looking at me now like I'm far away. Like I've stolen the last year from her and dropped it on the seat between us.

"Oh, please," she says, her voice sharp now, bitter. "I didn't ask you to come with me that night, remember? I was leaving."

That night. The skin under my arms and beneath my breasts slicks with sweat. No matter how many ways I walk away, that's where I am. *A hot August night. A maze of town houses. A game of manhunt.*

The second time I walked away from Jolene, we picked teams, dropped our cells in the basket (no cheating!), and ran into the web of connected buildings, concrete pathways, and rows of bushes that made up Cal's complex. In the souped-up version of hide-and-seek we called manhunt, the rules were simple: one team hunts, the other hides. If you get caught, you're escorted to home base, where you stay until the game ends or a member of your team beats the guards and tags you free.

But I wasn't worried about the rules.

Hudson had called me that afternoon sounding tense, desperate. His mom was on a plane over the ocean. His dad was deep in his drink. His brother was nowhere to be seen. I promised to meet him after the teams split. He said he'd find me.

So I pushed apart some branches and sank my sneakers into the dirt between two short bushes where the leaves kept trying to meet but never quite made it.

"You know you're hiding in plain sight, right?" Kris asked. She stood in front of me, arms crossed, red curls kinky and high from the heat.

"That was sort of the idea." I looked past her, scanned the silent grounds.

Kris had been quiet for a few weeks in the fall, after I'd forgiven Jolene for the ropes, but she'd never asked what had happened. She'd never asked about Hudson, either, even though she'd seen him fish a blade of grass from my hair the night we named stars. She didn't want to know every single thing like Jolene did. So I hadn't told her. Not because I wanted to keep anything from Kris, but because it didn't belong to her. Hudson had trusted me. He'd drawn me into his distant place. And I loved the dark, dense closeness of it. The shared secret. It made me greedy. I wanted him all to myself.

"As team captain, I should care," Kris said, separating the branches and stepping in next to me. "Lucky for you, I don't give a shit about winning." Our shoulders touched. The sticky skin on our arms pressed together. It had to be ninety degrees, at least.

"Maybe that's why Jolene chose you as opposing captain."

As if I'd summoned her, Jolene came around the corner: ballet flats soft on the cement, draped tank top swishing against her stomach, head swiveling left and right, throwing dark hair over her bare shoulders. I'd never seen her hunt. Usually we were on the same team. She reminded me of a cat: sleek, smooth, ready to spring.

When Jolene was a few steps away, Kris reached for my hand but hit a thin branch. It snapped. As Jolene's head whipped around, Kris and I took off in opposite directions. I ran flat out until I

*realized no one was behind me. Jolene must have gone after Kris,
which made sense considering Jolene's competitive streak, Kris's
hatred for any form of physical activity, and the fact that they were
opposing captains. So, with heavy breaths and a thin film of sweat,
I trotted back toward the last row of town houses and ran along
the path that led toward Cal's, where it would be easier to find
Hudson, and to tag Kris free once Jolene brought her back to base.*

But I never made it. Jolene appeared in front of me. Alone.

*"Lose something?" I asked. Jolene slowed to a stop, turned on her
heels. If she still cared about the game, she could have tagged me.
But she didn't lunge or run in my direction.*

*"Nope. You?" Her voice was light, pleasant almost, like I'd just
asked if she wanted a tall glass of lemonade.*

"Where's Kris?"

*"Trapped in a tower, waiting for a white knight." She motioned
to the sky, rolling her eyes. "Who cares?" she asked, holding out her
hand to me.*

I didn't take it. "For real."

"Real?" Jolene laughed. "Since when do you want that?"

*"Where is she?" I asked again, the temperature in my face and
cheeks rising way above the August heat.*

*Lightning bugs flew lazy circles in the dead air around us.
Screams and laughter sliced the night.*

*"I think you spend enough time with her already, working on
that poor excuse of a paper. If I didn't know any better, I'd think
you liked her more than me."*

Choose.

*Jolene slid the smashed half of our shared necklace back and
forth along its chain.*

Since I'd walked to her house at midnight, Jolene had fixed it so we were all best friends again. But it wasn't the same. Inevitably Bella would bring up something that had happened "back then," which is how she referred to the time I didn't exist. And if Kris and Jolene were opposing magnets before, they weren't anymore—sometimes off talking in a corner, other times eyeing each other in silence. I'd wondered once or twice what had changed to make them this way, but I didn't wonder for long. Obviously, things were different now. Including me. I'd lain in the grass with Hudson, star naming. I'd kept working on the paper with Kris. This wasn't the first time Jolene had mentioned it.

"That's for school." I tensed my neck, felt my own gold chain strain against it. "It has nothing to do with you."

Jolene dropped the necklace. It stuck to the damp skin on her neck. "This night calls for air-conditioning and ice cream," she said. "Come on." She reached for my hand again.

Choose me.

Cinnamon rose from her skin—the scent of our sleepovers. I didn't want to be real. Boring. Mapped out. Made of lists. The way I was before I met her.

I didn't want to be me without Jolene.

But I couldn't leave Kris, either. She'd never left me.

"You go ahead," I said. "I'm good."

Jolene snapped her hand shut and dropped it to her thigh. She lifted her chin until her eyes formed slits.

"I picked you, you know. Out of everyone."

A rare breeze blew through the thick air, lifted my hair like it did on the cliff that day when Jolene grabbed my hand and we ran above the streets so far below.

"I know."

"Well," she said, less a sound than a slow sigh. She lowered her chin. For a second her forehead creased and her thin-slitted eyes dipped at the sides. Then she took a deep breath, and her face brightened again, like a hard reset. "More for me, I guess," she said, before sauntering down the cement path back to Cal's.

It didn't sound like she was talking about ice cream.

The voices in the distance grew layered. Concentrated. People were gathering. The game was ending.

I pictured Hudson leaning against the wrought-iron railing in front of Cal's, tiny beads of sweat on his upper lip, hair puffed out and curly in the heat. Waiting for me. The last time I'd found him at Cal's, he'd been on the couch, bathed in blue light. An hour later I'd been with him, the two of us silent and fused in front of the TV. That's what Jolene had seen. She'd been looking for me. She'd found us. She'd find him, tonight. This time it would be Jolene who showed up first.

It was supposed to be me. I wanted it to be me.

Instead I stepped into the soft, wet grass and ducked into the narrow alley Jolene must have taken that cut through the town houses to the parking lot.

I told myself Hudson would understand. That he'd hear me out. But the farther I got down the alley, the harder it was to think. The distant murmurs of the group back at Cal's stoop faded, overtaken by the whirr and click of crickets and the plink of water dripping. Darkness and brick rose up around me. Half-way through I held my breath. The heat trapped between the town houses was thick as syrup and smelled like piss. When I reached the other side, I breathed again, then skipped down a steep angle of grass to the edge of the dimly lit parking lot in time to hear a flat slam, a loud bang, and the clicking sound of metal on metal. The few seconds that followed were filled with buzzing insects, grumbling garage doors, high-pitched barks, and girly squeals.

Then I heard it again.

Slam. Bang. Clickclickclick.

The storage shed. Of course. Nothing else in this complex was made of metal, or had a reputation worthy of Jolene. In intermediate school we used to dare each other to open its doors, take a step in, stay for one minute, two. We'd heard stories: A nest of bats. A haven for stray cats. The stink of rot. The rounded shape of an animal corpse covered in maggots.

I'd touched my nose to the cracked plastic of its single small window once, after cicada season. The inside of the window, usually obscured by a thick film of dirt and oil swirls, was covered in bug husks: the spindly legs and shed skins of millions of insects. As if they'd fled to the inside of the shed, known it was wilder and darker than any suburban summer night.

Slam.

I ran.

My lungs weren't used to it. Every sound got drowned out by the whoosh and blow of my breath in my head, and somewhere beneath that a steady beat: the bang of my heart, the slap of my feet.

A few minutes later they came into view: five small steel sheds. Four clean and strung with shiny combination locks. The fifth crooked, dented, dirty, its doors sunken and bowed into a sick smile, with rusted teeth biting a branch where the lock should be.

Slam.

The doors pushed against the branch.

Bang.

A hit from inside the shed. On the side. It shook the next shed over and swung its shiny silver lock.

Clickclickclick.

"Kris?" Slam. "Kris! Stop. I'll get you out, but you have to stop hitting the door, okay?"

Silence.

I pulled at the branch, but my hands slid right off, scraping over the rough bark. I wiped my palms on my jeans and tried again: a hand on either end of the stick, my feet shoulder width apart, pulling with my whole body. The stick didn't budge. Then, just as my hands started to burn from sliding on splintered wood, a thin strip of the branch peeled away, and the rest of it sailed through the metal slots. I flew back, then found my footing and dropped the stick. My fingers were stiff and sprinkled with bits of bark. My palms were raw and red, like my wrists had been from the ropes. I panted, sweat drenched, as the metal doors swung open.

Kris burst out—along with a matted brown rat and a swarm of mosquitos—swatting at enormous flies. They flew out of her curls and lifted from her scratched, bitten skin in fits and jags. When she was finally free of them, she found the stick that had locked her in. It lay near my feet. She picked it up, then smacked it down so hard, it split in half and skidded along the pavement.

"I'm leaving," Kris said. She dropped the end of the stick and stalked away. At the sudden movement, two more flies shot out of her hair.

"Me too," I called, running after her.

Kris spun around and studied me like I was a glass-trapped specimen.

"You sure?" she asked. "Because this is it. I'm finished. With her. With all of it. And Jolene can spread whatever brand of fucked-up shit she wants about me, because people might be interested now, but they won't be for long. I'm going to fall so far from popular, no *one will care what she says about me. No one will care about me at all. But it'll be my choice. It'll be perfect. Because I don't care about them. I care about me, and you, and getting through the next two years of high school on our terms."*

Was I sure? As if I still had a choice. I'd already made my decision, up on that cement path, when I'd left Jolene empty-handed. I'd chosen Kris. There was no going back. Not with Jolene. When she did something, she did it completely. Being her best friend wasn't a pinkie-swear kind of thing. It was rabid: a deep cut instead of a drop of blood; smashed glass instead of a store-bought necklace. It was thrilling, the lengths she'd go to for me. The violence. The intensity.

But dragging Kris into it, that was something else entirely.

I knew Jolene would be furious. That she'd turn on me as completely as she'd once clung to me. But I'd survive. I'd done it before, thanks to Kris—I owed her this.

"You were leaving. What was I supposed to do?" I ask Kris.

The bell rings, and suddenly the rest of the world exists again. The sweat on my neck turns cold and clammy. I swallow back the lump in my throat. Swipe my sweater sleeve across the stray tears on my cheek.

"You were supposed to make a choice," Kris says, "and congratulations! You did. You walked away all by yourself." She shoves open the car door to demonstrate.

CHAPTER 27

DOORS OPEN, CLOCKS tick, chalk squeaks, hands rise, people speak, bells ring, doors close. My morning classes pass in the usual sequence even though I feel out of sorts. After gym, sweat from the fitness tests coats my cheeks and beads on the back of my neck as I head to psychology. I let it drip.

Kris didn't wait for me after she slammed the car door this morning. We didn't walk into school together. She didn't meet me after homeroom or before history.

I wanted space. She gave it to me. But even though I ditched my routine weeks ago—even though Kris and I haven't been as close lately—I didn't realize how much I counted on certain things: an arm swinging beside me, a seat in the cafeteria, a sideways glance that no one else understands.

Without them I feel dangerously weightless, like if I take too big a step, I'll bounce up off the surface of the earth and into the atmosphere.

So when Hudson catches me in the hall before physics—rough

skin on my fingertips, the cuff of his flannel brushing along my wrist—and tells me he can't meet at the bike racks, I grip his fingers hard and press my heels into my sneakers.

"Come over after school," he says, cupping his hands around his headphones. "I've got something to show you." He squints his eyes and kisses my lips, and he's off again.

I walk into physics. I feel better in a desk, with a pencil in my hand, copying diagrams from the board. But as soon as I finish, I'm drifting again, through lectures and bells. I skip lunch—obviously Kris doesn't want to see me—and walk the halls, pretending I'm late for class, or going to the bathroom, or on my way to the nurse. I coast through calculus. It's not until I'm on my way to study hall that I realize I've felt like this before. It was during that first day after Thanksgiving break, when Jolene wasn't in school. I'm struck with a sensory memory so strong I stop walking: a whiff of spicy sweetness; the dead-weight of Jolene's arm around my neck; the night air, cool and brisk, with a burning tinge, the hint of true winter—a warning of the things to come.

A fluorescent light flashes over my head and blinks out, and I'm back again. I didn't stop walking after all. And that's what's different about how I feel now as opposed to how I felt then. Before I was untethered, a kite with a cut string. But this is different. I'm not floating aimlessly. I have a destination. And when I sink down with a squeak into the musty, faux-red-velvet seat under the eave in the auditorium, I feel anchored. This is what's left of my routine: A darkened hall. A stage full of scenery. A chorus of voices.

Jolene.

I close my eyes, rest my neck on the curved metal rim of the seat back, and wait. Jolene's always a few minutes late.

She's been telling me stories. Ever since study hall switched from the library to the auditorium, I haven't gotten any notes—nothing to clutch during classes and unfold in my car. No more memories. Something better. The old stories, the original magic, before fights and ropes and manhunt games. Before boys.

Queens and kings and talking things. Lorraine and Jane. The two little girls. I close my eyes. She plays with my hair. The world disappears. Sometimes songs seep in—lights, laughter, voices—but Jolene always makes them part of the story, a seamless landscape painted in the throaty tone of her voice.

At first I worried that other people could hear. I listened without speaking for fear someone could see. But no one ever turned around, no one found us. So I began to add details. Just a little something here or there. A whisper, a name, a shade of sky. They're never as good as Jolene's, but it doesn't matter. It's still our world. Our escape.

Something I need today.

There's a rustle in the row behind me. Feet. A soft squeak. The smell of cinnamon. I shift in my seat, sit up a little bit, making sure to leave my hair draped so she can play with it. My skin is already tingling in anticipation.

"Lorraine," she says. It's how she greets me now.

"Jane," I reply.

I wait for her voice, raspy and low, to take me to another place. But instead she grips the back of my chair with both hands and leans forward until we're cheek to cheek. She blinks, and I feel her eyelashes flutter. She smiles, and her skin curves a path up my cheek. She turns her head left, and it turns mine too.

We're facing the opposite corner of the auditorium, where the straight kids sit: straight spines, straight As, straight to bed.

"If you look hard enough, you can almost see their pointed ears," Jolene says. The sound reverberates through her cheeks; I can feel the words before they come out of her mouth. "And their noses, red. All of them, little elves, always working. So busy." She sighs. I inhale her scented breath.

Then we turn to the center, toward the trendy kids. They're in the first row, decorated with glitter and mousse and makeup. Even the boys. They aren't onstage, but they've got costumes and characters.

One of Jolene's long, dark hairs falls across my cheek and catches on my lip. I don't move it.

"And there," she says, the skin around her mouth lifting and tightening again, "see their wings and sparkling skin? The way they fly above everything? How they hide? Fairies. Obviously."

I laugh. Our lips lift together, touching at the corners.

"And them?" I ask, pushing my cheek against Jolene's until we're all the way to the right, facing the girls who clamored to sit with her when Kris and I stopped.

"Trolls, of course," she says, peeling herself away from me. I want to pull her back. Instead, I hide my hands inside the pockets of my half-zipped hoodie and run my thumb along the lighter.

"What does that make us?" I ask. I wait for her to dress me in gowns, crown me like she used to.

"It makes us Us," she says as the heel of her faded, brown cowboy boot descends next to me. Jolene slides her skinny jeans, narrow hips, and loose, turquoise sweater into the seat. We're sitting side by side for everyone to see.

My fingers grip the Zippo. It's hot and slick. My eyes dart across the auditorium.

Jolene keeps her face toward the stage as she slips her hand into my pocket, twines her fingers through mine, and locks the lighter between our palms. "Don't worry about them," she says. Then her hand is gone, and so is the lighter. Jolene holds it up, twirls it around. "They're not real."

"Funny," I say. But it's true. No heads turn. No eyes bore into us. Nobody's even noticed. It's like we're not here. Like Jolene knew—the night she called me to her house and I walked dark streets to get to her—that we'd end up in these seats, having this conversation. It's like she's always known: *Maybe we're both not here.*

"I remember it being the other way around," I say. "Us, not them."

I rest my arm on the worn bar of wood between us. Jolene does the same thing. Our forearms touch, our middle fingers link.

Hudson wasn't at lunch. Kris left me in the car. Jolene is here. She's real to me.

"Maybe there is no way around." She flicks open the Zippo with her free hand and hits the flint with a square, dark-blue nail. The bitter, burned smell reminds me of the bonfire. The party. The way I found her behind Bella's house. Passed out.

Jolene and I have talked about a lot of things in this auditorium, but she's never mentioned that night. How out of control she was. I'd never seen her that far gone before. Even when her mom would call for the third night in a row to say she couldn't make it home. Even when her dad walked in the door and went straight to his study, flat out ignoring her.

"Are you okay?" I let go of her finger and clasp her whole hand.

"Didn't know you kept this." She flicks the Zippo again. The metal top clicks closed, killing the flame.

"You gave it to me," I say.

"I did." Jolene pockets it. "It was my favorite."

"Jolene."

"What do you care anyway?" Her tone is flip, but her mouth is tight and her breath is quick. "You didn't seem to give a shit when you dropped me last year."

Her words are a punch: *You dropped me.*

Doesn't she get it? I walked away because she forced me. Because she gave me an ultimatum. On that cement path, in the sickening heat, Jolene had asked me to leave the one person who had never left me. And just like Kris said in the car this morning, I made a choice.

So yeah, I walked away from Jolene that day. But I didn't drop her. I knew we'd find our way back to each other eventually, like the shrimp to the goby fish. We always did. She'd call or text or show up at my house.

I just didn't know she'd show up with him.

"You didn't need me. You had Hudson." I pull back on my hand, but Jolene holds on hard. I swallow back the shame of that day, of finding them together after I'd been hoping that he and I could—

"I did," she says, and smiles, but it's not pretty. I see it in profile. The pain—plain, ugly—seems out of place on her face. "Seemed like a fair trade at the time. You for him. I had such high hopes, after everything you told me." Jolene juts her chin. Her eyes rise above the stage, to the scaffolding and lights, but she's not looking at them. She's not looking at anything. "He used to trace letters on my back and make me guess what they said. I was always cold. That open window." Hudson's window.

That's why it always seemed so familiar. It's one of the pictures Jolene texted me. "One night, after we trashed his dad's office, he spelled 'I love you.' It was the first time he said it. To my back, not my face."

She swallows slowly. The taut muscles of her throat bow and constrict.

Then it's like something clicks, and she's with me again. "Anyway, it didn't matter in the end, did it? He ditched me, too. Gave up on me as soon as his mom called. He said he hated her. He said he'd stay. But he left as soon as things got better. Didn't give a shit that nothing changed for me."

"Jolene."

In front of us the curtain closes, but it doesn't block everything. In the slim strip of space between the thick velvet and the scuffed wood floor, shoes and shadows scurry away from center stage.

"At least his mom said she was sorry," Jolene says. "You know what my mom told me the last time I asked her to tell me a story?"

I shake my head.

"She told me to make one up myself," Jolene says. "I was six."

Now I'm the one clutching her hand, holding us together. "Maybe he didn't know," I offer.

"He knew. He just wasn't you." She turns to me, her wide lips and wet eyes lit from the side.

The curtain opens. The cast lines up across a stark stage. Soft notes echo from the piano. Even though it's only rehearsal and we're no kind of audience, the whole place shushes.

"You had Bella," I whisper.

Jolene lets out a quick laugh, leans her head back, and lifts her eyes to the ceiling. "Bella's fun. But she doesn't have this." She loosens her grip, then skims her finger along the scar on my palm. "She's not best-friend material. Not like you and Kris."

"We're not best friends," I say. It's a reflex. *That's just a label. It doesn't mean anything.* "Never were."

"No?" Jolene cocks her head. A boy's voice floats across the auditorium.

"It's not like that with us." I can't explain Kris to Jolene. Just like I could never explain Jolene to Kris.

The entire cast begins to sing behind the boy. They're facing us—mouths open. I want to sing back at them. To let something out of me. It's too hard to hold Kris and Jolene in at the same time.

"I mean," Jolene says with a measured breath, "I *was* kind of surprised, after that whole thing with the ropes."

My lips stick at the mention of that afternoon. I pry them apart. "What do you mean? Kris was the only person who spoke to me."

"Oh," Jolene says, her voice low, her eyes down, her hand tight in mine again. "I thought you knew. I just assumed. You two— She never told you?"

The whole cast sings together now, including the boy. It doesn't sound pretty, like something practiced. There are no harmonies or separate voices. It's just one note, one voice, one full-throated sound, pleading with me.

"Told me what?" I ask. Kris is sleepovers and secrets, mind reading and fortune-telling. There's no way Jolene knows something about her that I don't. There's no way she had anything to do with the ropes. Heat rolls out from the center of my body to my fingertips. It's like when the stage light landed on me. So hot and bright, and suddenly I couldn't see, could barely breathe.

"Nothing," Jolene says, dropping my hand. "You should ask her." She glances toward the stage, stands, then spins on the worn heel of her cowboy boot.

She's leaving.

The song ends. The bell rings. The lights come up in the auditorium.

"Jolene," I call. Heads turn in our direction, but right now I don't care if they see us together. I have to know. I skip sideways down the row, thighs hitting each collapsed seat as I go.

Jolene stops in the center of the aisle and looks up, as if it just started raining and she's the first to feel the drops.

"Careful," she says, with a sideways glance to the rest of the class.

"This way." I grab Jolene's hand and pull her up the aisle, toward the back doors, leaving murmurs and open mouths behind us.

She falls into step behind me, so close it's not just our hands but our entire arms and half our bodies touching. That's how we are when I push through the door into what's usually an empty vestibule.

That's how we are when I see her, when she sees me.

"Kris," I say. The stack of student papers in her arms falls to the floor.

"You're fucking kidding me." She looks from me to Jolene and back again. "Her?"

At first I don't speak. Then I remember. There's no tape stuck to my lips. I can breathe and I can ask and Kris can tell me she had nothing to do with it.

"Ask her," a soft voice says, but it's not the one in my head.

That's when I notice strands of dark hair and hot breath on my neck.

"Ask me what?" Kris says with tight, thin lips. She looks at me, even though Jolene's the one who spoke.

"Hi, Kris," Jolene says.

"Screw you, Jolene." Kris doesn't break our gaze.

"Bye, Kris," Jolene says, like they hang out every day. And to me: "Lorraine." She raises my hand, squeezes it, pulls me close. "Ask her," she says again, soft enough to tickle my ear, loud enough so Kris can hear.

Then she leaves.

I turn back to Kris. Scattered holiday issues spread out around her feet like roots. It's like she's grown out of the paper, like she's made of it. That's how fragile the last year suddenly feels. Like something I could crumple in my hand.

I was kind of surprised, after that whole thing with the ropes. She never told you?

Kris is waiting for me to say something. But Jolene's words burn my throat, cover my lips, loop around my wrists. If Kris had anything to do with that afternoon . . .

Ask her.

"I should have known." Kris shakes her head. "Hudson. Those clothes. I'm so fucking stupid. But, god, Mattie. Jolene? Really? She's using you."

My hand—the one Jolene just released—closes into a fist. "It's not like that."

Kris laughs—a short, high sound of disbelief. "Really? What's it like? No, wait. Let me guess. She told you things about me. Hudson, too. Please, tell me you don't believe her."

I dig my nails into my palm so hard I know I'll see marks.

Ask her.

Kris shuts her eyes, takes a long, deep breath. "Mattie." My name comes from her throat like a groan.

"She needs me."

"I'm sure."

"She tells me I'm pretty." It sounds so stupid and grade school, but it's true. When's the last time Kris complimented me? Told me I was too good for someone? "She thinks I can be something better—"

"Better than yourself?" Kris asks, incredulous.

I stare at Kris without blinking, even though I can feel a tear form and fill my lower eyelid. Doesn't she get it?

"Jolene's not going anywhere," I say.

"Not while she still needs you for whatever it is she's planning to do."

"All you've ever wanted to do is leave." The words come out loud. Louder than I thought they would. But when Kris answers, she's even louder. She's shouting.

"This town, not you!" Kris crushes copies of the paper under her sneakers as she steps toward me. "Can't you see? She's doing it again. Remember the manhunt game? The ropes?" Kris knows what I do when she mentions that afternoon. What I did before Jolene said:

Ask her.

"Jolene did mention something, actually. About that afternoon with the ropes."

Kris freezes. Her skin pales next to her red curls. "Bitch," she whispers under her breath.

"I didn't believe her."

"You don't understand," Kris says, "you don't know what happened."

"Obviously."

"No, I mean—" Kris's chest goes red. I've seen it happen one other time—when we left the shed. But right now it's all I can focus on. Her skin blooming. Because if she had something to do with that afternoon and she didn't tell me—after a whole year of isolating ourselves, after all the hours I've spent alone, wondering what I could have done differently, after everything I've given up since that moment I got her out of the shed—then I want to hurt her. I want to cover her in that color, a full-body bruise.

"Look." Kris touches her fingers to her chest. When she takes them away, she lowers her shoulders and raises her chin high, resigned. "I knew Jolene before she moved here, okay?"

I shake my head. I thought Kris said—

"Remember that time after fifth grade when we moved across town and my parents sent me to camp for the summer to get me out of the way? That's how we met," she says, faster now, like she wants to get it all out in one breath. "She seemed cool enough, at first. She had a stash of candy and random comics she'd let me borrow after lights-out. Then halfway through the summer she decided to pick on this skinny, homesick girl with straight bangs named Melissa. By that time we were best friends, or at least that's what she called us to everyone else. You know I hate that phrase. I mean, I didn't like it before, but after that I couldn't stand it."

Kris pauses. She's waiting for me to say something, I guess. But I don't. Because she knew Jolene. She knew her.

When it's obvious I'm not going to say anything, she picks up the story again.

"Anyway, so one night Jolene comes up with this plan. I'm supposed to slip a bunch of laxatives into Melissa's drink at dinner so we can watch her shit her pants during evening activity.

Only I don't do it. So Jolene comes for me in the middle of the night—wakes me up, leads me to the bathrooms at the back of the bunk, and hands me a cup. 'I thought you'd like some water,' she says. But the liquid in the cup isn't clear. It's cloudy. And I know what's in it. But I take it from her and chug it anyway, because screw her, you know?"

Kris stops to catch her breath. It's not just her chest that's red anymore. The rash has crept up her neck to her chin and across her cheeks. Just like the heat inside me. Kris and Jolene shared a bunk and a bed and a summer. They shared all those things, and Kris never told me. Neither of them did. I feel left out again. Like I'm in the backseat of Kris's car watching Jim's hand creep up Kris's leg before she slaps it away. Jolene didn't just get Hudson first. She also got Kris.

I feel sick.

"That doesn't explain anything," I say, which isn't exactly true. It explains some things—why Kris and Jolene always seemed like opposing forces—but it doesn't explain everything.

The tendons in Kris's neck tense before she speaks again. "When Jolene moved here, we were good friends, you and me, remember? I mean, not like the last year, but good. Solid."

I swallow, nod. Nothing feels solid. Not the ground beneath my feet. Or the last fifteen months. Not Kris, or me. Everything feels slippery.

"I warned her not to screw with you," Kris says.

"I didn't need your protection." My voice feels far away again, like my ears are underwater but my mouth is out, and the sounds I make can't reach me, not completely.

"But you had it." Kris says, her breath fast, her stare sharp. "When I told her to stay away from you—"

"You had no right—"

"When I told her," Kris says again, sounding out each syllable, "she said it was *you* calling and texting *her* all the time. She told me you'd do anything for her."

Something inside me loses its white-knuckled grip and slips.

It's one thing to know you'd do anything for someone. It's a secret, dark thing that's hard to admit, because most of the time you don't think about it. You just do the things you need to do. You run with them over rocky cliffs, go to their house at midnight, stroke their hair, and hold them close. You carry them away from drunk boys on your shoulder. You take them home. But you don't say it out loud, and neither does she. Because it makes you feel weak. Because you don't know what it means.

My skin tingles, and my head hammers at the thought of them talking about me like that, taking the deepest parts of me and airing them out. Of Jolene saying it out loud. But I still need to know how the conversation ended. "And you said?"

"I told her it was bullshit," Kris says, "that if she went too far, you'd see her for who she really is, just like I did."

"I'm not you." This one thought keeps my head above the water. I'm not her. Whatever she had with Jolene doesn't matter. It's different with me.

Kris looks at the crushed paper at her feet—the issue I know she's been killing herself to finish for the past three weeks—and smiles. But it doesn't look like a smile. It looks more like our school mascot, the blue devil baring its teeth under her sneakers. "That's what *she* said." Kris drops the smile, lifts her head. "But I told her it didn't matter. That there were just some things you wouldn't do. 'Name it,' Jolene said to me. 'Tell me.'"

"*You* came up with the ropes?"

"Only because in a million years I never thought you'd actually go through with it!"

"But it was your idea."

"Yeah. Fine. It was my idea. But I didn't do it. Jolene did. And you let her."

Yes, Jolene did it. And yes, I let her. And I know Kris will never understand why—for the same reason she laughed when I said I wanted to be something new. Because Kris likes everything just fine the way it is. Including me. She won't give me gills or gowns. She doesn't think I can change. *I told her . . . there were just some things you wouldn't do.*

But Jolene had listened. She'd taken me seriously.

I'm back in that room, wrists bound, mouth taped, pulse racing. I'm screaming. Bella's laughing. I'm leaving, eyes wet and blurry. I won't speak to Jolene. And nobody will speak to me, except for Kris. "You'd been my only friend after the ropes thing, so I went back for you. I found you in that shed. I thought I owed you. But you only kept talking to me then because you felt guilty."

"No," Kris says, eyes wide, cheeks red, curls loose.

I step toward her. "I gave up Hudson. I gave up everything for you. And you couldn't even tell me the truth?"

At least Jolene had come clean. The night she'd called me to come over, she'd admitted that what she'd done was fucked up, even if she had done it for me. She also told me how easy it had been to turn my "friends" against me. *But not Kris,* I'd said to myself. *Kris didn't quit on me.*

No. She didn't quit on me. She lied to me.

"Why are you even here?" I ask Kris, scanning the pile of papers on the floor. "Shouldn't you be delivering those?"

"You said you'd help me." Kris's cheeks have gone from red to pink to pale. "I was in the journalism room all morning stuffing the inserts," she says. "I said I'd find you."

This morning, in the car, as the snow fell. That's right. She said she'd find me. Like the time I found her in the shed. And the time I didn't, at Bella's party.

"Well, I guess you did."

"I guess so," she says, squinting. I wonder if I look different to her, the way she looks different to me. Not because of the clothes, but because of what we now know.

Kris doesn't pick up the papers when she goes. She leaves them strewn across the floor—headlines about the holidays, black-and-white photos, pixelated people. I think. It's hard to tell from this distance. I bend down. Each senior in the picture smiles crisp and clear; the problem is, they do it twice.

Two mouths, two sets of eyes, two heads. One exposure dark, the other light, and a fraction of an inch to the right. It must be a printing glitch. Whatever it is, the effect is eerie: bright smiles broken, clear eyes clouded, perfect hair pulled.

Two people where one should be.

CHAPTER 28

I HAVEN'T WALKED anywhere in over a year. I used to walk home from school every day, starting in fifth grade. I complained about it to my mom, but the truth is, I liked walking the streets I'd seen on my map, and the ones that didn't exist then. Even in the snow and cold. Especially then, actually. I liked the way the white flakes covered everything and made it even, like a fresh canvas I could paint with my own colors and shapes.

Today it just looks blank.

My feet crunch over salt in front of the school and sink into slush as I cross the street. An icy stream seeps through the tops of my sneakers and into my socks. Then it stops, and I fall into a rhythm. Me. My breath. My legs.

It's not snowing anymore, but it's cold. A clear crust covers the white lawns along Lenox, some still dressed for Thanksgiving with paper Pilgrims and plastic turkeys, others looking forward to Christmas with blinking bushes and ribboned wreaths. Ice covers each needle on the evergreens—the trees that refuse to give up their leaves, that can't bear to let them turn beautiful because it also means losing them.

I walk faster. I can't feel the tips of my fingers, though when I press them to my lips, they're hot. Burning. I wipe my nose and sniff. Instead of charred winter air, I inhale something heavy and wet. Humidity. My shirt clings to my back inside my jacket. The snow sinking under my sneakers is fresh dirt. The trees have leaves, bright and green. I'm between buildings at Cal's complex on the night of the manhunt game. But this time I don't choose Kris. I'm hand in hand with Jolene, on my way to home base, where Hudson sits, waiting for me.

The game is over.

CHAPTER 29

HUDSON OPENS THE door in a plain white tee, worn and tight at the sleeves, and baggy jeans. The sconces in the foyer light him up from behind and throw a yellow glow through the doorway. The day went dark on my walk over.

"I've got something to show you." He grabs my hand and pulls me in. I want to tell him about Kris, but that means telling him about Jolene, so instead I follow him up the stairs to his room without telling him anything. Though I can't help noticing how his fingers, which have slipped between mine countless times, feel bigger this afternoon, his skin rougher than usual.

Hudson flicks open the door with his free hand. At first I think he's taken one of my maps. But when I look closer, I see it's not a single map but a book of them. And the pages aren't ancient, just old. It's an atlas. And it's enormous. It covers the length of his desk—spine soft, covers flush against the wood, like it's used to being open, handled, read. There are more on his bed.

"What is this?" I step first to the bed and then the desk to run my fingers over the pages, faded white with use, ripped and rescued with Scotch tape. It's strange to see such oddly shaped borders, so many new routes. I'm used to looking at maps of Westfield.

"This is me not giving a shit," he says. Hudson's leaning against the doorframe, hands shoved into his jeans, smiling at the atlases like old friends. I know how he feels. Even though I haven't taken out my Sanborns in weeks, I haven't forgotten why I wanted them, why I wanted any of them: maps are so much easier to read than people. I just didn't know anyone else felt the same way. For a second I see us from above: two dots in this room, in his house, on this street, in Westfield. Together. The same. Until I remember what he said.

"Not giving a shit about what?"

"College. Plans. What people expect."

That's when I notice the highlighted lines weaving their way across every open page. None of them stop. Each one falls right off the edge. They're escape routes.

"You mean you're actually going to these places? And your parents are cool with it?"

"Not even close," he says. "My dad doesn't know. I told my mom. She's not thrilled, but she gets it. I mean, she left him. She's split her time between here and the road ever since." Hudson shrugs. "She's half the reason I came up with it." He motions toward the atlases.

"Half?"

"Well, yeah, I mean . . ." Hudson pushes off the wall and walks to the bed. His arm hangs next to mine. I can feel heat radiating from it and, on the other side of me, a chill from his always-open window. "You gave me the idea to begin with," Hudson finishes.

"I did?" It doesn't make sense. I've never told him about my maps. He's never been to my room. And anyway, mine are nothing like his.

I follow a jagged red line across the page, imagine expansive skies and an open road. Then I drop my eyes to the yellow line in the middle of that made-up concrete. Because even in my imagination, looking into something infinite makes me dizzy. Disoriented.

My maps are familiar—places I've been, where I live.

Hudson's maps are a way out. Mine are a way in.

"Yeah." Hudson threads his fingers between mine. "You and Kris. If you two ditched everyone, I figure I can do it."

But I guess no matter how many times you draw yourself out of a place, you're still in it. It's been a year, but we're both back at the manhunt game.

And I came over here with words in my head, in my mouth. I came over here to tell him something.

"Kris isn't what you think," I say, shifting my hand in his. It feels too big.

"Good thing I'm not in love with her then."

"No, I mean the night of the manhunt game. Me and Kris leaving—" *Ask her.* "Kris lied to me. About the ropes. It was her idea. She said she was trying to protect me from Jolene—"

"Mattie." Hudson grips my shoulders, forces me to face him. I had it all figured out on the way here—how to tell him—but then he showed me those atlases, and now something's wrong. Hudson's holding me too tight, he's breathing too hard, he's creasing that spot between his eyes so deep his freckles meet. "I just told you I love you, and you're talking about *Jolene*? *Still?*"

"You're the one who started talking about her in the first place!" I was fine. I was sealed.

"I talked about her. Fine. Then I stopped. When are you going to stop?"

"But this changes everything."

He throws his hands out to his sides. "No, it doesn't. Who gives a shit whose idea it was? Jolene still did it."

An engine revs outside. It roars, then fades, and the room is quiet again.

"But Kris lied to me. She admitted it."

"To protect you. You said so yourself."

"*Kris* said that. Not me. And, really, what did she end up protecting me from anyway? The truth? If I'd known what she did, I wouldn't have left—"

"And I never would have known you like this. Why do you think I'm showing you these?" He motions toward the atlases. "I never thought, when I left this place, I'd want anyone to come with me. But you . . . I'm telling you I love you. And you still haven't said anything back."

I used to imagine this: Hudson telling me he loves me. Sweet words hot in my ear as we lie between his sheets. One hand on the small of my back, the other on my cheek. How it would make everything perfect.

But it doesn't. Because the girl Hudson is in love with is the one who leaves. It isn't me. It's who he wants me to be.

Something pounds inside me. It can't be my heart, because it's not just in my chest. It's in my ankles, my thighs, my throat, my gut.

I step away from him. The backs of my knees hit his bed. "You don't love me."

"I do." Hudson tries for my hand, but I pull it away.

"You don't know me." I've pretended long enough. But he's going to find out at some point. Just like Kris did. It may as well be now. It may as well be from me. "I took Jolene home from Bella's party."

"What?" Hudson stiffens. He narrows his eyes. And it's a relief, the way he looks at me. Like I'm strange. Like he can finally see down to the darkest, dirtiest bottom of who I am.

"Jolene. I dragged her drunk from Bella's party after you broke up with her."

Hudson presses his lips into a line. "Listen, if you don't feel the same way about me, fine. But don't lie."

"You don't believe me?"

Hudson's eyes go hard. His nostrils flare. He shakes his head once. *No.*

Figures. I'm finally telling the truth, and he accuses me of lying. But it doesn't matter whether he wants to believe me or not. I have proof.

"Give me my phone." I hold out my palm. I can feel my blood race through the blue tracks in my wrist, pulse in my fingertips. Not a pounding anymore, but an energy.

Hudson backs into his desk, forearms and fists tense. He's not going to do it. He doesn't want to know how wrong he was, how badly he misjudged me.

For a year and a half I've wanted him to love me.

But now I just want him to see me. The real me.

I push my upturned palm toward him.

Hudson jerks open the top drawer of his desk. The bronze

handle claps when he slams it shut and slaps the phone on my palm. It covers my scar.

I turn it on. The battery's low, since it's been in his desk for a while, but I don't need much. I pull up Jolene's texts—the entire string, beginning last year—and hand it back to him.

Hudson's eyes move side to side, up and down, but he doesn't lift a finger to the screen. "There's more. You can scroll," I tell him.

He gives my cell back and shoves his hands in his pockets. "I don't need to see anything else."

"So you believe me?" I find his eyes. They're dark and light at the same time, like the ocean: turquoise on the surface where it's shallow, layers of navy underneath where the floor's too deep to see. He doesn't look away. And as I wait for him to answer, the pulsing that's been pushing me forward stops. In its wake is silence, like my blood itself is holding its breath, wanting him to say yes, that he sees me for what I am—not strong and hard-core, but weak and soft—and also hoping he won't.

Because I know after this he'll never look at me the same way.

"I believe Jolene sent you those texts. And that you never wrote her back," he says.

I nod. Swallow.

He sits on the edge of his desk and cups one of his hands over his mouth like he's trying to figure something out.

He still wants to believe in some other version of me.

"I didn't write back. But, like I said, I took her home from Bella's party, and I've been talking to her in study hall."

"So you did cut her off." Hudson's moving his fingers along his lips as he speaks, but behind them I can see a quick curve, the beginning of a smile. It sets off the heat in me again. The pulsing.

"But she kept sending texts. And I kept reading them. She never gave up."

"Not one of her strong suits," he adds with a smirk. Like it's a cute trait on a dumb puppy. Something he can laugh at. But it's not. Jolene never gave up on me.

"Right," I say, angry now. "You're the one who gives up. You stopped calling me when you were with Jolene. You acted like I didn't exist. And then you made up some story about me, and you believed it. You got me to believe it, too. But I'm not brave or amazing. And I do give a shit." My throat hurts when I'm finished. I must have been screaming. I swallow hard and feel something hot streak down the side of my nose. I pull my sleeve over my fist and get rid of the tear before it hits my lips.

"What if it's not a story?" Hudson asks. He stands up, wipes his palms on the thighs of his jeans, and leans his whole body toward me. "What if everything I think about you is true?"

"It's not. You don't love me." I take a step back.

See me. Please.

Hudson walks forward. I can't get any farther back. He comes so close, I think I might fall onto his bed, or he might push me down if I don't. When he stops, there's half an inch between us, maybe. I can count the freckles on his nose and see the brown specks in his eyes. I can smell him—mint, winter— when he traces my jaw with his finger, tilts up my chin, and asks, "What if I did?"

I squeeze my eyes shut. Two more tears race down my cheek. I lick the salt from my lips.

Hudson drops his hand from my face. "It doesn't matter,

does it?" he asks. "Because you're not in love with *me*." Hudson clutches the back of my hand and turns it over so I can see my phone. Then he presses against my thumb and lights up the screen. Jolene's face stares back at me. The thumbnail of her getting ready for the freshman dance. She's looking at me over her shoulder, sleek brown hair with auburn streaks cascading across her cheek, wide lips spread in a suggestive smile. Hazel eyes rimmed in black, catlike.

But it's not the picture I see. It's every time she looked at me in the hall. It's every text she sent and note she wrote. Every night in her bed. Every breath on my neck.

It's why I couldn't look away when she was kissing Hudson.

I feel like I'm picking at a scab. Lifting, tugging, pulling up the crusty parts that cling to my softer skin protectively. It hurts, but I keep picking, lifting, pulling through the pain. Even though I have to hold my breath. Even though my eyes sting. And when the last piece finally releases, when I rip the scab off completely—there she is, red and slick and streaming. Jolene. Underneath everything.

Inside me.

All that time I thought I was building a new skin—I wasn't keeping her out; I was sealing her in.

I look up from my phone. I don't tell Hudson he's right, but I don't tell him he's wrong, either. And that tells him everything.

"You two deserve each other," he says, disgusted.

Hudson drops my hand, and as it falls to my leg, carried by the weight of my cell, everything seems to make sense. As if this is the way today was always going to happen. As if it's happened before. As if it's the only way it could ever be: Hudson dropping his gaze, clenching his fists, turning away. Leaving.

"Find your own way out," he says.

I pick up my bag and coat with one hand—the other's still clutching my phone—and do what he says. When I pull the door shut behind me, I take in the crisp night, the black sky, the spots of light; but as I walk home, I grow heavy with wet heat. Bushes and town houses surround me. It's August. Kris has gone home. Hudson isn't waiting. But I'm not alone.

Jolene's got my hand, and she won't let go.

CHAPTER 30

I WAKE UP in my underwear. I have a vague memory of coming home, stripping off my clothes, and curling up under the covers around some unseen center—pulling my knees tight to my chest until my body circled itself like a shrimp. I must have stayed that way all night. I'm sore and sweating.

I try to unfurl myself, but I slept on my arm and now it's stuck, numb, a foreign limb in bed with me. I roll onto my back and wait for it to regain feeling. First the pins and needles, then the heat. And then it's mine again. I open and close my fist. Something's in it. My phone. With a text from Jolene.

```
Two little girls all alone.
```

At first I think she forgot to finish the line; but when I blink, I see the period. She meant what she wrote.

I didn't call her last night to tell her what happened with Hudson, but she knows.

I hook my phone up to the charger, throw on one of Jake's old sweatshirts, and head for the shower. The water burns my skin, but it doesn't rinse away the dream-feeling. I get dressed, eat breakfast, turn on the ignition. But it's like the cloud of steam from the bathroom—the cloak of sleep—follows me.

It's not until I'm walking into school, well after the bell, that I realize I felt this way before I got in bed, when I was still awake.

I think back to yesterday, then last week, trying to find a time when I felt crystal clear—real—but each image I conjure shimmers and vanishes. None of them will hold still.

Señora doesn't say anything when I walk through the door ten minutes late. Instead, she slides her glasses to the tip of her nose, stares me down, then pushes them back up and continues her review of the subjunctive. I'm lucky it's her favorite tense. Señora says it will change our Spanish lives as we know it. I used to think she was taking grammar a little too seriously, but the longer I stare at the board, the more I think maybe she's right. Maybe the subjunctive *is* the crowning achievement of language itself, the root of desire, as unpredictable as the future it describes. Maybe that's why I can't complete the sentences. Because after four years of Spanish, I know how to conjugate the subjunctive. That's not my problem. My problem is that I can't seem to get past the part we've been given—the first word of each thick, white chalk scrawl across the board: *Quiero. Deseo. Espero.*

I want. I wish. I hope.

I tighten my grip on the pen. My paper is blank, my sentences unfinished.

Because I've done this before. *What do* you *want to be, Mattie?*

I stare at the thin blue lines on the page, willing the sentences

236

to write themselves. To tell me what I want to be and what it means.

"*¡Chicos!*" Señora says, bringing her hands together in a brisk clap. Heads rise around the room. "Let's see what you've done to my darling, the subjunctive!"

When the bell rings, the hallways buzz with manic laughter and excited chatter. It's only the end of first period, but everyone's already frantic with the idea of a week and a half of freedom, like we're on the verge of something huge and uncontrollable instead of Christmas break.

I wait for the rest of the class to shove through the doorway before making my way into the hall. When I get there, the crowd has thinned, leaving Kris. I didn't expect to see her after what happened yesterday. She stands up from her slumped position against the lockers. We stare at each other across the hall. Then an arm loops through mine and I'm swept away.

"Can you believe she's here?" Jolene's warm whisper in my ear.

"She's my—" I don't finish the sentence, because I can't. What is Kris to me now?

"She was never your best friend." My words from Jolene's mouth. It's not what I meant, but I nod anyway. Jolene tightens her grip on me. "She was never like us."

The few people left in the hall are watching. They're always watching Jolene, but now they're also watching me. I'm not sure if it's because I haven't been seen anywhere near Jolene in over a year or because she's barely been seen for the past few weeks, or if it's how we're intertwined; but when Jolene notices, she angles at a small crowd standing to our right, tells them to fuck off, then tilts her head to mine and says under her breath, "They wish they had this."

I wish. We wish. They wish.

We walk. All day long, before and after class; as the anticipation of vacation builds with the end of each period, Jolene and I walk together, hand in hand, hip to hip, ears to lips. She tells me things. How the dark-haired skater hanging out in the corner proposed to her one weekend, asked her to run away to his family's vacation home in Hawaii; how she said no because she didn't like his nose. How the pale-faced president of student council sitting in the back of the cafeteria eats nothing but Honey Nut Cheerios; how she shows her jutting bones in the gym locker room and stares at Jolene when they're changing. How the quiet kid in the black T-shirt and jeans in study hall fills his notebook with hit lists.

Jolene's words work their way around me like music.

When Hudson passes us in the halls—headphones up, eyes down, jaw set—Jolene tells me the story of a boy who loved us both but couldn't choose and so we dated him together, twin fair maidens, and broke his heart before he could break us in two.

I turn back and catch sight of the flapping flannel at Hudson's wrist. He seems far away, suddenly strange. I can't remember the temperature of his skin, the feel of his hair, the sound of his voice over my shoulder after we finished but before he fell asleep.

I get the same feeling after the final bell when Jolene and I walk, clasped hands clutched between us, past the squeals and shouts in the parking lot. It's as if the whole school—walls and windows, hoops and handles, desks and everyone who sits in them—slides away, fades to black and disappears behind our backs.

CHAPTER 31

WITHOUT SCHOOL TO deal with, Jolene and I fall back into our old summer routine: her place during the day, mine at night. When she leaves, she calls me on her cell and then we text until we go to bed. The days of winter break pass by in a stream of stories, cinnamon, and magazines. And even though I haven't heard from Hudson or Kris, I don't miss them. I'm too busy. Jolene needs me for makeup consultations, breakfast decisions, company. I forgot how sometimes she wants to stay on the phone without talking so she knows she's not alone. And I like being the person at the other end of the line. In a way, I feel like that's who I've always been. Even the past year and a half, when I wasn't texting her back, she knew I got the messages. She knew I looked at them, that I saw her. That even if we weren't speaking, our breaths would eventually fall into the same rhythm across the silence.

Then one night Jolene doesn't leave. The *SNL* rerun we were watching ends, and she doesn't get up from my bed. Instead, she rolls off the edge, opens my dresser drawer, skims her fingers along my clothes, and picks out one of my brother's oldest shirts: a soft black tee with letters so cracked and faded, you can barely tell they spell *Foo Fighters* anymore. With her back to me, she strips off her beige sweater and black bra, then slides the shirt over her head.

Jolene lifts her long, dark hair out from underneath the scrawl of tour dates on the back of the shirt and—after she finds my favorite light-blue cotton pajama shorts—peels off her jeans and threads her long, bronze legs through them. Then she crawls under the covers and curls up like a cat near my pillow.

She watches me change into a tank top and yoga pants, then turns away when I get into the bed. I lie completely still next to her, unsure of what to do, until she finds my hand and pulls me forward, into the curve of her back. Her skin is hot. Her hair smells sweet.

She looks at me over her shoulder. At first I think she's going to speak—a line from "The Two Little Girls," like we used to. I'm already forming the words in my head when she leans forward and presses her lips to mine. They're soft and smooth. And then they're gone.

A few minutes later Jolene's breath is light and rhythmic.

And even though I haven't spoken to Hudson in over a week, his words come to me through the darkness like a dream.

You two deserve each other.

I don't know why Jolene chose me that day on the cliff, but I'm happy she did. I'm not special, but I'm essential to her.

She needs me. I don't know what that makes us. Best friends? Something else? Hudson and I did a lot more than kiss, but sex with him didn't compare to this feeling.

Jolene twitches in her sleep, relaxes into me.

I don't know what I deserve, but I hope Hudson was right.

I hope it's this.

CHAPTER 32

I WAKE TO the smell of onions and potatoes, the clatter and clink of my mom putting pans on the stove downstairs in the kitchen. In my half-awake haze I forget what day it is, what year, and I wonder when Kris will be over for Hanukkah dinner. Then something dark sinks down my chest and anchors in my gut as I live it all over again, Kris lying to me about Jolene.

Jolene. Where is she?

I flip up the covers. There's nothing but creased sheets.

Then I hear her hoarse, morning voice in the hall. "Don't you think it looks good on me?"

A deep voice answers her. "Looked better on me." Jake. How did he get off work so early? I check my clock. It's barely eleven. Mom said she wasn't even sure he'd make it for dinner. She was hoping for dessert. Never mind that this isn't even officially Hanukkah—that's still two days away. It's just the day Jake could *probably* make it. Like he's the miracle, instead of the oil lasting for eight days.

I'm about to open my bedroom door and save Jolene from my brother when she says, "Do you want it back then?"

My fingers halt on the handle. I picture Jake in the hallway in a white undershirt and warm-ups even though, lately, I only see him in suits. I imagine his lips rising at the sides as he considers Jolene. Her dark hair and hazel eyes. Her long legs. Her smile.

I twist my hand and push open the door before he can accept her offer.

Jake's in cargo shorts and a collared shirt. Jolene's leaning against the banister, arms spread out behind her, one knee bent.

"What are you doing here?" I demand.

"Hi to you too," Jake says, without looking up from his work cell. "Happy Hanukkah." He sighs, then types.

I stare at Jolene. *What?* she mouths.

"Stop giving my stuff away," Jake says, tucking the phone into his pocket as he heads down the stairs. "I liked that shirt."

"I'll take good care of it," Jolene says, bending over the banister.

But Jake is already in the kitchen, talking about his wonderful life. I can tell because Mom is laughing. It's a sound I haven't heard in a while.

"What was that?" I ask.

"Had to pee."

"That's my *brother*, Jolene."

"We were just *talking*, Mattie." She grabs my hand and drags me into my room.

We change in silence. Until I slip on my white bra. Jolene spins me around by my shoulders and looks me up and down. My cheeks burn as her eyes move over my skin, pale compared to hers, and goose bumped.

"You have to keep this," she says, pinning her beige sweater to my body. It's soft and see-through thin. There's a delicate design stitched near the neck, above my breasts. "It'll look amazing."

"Okay." I hold it against my chest and peer down over my chin. It smells like her. "But it's not like I have anywhere to go."

"Yeah you do," Jolene says, with gleaming eyes and a satisfied smile.

I blink my eyes. I've seen that look. It's the same one she gave me when we were sitting on the floor of her room, listening to the storm, leafing through magazines. It's the way she settled her eyes on me right before the ropes.

My hands tremble. In anticipation. In fear. I set her sweater on my pillow and grab a gray V-neck from my bed.

"And where would that be?" I ask as my bedroom door swings open.

"Mattie, I have to go— Oh!" My mom pauses in the doorway. "Jolene. I didn't know you stayed over."

"You could have *knocked*, Mom." I turn my back to her as I wrestle my shirt over my head and tug it down my torso.

"It's okay." Jolene takes off my light-blue shorts and tosses them to the corner of the room. The only thing she's wearing now is Jake's shirt and her black bikini underwear. "We were just talking about what to wear for New Year's."

I snap my head in Jolene's direction, but she's too busy smiling at my mom, whose mouth is stretched into an O of delight and surprise.

"New Year's Eve? You're going out, Mattie?"

Every year my mom asks if I'm going out on New Year's Eve, and every year I stay in with Kris. New Year's Eve was our very first sleepover, in fourth grade, and we've kept the tradition ever since.

Before that, my mom used to stay up with me until midnight, while my dad slept on the couch. We'd play cards until the ball dropped. Solitaire. Spit. War. She'd tell me about all the parties she used to go to and how I'd go to them one day, too. She'd tell me how New Year's Eve was her favorite night of the year. And I agreed. Until Jake was old enough to babysit, and she started going out again.

Jolene and I answer at the same time.

I say: "Maybe."

Jolene says: "We're going to Bella's party."

My mom hears Jolene.

"How nice! All you girls together again. Well, I won't interrupt." My mom beams at Jolene before turning to leave. "I've got to go to the store. I'll be back in a bit," she calls over her shoulder, and clicks the door shut.

Then it's just me and Jolene again.

"Why did you say that?"

"Say what?" Jolene faces herself in the mirror, gathers the front of my brother's shirt in her fists—which lifts until I can see the tiny pearls on the front of her black underwear—and leans into her right hip. But she's not looking at herself. She's looking at the reflection of my room, searching it.

"That we're going to Bella's." The thought of going to Bella's party with Jolene makes me nauseous. I reach my hand up to cover my mouth and remember the gloss Kris wore to the bonfire, the lip balm I borrowed when we got there. How she looked at me before we went in to Bella's, to make sure I was okay.

I wonder now if this is how Kris felt at the end of that driveway: protective, scared, like she didn't want to share me. I wonder if she asked herself why she wasn't enough.

"Because we are." Jolene finds what she wants on my floor. She strips off Jake's shirt and pulls on the pale-blue sweater my mom gave me. "And I'm going to wear this. It's perfect," she says to her reflection.

I run my fingers over the fuzzy blue threads on her back and notice a catch in the stitch. It must have happened one night at Hudson's. "It looks great with your skin," I say. She smiles, pleased. "But"—I sit down on the bed and cross my legs—"why are we even going?" I smooth the small piece of comforter in front of me. "We don't need them."

"Of course we don't," Jolene says. "They need us."

CHAPTER 33

THE LINE AT the Bagel Place snakes around the counter and between peeling plastic tables full of people. Jake's in front of me, studying the chalkboard menu hanging on the wall as if it's changed since he's lived here. As if he's not going to get a toasted sesame bagel with vegetable cream cheese, tomato, and lox. I lean on the rounded glass counter that houses the smoked fish, salads, and more exotic cream cheese combinations, right next to a sign that says "Don't Lean on the Glass." But who cares? I didn't want to come anyway. I was supposed to spend the day with Jolene. But Jake didn't ask me before he told Mom we'd take care of breakfast. He just announced we were leaving. Now I'm standing in line behind moms with loud little kids, middle-aged men with beer guts, and a few kids from school—some guys I recognize but don't really know. I think they're juniors. Either way, I'm not friends with them.

I shuffle forward a few steps and lean on the glass again, but a woman behind me with a frosted helmet of hair taps the sign with her manicured nails and pinches her lips. So I stand up, shove my hands into my pockets, and bounce a little on the balls of my feet.

I'm not used to being alone. For the past week I haven't left the house without Jolene. When we're together, there's always a hand to hold or a shoulder to lean into. People look at us—at least, they look at Jolene—but the best part is, she looks at me. We make up stories about the woman spraying perfume, the man selling shoes, the guy buttering popcorn. I've tried to do it alone, but without someone else there to listen, the story doesn't feel true.

When Jake and I reach the front of the line, the round-faced guy behind the counter with sweat rolling down his stubbled cheeks asks us what we need. Not what we want. It's like after years of working in the Bagel Place, he's come to the conclusion that humanity *needs* bagels. That we'd suffer without them.

After Jake gives our order and pays, we stand against the opposite wall and wait for the warm brown paper bag with our name on it.

"Are you wearing perfume?" Jake asks, sniffing the air around my face.

"No," I say, bringing my arm to my nose. It tickles with cinnamon. Jolene. The sweater she left in my room.

"Okay, whatever." Jake reaches for his work cell again. "So, what's up?"

"Abby!" yells the skinny kid handing out the brown bags. A tall blond woman in a tight white tank top with a fluorescent iPod strapped to her biceps bounces toward the counter. "That's me!" she says to the rest of us. As if we'd challenged her identity.

"Nothing," I say, with a one-shoulder shrug. "Senior year. You know how it is."

"Totally," he says with a quick laugh. He looks up from his phone. From the faraway look on his face, I can tell he's flipping through memories. Parties. Soccer games. Friends. Girlfriends. But the things he sees, they have nothing to do with me. He's had tons of people in his life, but he's never had one. He has no idea how it is.

"Mike!" the skinny kid shouts. A dad in sweatpants and a Vanderbilt sweatshirt reaches across the counter and hands the kid a tip before grabbing his bag. "Thanks, Chief," the dad says, "take it easy." The kid gives a quick nod before stuffing the bill into his jeans and disappearing behind the bagel racks.

"You've been working a lot?" I ask. I don't want to hear another one of Jake's stories—or worse, his lectures—and this is the only question I can think to ask him, which is really sad.

"Yup," he says, running his hands over his hair. It's a habit from when it hung down to his shoulders in high school. Now it's short and cropped close to his head. "That's why they pay me the big bucks." He shoves his cell into his pocket and crosses his arms. "So who's the new Kris? She looks familiar."

"Her name is Jolene," I say, pressing my back flat against the wall as a huge, sweaty boy pushes between everyone who's waiting. No name was called, but when the boy gets to the counter, the skinny kid hands him a bulging bag with one hand and slaps him sideways with the other. Then the huge boy is on his way out again. "And she's not the *new* anything."

"Oh, riiiight." Jake tilts his head and rolls his eyes. "I remember that chick from back in the day."

Two girls walk past outside. I miss their faces but catch their hair—teased curls next to straight, dark-brown locks.

Jake nods his head. "Makes sense."

"What's that supposed to mean?" I ask, craning my neck to see the girls better. But they're gone.

I turn back to Jake. He rubs his eyes, and for the first time in years, it occurs to me that he's tired. I've never noticed the sinking yellow skin beneath his eyes, or the fine lines on his forehead. "Don't tell me you don't see it," he says, blinking quickly. "I know you're a girl and everything—"

"I am?" I say, my eyes fake-wide.

"Maybe," he says, smirking, "but not like her."

"Gee, thanks." I force a tight smile and turn away from him. The little girl spinning in circles next to us stops and stares up at me. She's got blond curls and Bambi-wide blue eyes. Even at four, she's gorgeous.

"That's a compliment," Jake says from behind me. "Jesus." I feel his hand on my shoulder and follow its motion around until we're facing again. I look down so he can't see my eyes. He shakes his head and shifts his weight before reaching for his phone again. His eyes fly left to right across the screen as he speaks. "If you were anything like Jolene, you'd be getting a sit-down with me. You don't want to be that girl, Mats. Trust me."

Leave it to Jake to tell me who I want to be. As if he knows anything about me.

For a second I wish he did. In this small space that smells of rising bread, I have this searing need to be his little sister again, to tell him everything in exchange for his protection from monsters and scary things. Then I remember his glance at Jolene's legs this morning. We're not little kids anymore. He's just another guy talking about girls.

"Jake!" the skinny kid yells. Jake leans over the counter and grabs our bag. The little girl starts spinning again. We head home.

After dessert we exchange cards and presents and kisses. Then Jake and I clean up the crumpled wrapping paper and ripped envelopes and head to the den while Mom and Dad clear the dishes.

Jake turns on an old sitcom and sinks into the couch. I sit in a separate chair. We stare at the screen and listen to the studio audience laugh. When the commercial comes, I expect him to go for his phone, but instead he stretches his arms to the ceiling and rests his head in his hands.

"Is Jolene coming over?" he asks.

"Not to see you," I say, even though I've been wondering the same thing. I texted her a few hours ago, and I still haven't heard from her.

"Not interested," Jake says, picking up the remote. "Just trying to figure out when to leave." He looks at his watch.

"Well, don't stay for me," I say to the screen. The sitcom is on again. I recognize it now. Jake used to watch it after he put me to bed, back when I needed a babysitter.

"Why else would I?" he asks with a lazy shrug.

I don't answer. It never occurred to me that he'd come home for anyone other than our parents, the people he entertains with stories the entire evening.

"You may be slashing my favorite shirts, but you're still my little sister," he says. "And anyway, word on the street is you've got a boyfriend."

"Did," I say, reaching for the memory of Hudson, even

though it's hazy now, the whole relationship ghosted—woven into something else by Jolene's words.

"Sorry," he says, pressing his lips together in sympathy. "Sucks."

"Yup," I tell him. Not because it does, but because that's what I'm supposed to say. The truth is, when I think of Hudson I feel numb. I check my phone again. Where is Jolene? We haven't spent a night apart since break started.

"Well, stop taking it out on Mom." Jake palms the remote again.

"She told you?"

"Yeah," he says. "I do talk to her, Mattie. Something it sounds like you aren't doing these days."

"I talk to her."

"Not much."

"Well, no one talks as much as you do."

Usually he'd answer this with a joke. But not tonight.

Jake's eyebrows rise. "What was that?"

"Nothing," I say. "It's not like it's a secret, with all those stories you tell, how well you think of yourself." The sound of studio laughter fills the silence after I speak. I keep my eyes glued to the TV. Jake grabs the remote and hits the power button. The screen goes dark. The room is quiet.

"You think I'm conceited?" he asks.

I cross my arms. "Aren't you?"

He keeps his light-brown eyes on me. Even though they're a different color, they remind me of our mother's. "Okay, so maybe I am," he admits, planting his hands on his knees. "Do you want to know why?"

"There's a reason?" I ask. I can't wait to hear this. I lean back in my seat. "Yeah, sure, go ahead."

Jakes rests his forehead on his fingers and digs his thumbs into his temples. "Listen, you think anyone gives a shit about me at the firm? I'm one of a hundred people, all doing the same shitty doc reviews all day. You think anyone there cares? Let me answer that for you—they don't. They think I'm disposable." Jake slumps into the couch. He looks thinner than he used to. Nothing like the dazzling big brother he was at dinner. "So who's to say I'm not disposable, huh? Who, if not me? If I don't think I'm better than that, why should they? So, yeah, I talk myself up sometimes, and maybe I sound like I'm high on myself. But, seriously, somebody's got to be."

"I didn't know," I say, and it occurs to me that for the first time in our brother-sister history, I have something Jake doesn't: somebody who thinks I'm better than that. Somebody who's always on my side. I have Jolene.

I check my phone again.

"No, you didn't."

"Well, I'm sorry." I wait for Jake to say it's okay, but instead he picks up the remote again and turns on the TV. The show ends. The credits roll. Another episode begins. I watch Jake's shoulders sink into the tan couch pillow—the same ones we used for walls in our pillow forts when we were younger. Jake would build them, and I'd get in when he was finished. Even then he was the practical one, planning in advance so I could play.

"Look, I'm sorry," he says. "I've just been working a lot. It's not as cool as being a senior in high school, you know. Party while you can."

"I will," I promise.

Jake searches the guide for something to watch. He yawns, blinks; raises his eyebrows high, as if he can force himself awake. "Nice," he says. The TV flips back to full screen. "*Caddyshack* is on. Now this," he tells me, "is a solid flick." We watch the first fifteen minutes together before he says he has to get back to the city.

CHAPTER 34

"NOW PRESS THEM together like this," Jolene says. She slides her wide lips together, then pulls them apart with a pop. I try to do the same thing.

Jolene shakes her head. "I'll do it for you." She takes my face in her hands and tilts it up. As she leans over me, her dark hair falls forward and skims my shoulders, shutting out the light, her room, the chair I'm sitting in—everything but her face. She licks her thumb and smoothes it across my lips, then dabs her index finger at the dip in the middle. When she stands up to see how it looks, her hair goes with her, letting the light back in, along with her quilted white bedspread, her hand-painted dresser drawers, her open jewelry box, and her sand-colored wood floor, which is papered with open magazines—possible looks for Bella's party. I glance up at her from beneath my heavy black lashes and lift the corners of my lips the tiniest fraction of an inch, like one of the models on the glossy pages, as Jolene examines her makeup on my face. She smiles.

"Perfect," she says. "You're ready."

"Then let's leave." I get up. I didn't want to go to Bella's at first, but talking to Jake made me realize this is it: senior year, New Year's Eve. I won't ever get to do it again.

Jolene flips over her wrist and checks her watch. She wears the face on the inside because the band is black and thick, like a cuff bracelet. "It's still a little early," she says, even though the party started an hour ago, "and I've got to pee. After that we'll leave." Jolene grabs her studded black clutch off the bed. I watch her disappear down the hall in my sweater. It fits her perfectly.

I grab one of my boots from the floor and tug it on. When I reach under Jolene's bed for the other one, my hand hits something hard. At first I think it's the heel of my boot, but then I see it—the jewel-encrusted box. It looks so ordinary, sitting there on the floor, without Jolene's closed, cupped hands retrieving and replacing its secrets. I hesitate for a second before picking it up and peering inside. I don't know what I expected to find: gold coins, strange creatures, the Zippo, maybe. But what's actually there is this: an old check, a small metal pellet, and an impossibly thin, brown thing shaped like a wing. I touch it, and it crumbles in my fingers, leaving a dusty film.

I hear Jolene's voice down the hall over the rush of the faucet. I cover the box, kick it beneath the bed, and get to work on my second boot. By the time Jolene's back, I'm ready to leave.

Cars line both sides of the street, but Jolene doesn't crane her neck searching for a spot. She drives straight to the brick house next to Bella's and pulls into a wide-open space, the only one on the block.

"That was lucky," I say, slipping my purse strap over my head.

"Luck has nothing to do with it." Jolene looks sideways at herself in the rearview mirror before turning her hazel eyes on me. They glow with shimmery gold powder. "Look at me," she says.

I do.

"You're beautiful," Jolene says, like it's the truth. And that's the part that sends a warm wave through me. Not the word, but the way she says it.

"You too," I say.

"Then we're ready." She cuts the lights. "Shall we?"

When we turn down Bella's driveway, there's no hesitation, no conversation. There's no Kris, asking me whether or not I want to do this. There's only Jolene's arm in mine, the click of our heels on the cement, the smell of dead leaves and something sweet. Small white lights are strung through the trees that line the winding drive, not on the tips of the branches, but farther back, in a second layer of darkness, floating like winter fireflies.

The last time I walked to Bella's house, I pretended to be brave, but I was really afraid. Of Hudson. Of Jolene. Of everything I hadn't done. But tonight, with its glittering trees and crisp energy, feels right. Like a continuation of me and Jolene from the past couple of weeks: our breath mingled in sleep; our fingers twined when we walk down the street, through the mall, past the school; our hair blown and tangled like our words—the silk threads of a story we spin around us like a chrysalis.

I'm not mapping the house. I'm not naming the streets. I'm not anxious.

I'm protected.

Halfway down the drive, as the music seeps through the trees, Jolene straightens her arm, finds my hand, and squeezes it hard. Then Bella's house rises above us—the same combination of blocks it's always been, with its thick walls and right angles burning white into the black night. Except tonight the sky is clear and the stars are out. So many of them I can't count. By the time I look down again, I feel dizzy, and we're at the foot of the stone stairs. Christmas creatures cover the large, sloping lawn. They're made of structured wire and sparkling lights.

We sparkle too as we make our way up the steps. I can tell by the way the small group of smokers standing near the front door looks at us. We walk right by them, through the soft, white puffs of our own breaths and into the house.

Jolene leads me through the living room to the kitchen. There's no turning my body to accommodate people this time. The crowd parts for us, and a minute later we're staring at the keg. But Jolene doesn't bother with it. She drops my hand and heads straight for the guys from the soccer team. They're circling the island in the center of the kitchen, shoving their glasses into a crowd on the counter, and pouring sloppy shots of brown liquor. The alcohol splashes all over the granite until Cal grabs the bottle out of some kid's hand and fills all the glasses to the brims without spilling.

He says something I can't hear, because the bass is thumping behind me, but whatever it is makes half the boys laugh and the other half drink. It also makes him turn to Jolene. He raises his eyebrows. She shrugs with one shoulder. He shakes his head, tips the bottle of thick, brown liquid again, and hands Jolene a full glass. She looks at me as she tosses back her head and downs the shot. The long stretch of her neck brings back a flash: her shirt off her shoulder, her lips a mess, her body limp on the lawn chair.

"You want some?" asks a hoarse voice. The boy standing next to me holds up a joint. I recognize him from when I used to meet Hudson at the bike racks. He'd cross the street with his friends smacking packs of cigarettes, which they'd smoke near the armory. Tonight he's wearing a gray-and-white-striped collared shirt with ballooning black jeans and neon-green sneakers.

I look for Jolene. She's gulping down another dose of the brown liquor, laughing. I lift the joint from the boy's pinched fingers, bring it to my lips, and breathe in. The smoke burns my throat. I hand it back to him. "It's cool," he says, nodding to the new beat blaring behind us. "Finish it." I take a few more hits and start nodding myself. The electronic notes come faster and faster. "You want to dance?" he asks, snaking his body side to side toward the strobe lights off the living room.

I haven't smoked in a while, but I can already feel it. The little lift. The sudden ease. The edges sharpening, coming into focus. I want to dance, but—

"She's with me," Jolene croons from behind me. She presses her chest against my back, throws the roach in a floater, wraps her arms around my waist, and guides me toward the island. Her breath heats my neck. Her glossy lips slick my ear. "We're playing a game."

I lean into her and laugh. Because of course we are. Aren't we always?

But Jolene isn't talking about us. She's talking about the shot that has appeared in my hand and the granite counter beneath it, which hits right under my ribs, where Jolene's arms just held me. She's talking about the half dozen people who complete the circle around the island and the interested eyes that have all landed on me.

I know stuff like this used to make me nervous. I know it the way you know the name of a song you can't remember: sure that it's there inside you somewhere, even as it hovers just out of reach, buried deep. But right now I'm lit up. And yeah, it might be the weed, but who cares when there's this energy inside me? The weird thing is, I recognize the feeling. I've had it before. Back then I called it restlessness. But I had it all wrong. It's anticipation. Something is about to happen—in the middle of this kitchen, between the keg and the near-empty bottles of liquor, surrounded by the stink of stale smoke, skunked beer, old deodorant, and fresh sweat.

"You know the rules, right, Mats?" Cal asks as he reaches across the table to top off the Hurley twins. I recognize them from school and Hudson's pictures. They play soccer, but they're built for football. Their plaid button-downs buckle at the biceps. Their baseball hats curve steep at the brims. Their sideburns drip wet with sweat, and the tips of their ears are tinged red. They remind me of garden gnomes, which makes my mouth open, which lets the energy bubble out.

I'm laughing.

Cal furrows his brow and tips his head toward me. At first I can't figure out why he's looking at me like that; then I remember—he asked me a question.

I bite back a grin and nod at him—*Yeah, I know them*—because I'm still thinking of the gnomes and feeling the energy, and if I open my mouth, it's going to come out again.

He brushes a lock of black hair out of his eyes, and his face breaks into a smile.

"Of course you do. But I'm going to offer a refresher any-way, since these jokers have been cheating for the past half hour." Cal ignores the halfhearted protests from the circle, caps the bottle, holds it by the neck, and slides it back and forth as he speaks, like a stick shift. "We go around the circle. Everybody talks. 'I never whatever.' If you've done the whatever, drink. If you haven't, don't. Or do it now. I ain't gonna stop you."

Hoots from the Hurleys. Eye rolls from the girls. A curved smirk from Jolene, who stands directly across the counter, surveying me. She glides the tip of her finger around the rim of her glass, then runs it across her lips. I lick my own—a reflex—and taste whiskey, even though I haven't had a sip.

The game begins.

"I never broke into Memorial pool," says Kristin Whelan—second-string goalie, first-string girlfriend. She bats her lashes at the bigger Hurley.

Everyone drinks. When they're finished, they push their glasses to the center of the island. Cal leans in to refill them.

"I never forgot my bathing suit," says the junior girl in the ivory, racer-back tank.

More shots. More refills.

"I never stole yours," Cal says.

"That was you?" She punches him in the arm.

I grip and regrip my glass, waiting for my turn to drink. But I've never broken into a pool, or skinny-dipped, or cut school to go to Great Adventure. It's starting to seem like I've never done anything. Like I'm not even here but standing on the other side of the kitchen again, watching.

Cal's mouth moves. Jolene laughs. They drink.

People pack into the kitchen in search of the keg and the cups and the half-empty handles of liquor.

My tongue sticks to the inside of my cheek and the roof of my mouth. So I swallow a few times, trying to work up some spit, make my lips wet, like everyone else's. I skim my fingers along the top of the syrupy liquid.

The faint music from the dining-room-turned-dance floor cranks way up, or at least it does in my head. A vibrating bass beat. Dizzying fades. The same words from different mouths around the circle, like lyrics over an endless loop of electronic music: *I never. I never. I never.*

Then hers.

At first I think it's in my head. Because isn't that how it's always been? A whisper in my ear. A pulse beneath my skin. A murmur in my sleep. The feeling of a forgotten dream.

Jolene.

But no. There she is, directly across the island from me—slender arm outstretched, shot of whiskey suspended between her thumb and middle finger. She extends the glass in my direction—an air toast—before she speaks.

"I never got tied up."

I lock eyes with Jolene. She lowers her lashes and curves her lips into a sly, knowing smile.

Eyes go wide around the circle, gazes volleying from Jolene to me. Waiting. It's not the naked break-in or the backflip off a cabana roof they were expecting.

It's better.

We're better than real.

I've guarded my memory of that afternoon for so long—locked it in an airtight case and shoved it into the darkest recesses of my safest place. But now that it's out there in the air, not just between me and Jolene, but on display at Bella's party, where it can live and breathe and everyone can see it, I feel . . . good.

I raise my glass to Jolene's. She tilts her chin and gives me a thin smile before our glasses clink. We throw back our heads and drink.

The liquor burns my throat and warms my chest. It lights me up again. Like the whiskey is kindling and I'm the fire, throwing sparks.

The Hurleys and their girls clap and cheer.

I wipe my lips with the back of my wrist and slide my glass across the counter.

"Tell me again why I haven't seen you at one of these things in so long?" Cal shakes his head like it's a shame and upends the bottle, but the brown liquor that's left barely fills my glass halfway. I make the whiskey disappear. Cal reaches beneath the counter and produces a pitcher of beer. Red plastic cups appear in front of us. Like magic.

They need us, Jolene said. And now I believe her.

Because as the game rolls on, the "I nevers" come fast, the beer goes down faster, and the laughter is manic; the circle spins like a compass, but it always stops on us.

Because they're playing for fun, and we're playing for each other. We're trading lines back and forth, the same way we have for years. We're used to this. The only difference is, tonight we have an audience.

First me: "I never got slapped."

Jolene purses her lips. Swigs.

Then her: "I never got suffocated."

I open my throat. Gulp.

With each piece of our past that's set free, I tip my cup to my lips and drink. And drink and drink and drink. Until there is only me and Jolene. Swimming, circling, submerged in a place that drowns out hollers and whistles and winks. Until I can swallow and breathe simultaneously, like the fish Jolene always knew I could be, if she pushed me.

My turn again. "I never felt like I wasn't real."

Jolene tosses her hair. The auburn streak underneath floats in the air for a second and catches a spotlight from the disco ball in the dining room before falling to her shoulder and settling on her sweater. My sweater. She lifts her cup to drink. The bottom blocks her face. I can't see her again until she claps the red plastic on the counter and licks the foam off her top lip.

When Jolene's up again, and she has everyone's attention, she lengthens her neck, like a cat stretching in the sun. "I never ran away from everyone. I never disappeared."

I feel the edges of my vision contract, go black, expand again. And then I laugh. If I could have disappeared back then, I would have—gathered up all my dark, scarred parts and folded in on myself until there was nothing left. But I don't want that anymore. I want to be here. I want to slice open the memories, peel back the skin, and let them bleed out in front of everyone.

I coat my throat with flat beer, let the voices recede and circle back to me. "I never wished someone would save me."

Jolene doesn't bother with beer this time.

"I never wished someone would love me," she says, her voice clear and cool over the slurs and shouts of the kitchen crowd.

Another part of me unearthed, released.

My eyes are locked on Jolene, but I don't need to see the rest of the faces in the circle to know they're looking at me. I can feel their eyes stuck to my body like a harsh August heat.

I breathe in the humid stink of the kitchen and breathe it out again.

I hold the moment.

Not because I can't think of a response, but because the response is so easy. It comes to me ready, willing. Like it's already been written. Which is actually sort of true. The line isn't mine; someone gave it to me. The same person I was thinking of when I made that wish, who my sophomore self hoped in her deepest, secret heart would love her, because she had no idea there'd be someone else—that there already was—someone who'd inhabit her heart, seep through her skin, curl up and take residence, poisoning her for everyone else. Even him. Especially him.

Hudson.

I say it to Jolene, because he said it to me. "I never begged my boyfriend to love me."

Jolene's eyes go wide. The tendons in her neck rise into ropes, and the corners of her lips pinch.

I'm afraid, for a second, that I've crossed a line—stepped into some invisible division.

Then I blink, and her lashes are lowered again, her neck smooth and slender, her lips imperceptibly curved in that Mona Lisa smirk.

But I can still see the other face underneath. The strand of auburn hair stuck to the sweat on her neck, the coiled tension cloaked in the posed slope of her shoulder, the flash of fire hidden in her half-lidded eyes.

One version of Jolene set over the other, like a piece of tracing paper. Or a double exposure.

I blink and blink and blink, but the two images won't line up exactly.

The effect is haunting. Disorienting.

I press my palms on the granite counter for balance, but when I shift my weight, the corner of my boot skids on something slippery and the room spins.

LOT 1
MB:46—865
MB:51—103
60' R/W
YOUNGBLOC

COS.
MB:46—865
MB:51—103
60' R/W
YOUNGBLO

EX. CB

CHAPTER 35

I FLAIL FOR something stable. Instead I connect with soft, supple skin.

"The twins love you, babe, but show some restraint." Bella flashes me a big, lip-lined grin. Then I realize where my hand is, and take it out of her cleavage.

"Bells, I—"

"Oh, don't worry about them." Bella waves one hand in front of her chest and lifts a champagne glass to her lips with the other. "They like the attention." She takes in the cups, the circle, the crowd. Then she sidles up next to me and rests the twins on the granite, between her elbows. "What are we playing?"

"*We're* playing I Never." Cal twirls his pointer finger in front of him like he's mixing an imaginary drink. "Those two," he says, wagging his finger back and forth between me and Jolene, "have got their own game going on."

I turn back to Jolene, who looks serene. Like she's in this

pristine, shimmering sphere while the rest of us are dirty, drunk, dim.

Maybe it's because she lines up again—one face, one expression. There's no overlay of thin rustling paper pinching her lips and roping her throat, just solid lines and strong strokes.

She stares back at me, still as a portrait.

"But you know me," Cal says, flashing Bella a million-dollar grin. "I'm game for anything." He brushes the same lock of black hair off his eyes and lifts the pitcher like it's evidence.

"Ladies first," Bella tells Cal, her doe eyes big and serious. Then she turns to us, and her hands fly forward, wrists bent, hands flexed, like two stop signs. "Okay. I was mad at you, Jolene, I'll admit it. But let's just agree here and now that we're all friends again. It's senior year, and we promised we'd be amazing things; and I can't take any more fighting." Bella tips her stiff waves of hair toward Jolene first and then to me. "I can do it. Can you two?"

"Of course," Jolene says—animated once again. She leans onto her forearms and drapes her hair on the granite, lifting her body over the counter in Bella's direction. "For you."

"Yeah," I agree. But Bella's already squealing.

"Yay!" Bella takes another sip of champagne. Imprints of lips overlap on the glass rim. "I've been wait-ing for this!" Bella separates each syllable into its own song and does a little dance in her stilettos. "I'm in!"

Cal hands a cup to Bella, and the game picks up again; but I have a hard time keeping track of whose turn it is, and when. At some point the original girls switch out and two more take their place. Then the Hurleys are gone too, replaced by more boys in hats, like they're a renewable resource.

Then Jolene is next to me—her chin skimming my shoulder, her fingers on my forearm—and everything's okay again. Maybe nothing was ever wrong. Because her head is on my chest. My cheek is on her neck. We're curling into each other.

What do you want to be, Mattie?

I want to be loved.

I lift my chin. My lips brush the lobe of Jolene's ear. She laughs at something Bella says and leans into me the slightest bit.

My skin pricks with adrenaline, the energy that was inside, pushing its way through my pores, to the surface. Turning my insides out, so everybody can see:

I want to be loved.

There's no order to the game anymore. Just drinking and shouting and more drinking.

"I never kissed a girl!" someone says. Is it me?

Jolene and I click our cups together and drink.

"Oh no you don't," Bella chimes in, catching the back of my neck. "I'm not going to be left out at my own party!" She smashes our mouths together. When she pulls away, her lips are half lined, and mine feel sticky.

Bella lifts her cup again. "I never liked it!"

We laugh into our beer.

We drink. As the beer flows down my throat, a sweet ache rushes up. This is how it should have been. All of us, together. The only thing that's missing is Kris. Even though she would have hated this.

Jolene pushes a hair out of my eyes with her middle finger and trails it lightly along my hairline. For a second her eyes flick up and above me, but before I can turn around to see what she's looking at, she's raising her cup again. She's talking.

"I never slept with a girl."

Shouts erupt around us. The house tilts, rights itself.

"Sleepovers, people! Deal with it!" Bella drinks.

We join her.

"I never slept with a boy."

It's hard to tell who's talking anymore. All the voices are so familiar, so similar. Saying things we all did. And then.

Red cups. Wet lips. Mine. Moving.

"I never slept with Hudson."

"Watch what you say."

Hudson. *He's here! I said his name and he appeared!* I think. It definitely looks like him—black thermal worn thin, flannel unbuttoned, dark hair pulled back, except for the strands that always seem to escape. I reach out to tuck them behind his ear, but my aim is off. My hand heads straight for his chest, but it never connects. Hudson catches it, a tight grip on my wrist. That's when I look at his face, which is the only thing in the room that isn't spinning, swimming.

It's his eyes that bring me back to the surface—a cool, cerulean blue. They pull me up from a deep, dark place, gasping. And changed.

I pry my wrist away from him and stumble backward, into Jolene's palms. She props me up.

"I've watched long enough, don't you think? I'm sick of watching," I tell him.

"It's not their business." His lips barely move when he speaks.

"It's my business. And I'm tired of hiding." I raise my cup again, and a surge streaks through me, soaks my skin. Or maybe that's beer. My neck is wet. So is my sweater. Jolene's sweater. "I never slept with Hudson!"

"You've never slept with anyone." Kris grabs my cup and takes a long swallow, then makes a face. "This is warm and flat, by the way."

I stare at her and wonder if I'm hallucinating. Can combining weed and beer do that? Because, Kris. At Bella's party. Standing shoulder to shoulder with Hudson? That doesn't happen. I squeeze my eyes shut, but that makes the room spin again, so I open them. But it's still happening: Hudson, Kris, Jolene, Bella, me, the party.

Bella bends at the knees and lets out a squee. "You totally came!" She stands tippy-toe on her stilettoes and throws her arms around Kris. "We're all here!"

Now that Bella has confirmed this is actually happening, I feel another surge stun me; but it's not the frantic energy this time, aching to get loose. And it's not the beer. It's Kris. It's everything we've been through and everything we haven't. It's drives in the reservation and Trivial Pursuit games and HaFTAs and Top Tens. It's her lying to me.

"Yes! You're here!" I announce. Ponytails and hat brims swivel in my peripheral vision. Chatter stops in the kitchen. But the quiet only makes me talk louder. "You *never* come to parties!" I grab Jolene's cup off the counter, shove it into Kris's cable-knit sweater, then sweep my arm in an arc across the room. "I never come to parties!"

Every red cup in the kitchen rises.

Kris crosses her arms. Hudson's hands curl into fists beneath his unbuttoned cuffs. Jolene's fingers press into the soft skin of my waist. I can feel her fingernails through the thin knit of the sweater. I can feel everyone watching. Their stares have a texture and weight I can wear. My skin pulses with it.

"It's a game, Kris. Come on! Have a little fun! We never do anything!"

Another wave of red cups.

"We never do *this*." Kris's voice is quiet and clipped in the hush of the kitchen.

"You don't. I do." I throw back my head and chug to prove it.

"So now you're lying too?"

"Nope," I say. "That's your department."

"You've never had sex." She's so sure. With her pursed lips and cocked hip. She's so sure I would have told her. But she shouldn't be.

I drink again.

Kris's lips peel apart and hang open. Then she clamps her mouth shut again and shakes her head.

"Fuck this." Hudson is a blur of dark hair and flannel as he shoves his way past the keg and through the packed living room. But isn't that how he's always been? Even when he was right in front of me? Even when I was touching him? Not so much a person as an idea. An apparition. A vision of what could have been. Who *I* could have been.

But not who I am.

When I step forward, out of Jolene's hold, every open mouth and roving eye in the kitchen follows me. They've eaten all my secrets, but they're still hungry. They want what comes next, and I'm going to give it to them.

I lean into Kris. "I never ran away from everything I was afraid of." Sip. "I never showed up at school each day wishing I was somewhere else." Sip. "I never thought I was too good for everyone, including my boyfriend." The peach in Kris's cheeks deepens, shifts to crimson. Not all at once but in rippling bits. I lean closer, until my lower lip hits her ear. "I never lied to my best friend."

Kris doesn't move.

"Come on now, Kris. You should be drinking. You know the rules, right? If you've done the thing . . ." I place two fingers on the bottom of her cup and flick it up.

She jerks away from me. "We're not best friends."

It's what we always said, but not the way we always said it—with a laugh in the backs of our throats and a shared history etched across our memories. With a confidence so deep, so sure, it drilled down to our cores.

No. When Kris says we're not best friends, I don't hear any of those things. The words are flat. Empty.

And this makes me angrier than anything.

We're not best friends.

"Exactly." I slam my cup on the counter and turn around.

Jolene is waiting. She snakes her arm around my waist. We make our exit together, hair and hips swinging through the white living room toward the dark, dense forest of the dance floor. But before we become a part of it, I hear a shout—three words thrown at my back, barely audible over the roar of the speakers—and unlike the last thing she said, this sounds exactly like the Kris I remember.

"Who *are* you?"

CHAPTER 36

THE MUSIC VIBRATES through my boots to the soles of my feet. It rattles my chest and takes over my head. My entire body thrums with it, as if now that I've let everything go—cut open my dark heart and exposed the stained and shameful things I hid there for so long—a physical space has been created inside me.

I'm light. My feet leave the wood floor and I'm airborne, over and over again. My hair swings in wet strings around me. The guy with the striped shirt—the one who smoked me up—is here too. He says something to me, but I can't hear him. We're right in front of a speaker. I shrug my shoulders and laugh. I think he shrugs too, but it's hard to tell in the flash of the strobe light. His movements seem separated. Choppy. Like a robot's. Which makes me laugh so hard, my eyes crinkle at the sides, my chin rises, and my neck comes unhinged. My head lands on something soft and hard at the same time: smooth yarn, solid bone. I'm surrounded by dark hair and cinnamon.

Because I'm light, but not empty. Open, but not alone.

Jolene sways behind me, her hands on my hips. The lit ball hung from the ceiling spins, and we're covered in tiny white dots. Like strung lights. Or stars. And for a second we're outside. We're the sky on a summer night. It reminds me of something. But Jolene spins me around and I forget, because she's laughing and we're dancing.

And I'm thinking, *THIS. This is what I've been missing.*

Then the song switches. The thumping stops. A few soaring notes fill the room. They float over us. And we wait with heavy breaths and nodding heads.

When the bass kicks in again, so do we. For a second it's like we're all suspended. Then our feet hit the floor, and the dining room explodes in a fit of waving arms and flying knees.

I lift my arms and close my eyes. Fingertips skim the swoop of my waist, my breasts, grip the back of my neck. When I open my eyes again, Jolene and I are nose to nose, hip to hip, lip to lip. Smiling. Then the strobe light flashes, and Jolene's hair flows forward. No, that's the back of her head. She's facing away from me. I recognize the small pull in my sweater, just above her shoulder blade. Until a boy's hand covers it. Another flash and there are hands on my back too. They aren't soft like Jolene's, but they're warm. And when they slip under the hem of my sweater and onto the slick skin of my stomach, I twist into them. They belong to the boy in the striped shirt. The girl from I Never. One of the Hurley twins. They are Kris's fingers twined in mine. Hudson's hand edging under the waist of my jeans. Jolene's palm on my pounding chest. Her lips against my ear.

Lips against my lips. Sweat gathers between my shoulder

blades and breasts, drips from the curve of my lip into a kiss.

It's like now that I've opened myself up, I don't want to stop opening. I'd turn myself inside out if I could; claw open my skin; expose my blood, my soft pink organs, and all the secrets stuck between them. So I'm not surprised when my skin seems to stretch away and snap. I'm not fazed when I hear the howl of material ripping. It's not until I feel a splash of air on my stomach and chest instead of the sweaty stick of thin knit that I realize what's happened. And who's watching.

The crowd has carved a circle around us.

Me and some guy I don't recognize. At least not with his mouth pressed against mine. I push him off me. He wipes his lips with the back of a doughy hand, and when his eyes finally focus on me, a mix of delight and confusion dawns on his half-moon face.

Jolene's sweater hangs in ragged folds along my sides, like curtains to a show.

"Oh, shit," he says. "Hard-core."

Hard-core. Not strong and sought after, but stripped down, rough, senseless.

The music turns shrill, a repeated scream. My stomach sours. Liquid climbs its way up my throat. It wants out like everything else. I swallow back a mix of bile and whiskey, but what's left in my mouth afterward is even worse: smoke, stale and bitter, stuck to my tongue. Not the earthy aftertaste of weed anymore. Something acrid.

I grab the jagged edges of my sweater, cover myself with a tight hug, and dive into the huddled crowd that surrounds us.

For the first time tonight I don't want to be seen. I don't want the crowd to cleave for me. I want to melt into it.

I want Jolene.

But it's impossible to see anything in the flashing dark other than a split-second freeze-frame of open mouths and closed eyes, nodding heads and slinking hips. Teased bangs. A shock of red curls. Bella? Kris? I turn around and get knocked forward. A girl in a tight white cami and loose cargo pants dances away from me, toward the boy with the striped shirt. My head pounds in time with the bass beat from the speakers. I turn sideways and shoulder my way through the moving bodies.

The air from the kitchen window cools the sweat on my forehead and tickles my uncovered belly button. Trembling, I angle my neck to see past the crowd and around the keg. Cups and hands and elbows cover the countertops, but none of them are Jolene's. I turn back toward the living room.

I've been in Bella's house a million times. I know the placement of each wall and the pattern on every floor. I try to bring up the map in my head, but I can't see it. Between the shots and the beer and the weed and the dancing, everything's fuzzy. I stop short of the thick living-room carpet and squint to see between all the people. I search from neck to mouth to face. I catch a flash of honey skin here and a dark-purple nail there, the slope of a shoulder, the curved corner of a wide smile, but never the whole of her. It's like Jolene's scattered around the room in pieces, and I can't follow any of them. Because it's thirty minutes to midnight on New Year's Eve, and the sequins and polos and cups of beer crowd closer and closer and closer together until they're packed and pulsing and pushing.

I squeeze the fine knit of Jolene's severed sweater in my fists and step backward. And back again. And then I hit something solid. A seam in the wall. The invisible door. Bunching both ends of the sheer material into my left hand, I pull open the white door and slip into the damp air of the basement.

It's quiet down here compared to upstairs, but I can still feel the music. The bone-rattling bass in my chest. The quick fades in my head. I dig my knuckles into my ribs and screw my eyes shut, but that only amplifies the sounds.

I sit down and clap a hand over my mouth as my stomach roils, convulses. When I'm sure I'm not going to be sick, I stretch the dangling sides of the sweater across my stomach again and force myself to breathe through my nose.

In. Smoke. The sticky, sweet kind.

Out. Techno beat and DJ fades. Go away.

In. Focus on each floating stair.

Out. *Hard-core.*

In. Jolene.

Jolene. Jolene. Jolene.

Where is she?

And then—as if I'm under the eave in the auditorium again, with her hands in my hair and her words in my ear, telling me—I know.

I know exactly where to find her.

LOT
MB:46—66
MB:51—10
60' R/W
YOUNGBLO

COS
MB:46—6
MB:51   1
60' R/
YOUNGBL

EX. CB

CHAPTER 37

I RUN UNDER the black-blue sky, crunching frozen blades of grass beneath my boots. One hand grips my gathered sweater, the other pumps back and forth. Icy air sweeps past me, filling my ears, until I can barely hear the faint noises from the house—a solo cheer here and there. It must be close to midnight.

When I get to the far end of the backyard, I drop the sweater, arrow my hands in front of me, and cut through the bushes. Pine needles scratch at my ribs, grab at the knit, pull at my cheeks like thin fingers. When I'm free of them, I see her— lying on the lounge chair, legs splayed, like after the bonfire. Except this time she's awake.

"I saw you in there," Jolene says to the single cloud that ghosts the sky above us and the stroke of stars to its right. "Everyone did." She circles her lips and blows her own cloud into the air above her face, watches it disappear. "Did you like it?"

I wrap my arms around my bare stomach.

"No."

Jolene props herself up on her elbows and considers me. Her eyes don't look hazel in the moonlight; they look like light. Like her irises are on fire. She stands up, walks toward me, and stops just short of stepping on my feet.

"No?"

I think of earlier on the dance floor: The lights becoming the sky above us. The music through my body. The collective energy. Her arms reaching for me.

"Yes," I admit.

Jolene nods, satisfied.

Shouts and noisemakers sound from the house. We turn toward the lit windows.

"They liked it too," she says, as if she's translating for them.

"What about you?" I ask.

"What *about* me?"

I face her. "Did you like it?"

She keeps her eyes on the house, her profile set off by a thin shine of moonlight. Until she turns and the light is behind her. The crooks of her face are dark caves as she lifts the loose ends of her sweater that flap against my waist. She rubs them between her fingers. I half expect her to rip them off and roll them the way Hudson does. Instead she holds both sides open so she can see every inch of my winter-pale skin. I breathe deep, feel the gooseflesh of my breasts press against my bra and go slack again under her gaze. I wait—chin up, eyes steady—as she makes her way back to my face.

Jolene drops the edges of the sweater, fastens her eyes on mine. "No."

The breath from her word warms my lips. Maybe that's why

I kiss her. To prove she's lying.

She kisses me back, at first: mouth open, tongue strong, lips soft. She tastes bitter and sweet, a mix of burned cocoa and sugar.

Behind my eyelids, the darkness folds and shifts, like covers for us to burrow under. I clutch her hand and curve into her. I tilt my head so I can taste her better. And when her chin doesn't turn with me, I claw at her jaw, dig my thumb into the skin on the side of her nose and force her head to the side. I push her, for all the times she pushed me. I'm the rope on her wrists. The hand on her mouth. The glass through her skin.

Until Jolene jerks back again, and I lose my grip. When she breaks the seal of our kiss, there's a hiss—a shared breath escaping.

"What?" I grab the tattered edges of the sweater and cross them like a cardigan over my stomach. "You want this."

Jolene smoothes her hair and squares her shoulders. "I don't."

"Then why—?" My head is spinning, and this time it's not from the pot or the alcohol. It's from the memories: her hand in my hair, her palm covering my mouth, the curve of her back as she pulled me close. Those things were real. They happened. She has to want me. She has to want this. But if she doesn't— "Then why did you do all those things?"

"What? Up there?" She flicks her head toward the crowd of silhouettes gathered in the living room, backed by blue light from the television. "I did those things because I can. Because that's what I'm good at. I can dance and drink and lie. I can give guys what they want. And girls too, apparently." She sighs. Her breath steams like smoke in the cold. "And now you can, too," she adds with a smile.

"No, I mean . . ." An ache grows in my throat, but I force the question around it. I have to know. "Why did you do all those things *to me*?"

Jolene's smile shrinks but doesn't disappear. It almost seems appreciative. "Because you like it."

"You think I like being tied up and suffocated and lied to? You think I like losing all my friends, and my boyfriend?" I'm shaking now, not shivering. It's almost like my skin is vibrating.

"Yeah. I do," Jolene says simply. "I think you like the fact that something finally happened to you."

"I like you."

"No you don't. You don't even know me, and you don't want to. Why did you want to be friends with me in the first place? Think about it."

I see the cliff, feel her hand, hear the rocks falling beneath my sneakers. I was scared and excited at the same time. I felt alive. But it wasn't just that, was it? It couldn't have been.

"Let me remind you," Jolene says. "It was because you hated yourself. When I met you, you were making lists and checking boxes. You had a million maps of the same place. You were trapped. You wanted out. You wanted to be new, and you figured I could give that to you. And you were right. Though I have to say, I think you made a real mistake running away on the dance floor like that. Not that it can't be fixed."

I wiggle my fingers. I haven't felt them tingling for the last few minutes, and I'm afraid they're going numb. Then I realize I'm having a hard time feeling anything. I let my hands go slack at my sides.

"So this is all a game to you?" I ask. "I'm just this thing you've been playing with? You saw that I was weak—an easy target—and that gave you the right to take advantage?"

"You're not paying attention." Jolene shakes her head and clucks her tongue. "I wasn't using you, Mattie. *You* were using *me*. You came to me every time you needed a little something interesting, and when someone else looked better, you left." She clamps her jaw shut, as if something big, or bitter, has landed on her tongue. Then she grimaces and swallows it whole. "You were only in it for yourself. *You* used *me*. And look what you got out of it!"

"What I got out of it? Are you kidding?" I pick up the ends of the ripped sweater. I think of Hudson storming out, and the tone of Kris's voice when she called after me: Angry. Shocked. Full throated. The same way I sound when I say, "I lost everything!"

"Not everything," she says, swiveling toward the house. And as if everyone inside can sense Jolene's attention, the hollers get louder. "You've got them."

"But they don't know me. They're not my friends. What I did up there—what they saw—that wasn't me."

"It sure looked like you."

"Okay, I mean, obviously it was me, but—"

"Then own it," Jolene demands. She huffs out a hard, impatient breath. "Do you really think what happened at Bella's party broke me? That I stayed home, sulking about some stupid fight, some dumb breakup, until I could drag myself back to school the next day to live in the shadows? That I just *let* it all happen?"

I open my mouth, but only air comes out.

What *did* I think when I slid into my old seat in the cafeteria and Jolene slid into the seat next to me in the auditorium? That we'd switched skins? That the world had finally righted itself, decided I'd served my sentence? That it was time I reclaimed what was rightfully mine?

Or was that just the version I wanted to believe?

I swallow a mix of whiskey, shame, and spit.

Because I knew, didn't I? That Jolene had something to do with it? As soon as she missed school on Monday, and then again when she came back changed, no longer full of bite and blaze. I knew, and I buried it. Because I wanted to believe it was mine. That I earned it. That I deserved it. That I was worth it.

But if she orchestrated it all, why?

And if that's not the real version, what is?

The questions kick at my closed lips, but Jolene's not finished.

"Tell everyone you were drunk and wanted to put on a show. Or tell them you went home with me. Tell them *something*, and it'll be your story instead of theirs."

"I don't care about the story." I step in front of Jolene, cutting off her view of the living room, where every arm is raised, black strips against the blue light. "It's not about the story."

She laughs. It's a sad, sorry-for-me sound. "It's always about the story, Mattie."

As soon as she says it, something in me settles, clicks, like the metal ridges of the flint wheel. Jolene and I, we've never been the real thing. We've always been a story. Our story. "The Two Little Girls." That's how we were born, and that's how we've lived. I think back to the auditorium and the early parties, where Jolene always made people into fantasies. I think of her face, grim and determined, as she stared at me in the bed and held her breath. I think of the ropes and the cliff and the shed and the texts. Hudson. Even these last few weeks when she played dead.

Jolene told me the night I walked to her house at midnight. She said it: *Maybe we're both not here. What if we're both not real?*

I look hard at Jolene—at the curve of her lip and the line of her chin, the angle of her neck and the bend of her elbow—trying to find something genuine. For a second I think I glimpse something—the rope-throated version I saw inside the party—but then it's gone, buried beneath a veneer of dark hair, auburn streaks, and gleaming teeth. It's a practiced pose, but not the real thing. More like some kind of covering. And it occurs to me now that maybe Jolene was right. Maybe I don't know her at all. Maybe I've never seen what's underneath. But if I could just lift the film . . . if I could just see—

I reach for her cheek.

She pulls back a fraction of an inch.

And suddenly I'm struck cold. Not from the weather or the wind but from fear—fear that the story is all there is. That she's as insubstantial as a collection of words and phrases I could erase. That if I reached out and pulled off the covering, she'd cease to exist.

Or, worse, that one pull wouldn't be enough. That I'd peel and peel and peel only to reach another layer. Another lie. Another story.

"Is anything about you real?" My voice shakes.

Jolene doesn't respond right away. She waits until the voices lift through the open living-room window and float across the lawn toward us.

"FOUR!"

"THREE!"

"TWO!"

But she keeps her eyes on me. They shine like wet paint when she smiles.

"You used to be."

One.

LOT √
MB:46-665
MB:51-103
60' R/W
YOUNGBLOOI

COS
MB:46-665
MB:51-103
60' R/W
YOUNGBLO(

EX. CB

CHAPTER 38

I STAMP THE snow from my boots, peel off my knit hat, and pad up the steps to my room, where hundreds of crumpled pieces of paper—yellowed at the edges, brittle to the point of breaking—carpet the floor. I step between the stacks, around clear, curled balls of packing tape piled like popcorn, and sit down on the only spot of open carpet. Then I reach into the worn cardboard box sitting next to me and slowly slide out the final sheaf of thin sheets.

Since Bella's party I've kept to myself, and so has everybody else. I drive to school. I eat lunch alone. And when I get home, I hang out with happyelizabeth's grandmother in 1901.

Turns out I won the auction. The beat-up box was sitting next to my bed New Year's Day, with a Post-it that shouted, "THIS CAME WHEN YOU WERE OUT YESTERDAY!" in my mom's handwriting. The caps alone had caused me pain. I'd woken with a raw throat and a heavy head, wearing a black thermal. I'd tried to crawl back into sleep, only to wake again with a bucking stomach, tasting whiskey and cocoa, fending off flashes of shot glasses and strobe lights, smoke and liquor, sweat and secrets. Me: dancing. Jolene: leaving. I'd turn over in bed, only to feel the cold creeping over my skin again. The hands between my back and the stretched rubber strips of a lounge chair. Kris's curls covering my face. Curses. A flannel shirt. The scenes had faded in and out like the music had on the dance floor. And for a few hours I'd felt like I was fading, too—skin papery thin, vanishing, then solid again. But eventually the sensation had gone away. It wasn't until noon that day, when I'd finally gathered the courage to sit up straight (elbows dug into my thighs, head in my hands), that I'd seen the stained box.

I'd opened it immediately—picked and pulled at each long piece of clear tape until it screamed with release, even though the sharp smell of glue and plastic turned my stomach.

My room doesn't smell like that anymore. Now it's a musty mix of oil and wood, grass and vanilla, same as my Sanborns. I haven't found any maps so far. I've sorted handwritten letters and transcribed telegrams. Loose pages of old newspapers. Medical information. Lists of food and supplies. Political flyers. Theater playbills. A pencil drawing of a farmhouse (on a piece of paper so old, I thought it might be woven, but no; when I brought it to my nose, it reeked of vinegar—a sure sign that the paper was wood pulp).

The small stack in my hand is the last of it. A few stuck-together pages. I set them on my lap and begin to peel them apart, starting at the corner. The first two don't release so easily, but the third comes away. And I see it. The map. There are more beneath. Hand-drawn plans of the house with floor layouts and measurements. A land survey with symbols for fences and farmland. Sales documents with plots and dollar amounts. Half-torn pages from a printed Colton atlas. Most of them only capture the southern part of the state, where the estate must have been located. But there is one that climbs north, detailing each county in central Jersey. It's not a Sanborn, but it's similar. Clear lines. Crossed boxes. Stark depictions.

I take that one to my bed, cross my legs, and smooth it flat with my hands. I don't worry about the oil from my fingers, because this map is already ruined. It's got color spots from the other paper it was pressed against in the box, not to mention the water stains and yellowed edges. So I touch it where I want, adding myself to the history of the page. I run my fingers up from Camden, through Mercer and Monmouth Counties, up to Union, and across the name printed on the yellow claw shape: *West Field*. Two words, separated by a space.

I get up and lean over my desk to lift my framed Sanborn off its nail, where it's been hanging since Thanksgiving. Then I set it on my blanket next to the decaying map from happyelizabeth. Both maps are from the early 1900s. Both are survey maps. But they're not the same. The northeast corner of Westfield, which stretches to meet Springfield, looks longer, narrower in my map. The dip in the middle looks steeper, as if Mountainside were dripping water into the top of Westfield and deepening the decay.

I always thought the Sanborn style was transparent, that it didn't have an agenda or a point of view. But looking between these two maps, it's obvious now that it's just a matter of style. Plain versus ornate. Informative versus illustrative. Detailed versus decorative. It all depends on the mapmaker, and what kind of story she wants to tell.

I hang the map back on my wall and step up onto my bed. From this height I can see the entire contents of the box spread out on my floor—a whole year of someone's life, laid out in scraps of paper. It gives me an idea.

After dinner that night I pack up all the pieces, laying each delicate page on top of another and slowly guiding the tall stack back into the bowed box. When I'm finished, I close the cardboard flaps and push the box into the corner of my closet. Then I gather the discarded balls of tape, some pieces still fuzzy with the film of cardboard skin that ripped away with it, and toss them in the trash. The room feels open and spacious.

I grab my cell from my nightstand and send Kris a text:

```
Talk at the reservation this weekend? Promise to
be your Worst Friend.
```

It's the first real communication we've had since New Year's Eve. She doesn't respond right away. I don't blame her, though. I've blamed her long enough.

After all, Kris didn't force me to leave the night of the manhunt game. She didn't ask me to walk away. I could have taken Jolene's hand. I could have gone back to find Hudson on those steps. I could have said no when Jolene showed me those ropes.

I had a choice. I chose this.

And I don't regret it. Despite the scars—the ones you can see and the ones you can't—I wouldn't change anything. Without Jolene, I wouldn't know how to run without looking down, how to laugh into the night, how to make my heart beat so loud it drowns out the rest of the world. I wouldn't know how to take control. I wouldn't know how to let go.

Of course, I wouldn't know the pain, loss, loneliness, or

confusion, either; but as hard as all those things were to live through, they were worth it. Because I survived them, and now I know that I can do that too.

I can survive.

About an hour later my phone buzzes. It's Kris:

```
Fine, but I'm driving.
```

I tap the letters on my screen.

```
Deal.
```

Then I lean back on my bed and stare up at the ceiling. I finally took down that cartoonish map my parents got me in second grade. Now when I look up I see pure white. A blank canvas. And when I close my eyes, I don't find intersecting lines. I'm not strung up in a familiar web of streets and houses.

I'm at school the next day.

Kris isn't waiting for me. It's not going to be that easy. Things between us might not ever be the way they used to be, but that's okay. I don't want to go back anymore. I want to go forward.

Jolene is at her locker. She's still with Bella. Still in front of an audience. Still lowering her lashes, tossing her hair, becoming whoever they want her to be.

Tomorrow's story.

But I know what's underneath. I know who she really is.

Not beautiful. Not even pretty.

Sad. Lonely. Desperate.

But most of all, separate.

I thought Jolene and I were the same thing: two hearts wrapped in the same skin. I thought she understood me. That she chose me. And in a way, she did. She wanted attention, and she knew I'd give it to her—that I'd scoop myself out to make room for her. She knew I'd give her everything, because I was desperate, too.

That's the thing I figured out about me and Jolene, after everything.

I wanted to be loved. She loved to be wanted.

It's not the same thing. And it definitely isn't love with a capital *L*. I'm not even sure I know what Love is.

Jolene said she loved me. I think she tried her best. It's the only explanation I can come up with. Why else would she have fought so fiercely for me? Why else would she have disappeared on purpose after break? That was her gift to me. It was the only thing she knew how to give.

Hudson said he loved me, too.

I never said it back to either of them.

Maybe because I couldn't separate the strands of love from need. Maybe because I was too intent on what could have been. Maybe because one was a boy, and one was a girl, and I wasn't sure what that meant. Maybe because we were all looking for something that didn't exist. Or maybe it's because love isn't what I was looking for in the first place.

What do you *want to be?* Jolene asked me. But that was the wrong question. It was Kris who got it right: *Who* are *you?*

I shut my eyes tighter.

I am ducking into the journalism room sixth period, not to find Kris but to collect samples of my layouts for a college portfolio. I am going to apply to some design programs, after Jake vets my essay. I am getting the issues I need. I'm locking up. I'm leaving.

Hudson is coming in from the bike racks with his headphones

up and his head down. We don't speak, but I remember what he said—that *I* walked away from *Jolene*, not because she forced me but because I wanted to. I know now that he was right. The same way I know that this time I won't go back, no matter how many times she calls.

I will flip up the hood of my sweatshirt and listen to my thoughts, which I've discovered have a flow and rhythm all their own. I will walk the route I want in the halls, not to avoid someone or run toward them, but so I can get where I need to go. I will choose a college miles from Westfield, not because I want to be far away from old friends, but because I want to hold myself closer.

I will test the jagged border of the space where Jolene used to be and feel a steady beat: warm, pulsing, blue—my own blood in my veins.

The threads of a tale only I can tell.

ACKNOWLEDGMENTS

THE FOLLOWING PEOPLE took the voices in my head seriously, and for that I'll be forever grateful.

To critique partners Jessica Fonseca and Cathy Castelli, for early reads, insightful comments, and constant cheerleading (and for never again bringing up the foot scene).

To Paula Stokes—friend, therapist, word doctor, professional adviser, writing machine. I would have jumped off many mental cliffs without you. Thank you for all the shared tears and celebrations, and for being there every single step of the way.

To I. W. Gregorio, for perspective. See you in Ocean City.

To Liz Van Doren, for Rolling Stones lyrics, Venn diagrams, and being the first person who really made me believe.

To Steve Raizes, for telling me about that writing class you were taking and making me wonder why I wasn't doing the same.

To Martha Lawrence, for authorly advice, words of encouragement, and telling me when it was okay—and necessary—to take a break.

To Deborah Moss, Sieglinde McKeown, Rachel Peachman, Liz Sadeghi, Katie and Gabe Bevilacqua, and all my friends and extended family, for unlimited support and unwavering faith.

To Sarah Lieberman, the sole member of my YA book club, for answering questions about school and being the type of reader I write for.

To the town of Westfield, New Jersey, for being home. I did my best to honor your history and streets. Any inconsistencies or mistakes made in the service of the story are mine and mine alone.

To the Fall Fifteeners, the Fearless Fifteeners, the Binders, and the bloggers. You are my people and my community. This journey would have been insurmountable without you.

To Jaime Primak Sullivan, for big dreams, positive energy, love, the lake house, and divine timing.

To Hillary Scarbrough, for texts about kissing, chats about the nuances of human behavior, and Totally Getting It; and for telling me I could when I felt like I couldn't.

To Mandy Tagger-Brockey, for plot help, the perfect advice in a crisis, and so much more than I could ever list.

To Judy and John Paul, my other parents, for always believing.

To Sara Sargent, for the best editorial letter ever, and for understanding exactly what I meant, even when I didn't realize I meant it.

To the entire B+B team, especially fearless leaders Alessandra Balzer and Donna Bray and editorial lifesaver Viana Siniscalchi. Thanks for bringing me back to 10 East 53rd Street as an author.

To Michael Bourret, who makes everything okay. Having

you in my corner has made all the difference. What can I say? I'm glad I waited the extra week.

To my older brothers, Lawrence—pillow fort builder, homework helper, fuzzy finder; and Bryan—creative ally and genuine rock star. Thanks for doing everything first.

To my parents: Mom, for telling me to invite another friend over when I was crying about what some fourth-grade girl said, for that trip to California, and for so many other things you did that got me through the hardest parts of high school (and life) and had me laughing on the other side. Dad, for telling me I could be whatever I wanted to be over and over again, even when I made faces and got all sensitive. Believe me, I know how lucky I am to be your daughter.

To Stephen and Alex, for reminding me how thin the line is between imagination and reality, and for going to bed on time so many nights so I could write.

And, finally, to Chris, who met me when I was Mattie's age and decided to stay. This book would not have been possible without you. Thanks for making ours a love story.